ALL THE LIES WE TELL

ALSO BY MEGAN HART

Lovely Wild
Precious and Fragile Things
The Favor
All Fall Down
Little Secrets
The Resurrected
Passion Model
Driven
Beneath the Veil
Seeking Eden
Exit Light
Beg for It
Perfectly Restless
Hold Me Close
Vanilla
Flying
Stumble Into Love
The Space Between Us
Collide
Naked
Deeper
Switch
Stranger
Tempted
Broken
Dirty

Tear You Apart

Captivated (with Tiffany Reisz)

Taking Care of Business (with Lauren Dane)

No Reservations (with Lauren Dane)

Order of Solace series

Pleasure and Purpose

No Greater Pleasure

Selfish is the Heart

Virtue and Vice

ALL THE LIES WE TELL

A NOVEL

MEGAN HART

Montlake Romance

This is a work of fiction. Names, characters, organizations, places, events, and incidents are either products of the author's imagination or are used fictitiously.

Published by Montlake Romance, Seattle

www.apub.com

ISBN-13: 9781503942776
ISBN-10: 1503942775

Cover design by Shasti O'Leary Soudant

For anyone who's ever thought of giving up the dream . . . don't.

Keep dreaming.

CHAPTER ONE

There might be worse things than looking out her kitchen window to watch her ex-husband smooching up on some tousle-haired blonde wearing last night's outfit, but it sure wasn't the first thing Alicia Stern wanted to see in the morning. Sipping her coffee with both hands warming on the mug, she leaned against the counter and listened to the soft plink-plink of her dripping faucet. Ilya had promised to fix it for her but hadn't gotten around to it yet. Of course. And no wonder, Alicia thought as the blonde drove off in a kicky little VW Bug with fake eyelashes decorating the headlights. He was too busy laying pipe to fix a leaking faucet.

Ilya waved after the car, put both hands on his hips, and arched his back. Then, with his arms flung wide, he twisted at the waist. He touched his toes. Did a couple of jumping jacks.

All in his leave-nothing-to-the-imagination boxer shorts.

Alicia's coffee slipped down a little too fast, too hot, and she coughed. The neighbors were getting quite a show, she thought with a shrug and a shake of her head. It wasn't any of her business what Ilya did in the mornings in his own front yard. She could no longer be held responsible for him or his helicoptering ding-dong.

She would be, though. That was part of the problem with living in a small town. Ilya could—and often did—bring home a different woman every night, but until he put a ring on one of their fingers, Alicia was still going to be the one everyone expected to keep him in line.

Her phone rang. The house line, which meant it was Dina Guttridge from the Cape Cod next door. The Guttridge family had moved in about eight years ago, their house a part of the new construction that had cropped up all along Quarry Street within the past ten years. At first, newlyweds Dina and Bill had been fine neighbors. Friendly without being overbearing. Then the children had come, one after the other, three in a row, and two years ago, a fourth. Bill Guttridge had taken a job driving long hauls.

Dina had started getting cranky.

Now she was the sort of neighbor who called about the lawn being too long on Alicia's side, about late-night loud noises, and about the motion-detector lights being too bright. Once about the smell of the barbecue grill making her precious tots "too hungry" when it was past their bedtime. Alicia had lost her patience a while back with Dina's constant nosiness and complaining, though she usually managed to keep her annoyances to herself in the name of keeping the neighborly peace.

"Dina. Hi," she said before Dina could even identify herself.

"He's almost naked! It's January!"

Alicia bit back a chortle and peeked out her kitchen window again. From this angle she could see only Ilya's driveway and not his front yard. Her answer wasn't a lie. "I can't see him, Dina."

"But you knew who I was talking about right away, didn't you?" Dina huffed and puffed.

Alicia imagined the other woman lifting a toddler onto her hip while she stared out of the gap between her living-room curtains. "I assumed. Yeah."

"You're going to have to say something to him. This is ridiculous. Go see what he's doing!"

Alicia topped off her mug and cradled the phone between her ear and shoulder while she pulled open the fridge to find the creamer. Her parents had done some nice things to this house before moving permanently to Arizona, but they'd never upgraded their landline to a cordless model. She was tethered to the wall by the phone's long, curling cord. So it was also not a lie when she said, "Can't see him from here while I'm on the phone, Dina. The cord won't stretch."

"The cord won't . . ." Dina huffed again. "He's doing some sort of . . . yoga!"

Of course he was, in his own way. It looked like he'd learned from a contortionist with an extra arm, and once he got into downward dog, he pumped his pelvis against the ground a few times, probably because he suspected Dina might be watching. Alicia didn't miss much about being married to Ilya, though occasionally—very occasionally, and usually only when she'd had a few glasses of wine—she did allow herself to remember fondly his flexibility and ability to control his breathing. "Look, Dina, if you're so worked up about it, you call him. I can't stop him from doing anything."

"He's *your* husband!"

"Ex-husband." Alicia thought, and not for the first time, how simple it was to say. It made her sad, sometimes, how easily she'd been able to stop thinking of Ilya as her husband, even if nobody else seemed to manage. "We've been divorced for almost longer than we've been married, Dina."

"So you don't care that he was practically humping some random woman in the driveway. Right in front of my kids."

"I don't care about what Ilya does with random women, no. I'm sorry he's a douche, Dina. What can I say? He's a free spirit. Holler at him, not me." Alicia put the creamer back in the fridge and added some sugar to her coffee, stirring it before sipping. "There's honestly not much I can do about it, and, frankly, I don't even want to."

That last bit slipped out a little harsher than she'd intended, but Alicia decided she didn't regret the words. Or her tone. It was the truth.

"Just say something to him, anyway. I know you'll see him at work." Dina's voice faded, and there came a sound of scuffling. A wailing cry. She came back on the line, sounding disgruntled and exhausted and irritable, and Alicia would have had more sympathy for her if the woman hadn't been so insistent that somehow everyone else take some responsibility for her woes. "Tell him it's . . . well, it's just not right that he lets his goods hang all out like that."

"Fine. I'll say something," Alicia promised, if only to get Dina off the line so she could finish her coffee in peace. "I can't make any promises about him changing his behavior."

Dina huffed and puffed again. "He should be more considerate of the people around him! I mean, he should just *think*!"

"That's Ilya for you. Not a big thinker." Alicia hated the tone of apology that had managed to creep into her voice despite her earlier abruptness. No matter how she fought it, she was still taking the blame for him. "I'll tell him to cool it."

After hanging up the phone, she punched in a familiar set of numbers for the house across the street. She'd been calling that number since they were kids. Like her, Ilya had kept the same phone from the time he'd been growing up. She had his cell number, too, of course, but if he was out there on the front lawn doing half-naked yoga, he didn't exactly have a pocket to keep a phone in. He'd hear the old-fashioned jangling, though, and maybe he'd at least go inside before Dina completely lost her mind.

The phone rang ten times without an answer, but a knock on her front door a few minutes later revealed an unapologetically grinning Ilya glistening with sweat. It had slicked his dark hair back from his forehead and sparkled on his upper lip, until he licked it away. January had been unseasonably warm, but even so, he must've been putting on quite the show after she stopped watching.

"She called you, huh?" Ilya said.

Alicia stepped aside to let him in. "Yeah. Do you have to be such a dick about everything? You know she gets all worked up about that stuff. We don't live alone on this street anymore. It's not like it used to be. You need to remember that."

He moved past her and into the kitchen. He poured himself a mug of coffee, as at-home in her house as she'd be in his, even after being divorced for so many years. One of the hardest things about them splitting up had been enforcing boundaries. This was *her* house now, not her mom and dad's, but apparently even almost a decade of not being married couldn't cancel out a near lifetime of being somehow intertwined.

This was one of the many times Alicia thought it would have been a better choice if she'd sold her childhood home and moved away when she left him. Across town, or even farther. Canada. China. A house near a loch in Scotland. There were thousands of places she might have gone instead of staying in Quarrytown, but here was where she'd always been, and here was probably where she would always stay. Anyway, moving away would have required money. It always came down to money, and hers had been tied up in the business.

"She's a busybody. You got any eggs?"

Alicia reached around him to shut the fridge door he was attempting to open. "Out."

Ilya gave her puppy eyes, but she'd grown immune to those charms long ago. "C'mon, Allie, I haven't made it to the grocery store yet this week."

"Starve," she said unsympathetically, and stood in front of the fridge with her arms crossed.

Frowning, Ilya took a few steps back and drank his coffee. "Wow. Harsh."

She couldn't let herself feel upset about hurting his feelings. If she let him, Ilya would simply continue to walk in and out of her kitchen the way he walked in and out of her life. "When are you going to grow up?"

"Harsher," he said, brow furrowed. "Shit, Allie."

She couldn't let him guilt her into anything, either. He was a master of that, too. Charming, insistent, oblivious to anything beyond himself. It had stopped hurting when she'd come to accept that Ilya's self-absorption had nothing to do with anything lacking inside her—it was all him. Still, there would always be that tiny sting when she looked at him and remembered that once upon a time she'd loved him enough to marry him and take his name. Once upon a long time ago.

When she didn't answer, he shook his head, then muttered, "Sorry. I'm hungry, that's all."

"Your girlfriend didn't make you breakfast in bed?" The words slipped out sounding angry, even though she wasn't. Not really. Not about the blonde, anyway.

Ilya laughed. "R-i-i-i-ight, girlfriend, right. And she couldn't cook me breakfast if I didn't have anything to eat."

"So go to the store," Alicia said without moving. "Or get a girlfriend who will go shopping for you."

"Jealous?"

She laughed and rolled her eyes. "Oh, yes. So, so jealous."

"I'm sorry," he said again, this time sounding more sincere.

She paused, eyes narrowed. "Uh-huh. What's going on?"

"Nothing." He sipped his coffee and went to the window to peek out, as though checking on what she'd been able to see earlier. He glanced at her over his bare shoulder. "Think Dina would let me borrow some eggs?"

Alicia grinned. "Why don't you go over there and ask her?"

They both burst into laughter. If it felt a little mean, it also felt a little nostalgic. It felt a little melancholy, and she wasn't about to go there with him. Too much had passed between them for that.

"She doesn't mean anything to me," Ilya said suddenly to her back as she emptied her mug into the sink and moved to put it in the dishwasher.

Without even a glance, Alicia answered, "Who? Dina?"

"Not Dina."

Her back stiffened, and she almost dropped her mug but managed to settle it onto the top rack before she did. When she heard the clink of his mug on the counter, she said, "Ilya. Don't."

He moved up behind her and put his hands on her hips. His fingers squeezed her lightly. His crotch pushed against her ass. She tensed at the gust of his breath on the back of her neck. He had not touched her that way in years.

"Allie . . ."

"I said 'don't,'" she repeated firmly, willing her voice not to shake. He couldn't see her closed eyes or the way she sealed her mouth tight to keep herself from crying, her tears as unexpected as his come-on had been. "Stop it, Ilya. It's not going to work. I'm not one of your pickups, okay?"

His fingers gripped tighter for a second or so before he stepped back, putting distance between them. His voice, low and rasping, tried to turn her, but she kept herself facing away. "I know that. I just thought . . ."

"You want what you want," she told him as coldly as she could, which was barely lukewarm, because this, after all, was Ilya. Her worst mistake. The one man who had never been meant for her.

He snorted soft laughter that had no humor to it. "Doesn't everyone?"

"It's getting late. Are you coming in to the shop today?" She didn't turn. Didn't look. She breathed through the threat of tears and forced them away.

After half a minute or so, she heard him sigh. "Well . . . yeah. Of course. I'll stop in before I head over to the Y for the beginner classes."

Carefully, she closed the dishwasher and rinsed her hands at the sink. The beginner sessions consisted of a bunch of paperwork, a few lessons on technique, and some preliminary work in the pool. The advanced sessions were all in the water, and they'd also take place in the pool since Go Deep didn't allow winter diving. All of them were Ilya's responsibility.

She turned to face him. "Don't forget the advanced sessions later this afternoon—both of them. You need to get them all their certification before you take them on the trip."

"Yeah. I know. It'll happen. Don't worry about it."

"They've all put down deposits and bought their flights. I've paid the hotel. We can't afford to be late on any of this—"

Ilya nodded, his normally open expression unreadable. He glanced down at his boxers and seemed uncomfortable, at least in the way his gaze cut from hers. He scuffed a bare foot along the faded linoleum, then looked over at her sink.

"Hey. Your faucet," he began.

Alicia cut him off with a small wave. "Don't worry about it. I'll call someone to come and deal with it. It's not your problem. We're not . . . it's not your problem."

He nodded slowly. "Okay. Sure. But you know I wouldn't mind."

She looked him in the eye, both of them full of words that neither of them seemed willing to say. "I'm going to be late. We have a delivery scheduled. I need to be there for it."

"Sure. Right. Yeah," he said and backed away. "I'll see you there in half an hour."

That meant easily an hour or longer, but Alicia didn't say so. It would start a fight and not change anything, in the end. Ilya would still be there late, and she would still be irritated, and around and around they'd go. Instead, she smiled and nodded and showed him to the front door. She closed it after him and leaned against it, eyes closed, breathing in and breathing out. Most of the time it was so easy not to love him anymore, she thought as she shook it all off, got her chin up. Most of the time it was so easy, but sometimes, it was so, so damned hard.

CHAPTER TWO

Ilya didn't have to erase the blonde's number from his phone, because he hadn't even typed it in when she gave it to him. He'd meant for her to be as easily forgotten as all the women had been in the past few years. This one, though, had left her scarf on the dining-room table. He hadn't even remembered her wearing a scarf.

Now he lifted it to his face, breathing in the scent of her perfume, to see if that would help him remember her name. *Amber. Her name was Amber.* Well, he could put the scarf in his "Lost and Found" box, and if they ever hooked up again, she could sift through the discarded lingerie, sunglasses, and lipsticks. One day he was going to get rid of all that junk, those mementos of his wild nights out, but for now he tossed the scarf on top of everything else and slid the cardboard file box back into its spot on the shelf in the front closet above the winter coats.

Stripping out of his boxers on the way to the shower and kicking them in the general direction of the pile of dirty laundry near the basket, he thought about running out onto the front lawn totally naked for a few minutes just to get Dina Guttridge's motor running. If she had a hissy fit about him doing a few downward dogs in his boxers, she sure as hell wouldn't like him doing it in the nude—but ultimately, it wasn't worth the hassle. Sooner or later, he figured she was going to quit spying on him and get over the fact that once a few years ago they'd had a couple of glasses of wine while her husband was away. Not much had happened. A little making out, a little finger banging. As far as Ilya was concerned, it was only cheating if someone came. It had been a mistake, though, and not because she was a married woman living next door to his ex-wife, with whom he still owned a business and worked with every day. Nope, he should never have fooled around with Dina, because she was flat-out crazy for the D, and she couldn't seem to get it through her head that Ilya was not interested in being anyone's side piece—at least not more than once.

He wasn't interested in being anyone's front or back piece, either. Him and relationships? No, thanks. He'd done that already, all serious and committed and monogamous, and look what had happened. The sour sting of that experience still lingered. Probably always would. And why? Because he'd done his best to love Allie and be good to her, and in the end all he'd done was make a mess of things. That was all he was good for: screwing up.

He couldn't blame her for it. Their relationship had been doomed from the start. Tumultuous and emotional and stupid. It had ended as abruptly as it had begun; he'd come home one day to an empty house and a note telling him she'd moved back across the street into the house her parents had left behind when they moved to Arizona. There'd been no counseling, no "working it out." Ten years and it was over, yet they were still a part of each other's lives and would likely always be. They were family.

They'd once filled an empty space within each other, one that nobody else could ever understand.

Maybe that was why he'd been an asshole and tried to come on to her this morning, he thought as he stood in the shower under water still too chilly for comfort. Because, despite last night and Amber, all Ilya had was a still-empty space. He pushed those thoughts away because, damn, it was too early for self-contemplation. Hissing at the sting, Ilya twisted the faucet handle sideways, to get beneath the water so he could scrub his armpits, still rank from the night's acrobatics and not helped by his morning exercise. The showerhead had come off a few years ago, and he hadn't replaced it, which meant the water shot out of a single pipe sticking out of the wall with enough force to abrade him in every tender place if he didn't stand at just the right angle. He winced at the scratches along his back and sides. Next time, he told himself, he'd make sure to pick up a woman who didn't have talons.

He heard the muffled sound of the landline ringing again but didn't bother to get out of the shower to answer it. The only calls that came through on that number were solicitors or scams. Or his ex-wife, he thought, calling to chastise him about naked front-lawn yoga. He took his time scrubbing and rinsing, then stepped out of the water and rubbed his hair dry with a towel that smelled faintly of mildew—shit, he needed to do laundry. Again. What the hell was up with that?

Ilya tossed the damp towel toward the basket and went, still naked, down the hall into his bedroom, where he dug through another pile of clothes to give them a sniff test to determine whether they were clean enough to wear a second time. He was going to be in his scuba gear most of the day, anyway, or a pair of trunks and a T-shirt, so what difference did it make that he picked out a pair of grass-stained cargo pants and a tank top with a hole in the side? He wasn't entering a fashion show.

His phone buzzed from on top of the dresser, then went silent, which meant he'd missed a call. A moment later, the landline rang again, sounding louder this time, since there was still a handset hanging in the hallway outside his bedroom. Pulling up his briefs with one hand and hopping on one foot, Ilya headed for the doorway. His shoulder connected with the door frame hard enough to bounce him backward, and he let out a curse of pain as he managed to unhook the phone from its cradle, but then dropped it and kicked it out of reach when he bent to lift it.

Behind him, on the dresser, his phone buzzed again.

"This better be important!" he barked into the landline when he at last was able to snag it.

"Mr. Stern?"

"Mr. Stern's my dad," Ilya said, ever the smart-ass, and unable to stop himself. His father had died when Ilya was two. He didn't even remember him. "Who's this?"

"Ummm . . . I'm trying to reach Ilya Stern?" Whoever it was pronounced the name as "Eye-lah" and not "Ill-ya," which set him directly into telephone-solicitor territory.

"Wrong number." Ilya slammed the phone back on its cradle, hard enough to shake it on the ancient screws barely securing it into the plaster.

His cell hummed with another call, this time adding a few beeps to indicate a voicemail. Damn, he was popular this morning. Throwing on his pants and tugging his shirt over his head, he thumbed in the code to listen to his messages. There were three. Two from a number he didn't recognize, with nothing but the empty hiss of air for a message.

The third was from his brother, Nikolai. He hadn't heard from Niko in a couple of months—nothing unusual about that. Niko had been living overseas for the past few years. Niko hadn't been stupid enough to get married too young. He'd been smart enough to get the hell out of Covey County and see the world instead.

Without listening to more than the first few words of Niko's message, Ilya thumbed his brother's number instead. "Yo. What's up?"

Silence.

"Niko?"

"Ilya . . . you didn't listen to the message, huh?"

"No." Ilya paused his search for a pair of shoes. He straightened. "What's going on?"

"The nursing home's been trying to get hold of you for like an hour, man. They finally got me on my cell, but that was a lucky shot. I just happened to be taking a break from work and checked my messages."

Ilya sat on the rickety chair in the corner, knees suddenly weak. "You sound bad. What is it?"

"It's Babulya," Niko said with an edge in his voice. "She's . . . they say she doesn't have long to live. You need to get over there right away."

CHAPTER THREE

Alicia had seen Ilya cry only once before, and that had been the first night they'd ever had sex. She didn't like thinking of that night at all, but especially not now, not here in Babulya's sparsely decorated room in the nursing home, as they'd all gathered around her bed. The old woman had been as much a grandma to Alicia and her older sister, Jennilynn, as she'd been to her own two grandsons. The only one Alicia could remember, as a matter of fact, since her own grandparents had all passed away when she was a toddler. And now Babulya was dying, too.

Nikolai was here, travel-worn and exhausted. It had taken him a day and a half to get home from whatever far-off adventure he'd been having, and Alicia hadn't even had time to say more than a quick "Hey." Not that she had much more to say to him than that.

Her former brother-in-law had taken charge quickly enough, stepping in where Ilya had faltered, and Alicia supposed she ought to be grateful that someone had, if only because it meant *she* didn't have to. Babulya had fallen silent an hour or so ago, but before that she'd been only vaguely alert and scolding all of them for tracking dirt into her kitchen. She'd promised Nikolai some chocolate-chip cookies if he was a good boy and ran to get the mail for her, and though Ilya's younger brother had stopped being a boy, good or otherwise, a long time ago, he'd nodded and patted Babulya's hand with a promise to do just that. The old woman had also given Alicia a wavery-voiced bit of advice on how to take stains out of a white tablecloth. Then she'd launched into a muttered jumble of Russian that none of them could understand.

Now Alicia held Ilya's hand as he sat by Babulya's bedside, his head pressed to the blankets. She didn't want to be the one offering him this comfort, but who else was there to do it? She rubbed his back slowly between his shoulder blades as he hitched in silent but sobbing breaths. Alicia caught Nikolai's gaze from across the bed. His gaze followed the circle she made with her hand on his brother's back. When he looked back at her with a small, enigmatic smile, she didn't return it.

Screw him, she thought. Nobody in their families had been super thrilled when she and Ilya had decided to get married, but Nikolai had been the only one to actively speak out against it. The two of them had always had their tiffs as kids. One-upping each other. Pranks and teasing and occasional mean-spirited taunts. But he'd been ballsy enough to accuse her of trying to step into Jennilynn's shoes and, worse, of being insufficient for the task. Alicia and Nikolai hadn't spoken more than a few icy words since then; she had never told anyone, not even Ilya, what his brother had said or how deep those wounds had cut. She'd never forgotten, though. Not the accusation, and not how right he'd been that she and Ilya should never have gotten married. She'd never forgotten anything about Nikolai.

She leaned to speak into Ilya's ear, wrinkling her nose at the faint waft of sweat and fried food. They'd all been taking round-the-clock shifts for the past two days, but Ilya was the only one who'd refused to leave, even sleeping on the uncomfortable chair next to his grandmother's bed. None of them were happy about Babulya's decline, of course. They'd all adored her. Still, there was no denying that Ilya had been closer to her than any of them. Her first grandchild. She'd raised him while his mother had worked to support them after his father was killed, when Galina was pregnant with Nikolai.

Alicia wanted to admire his current dedication, but it faintly annoyed her, this sudden show of devotion, when he'd gone to see

Babulya no more than a handful of times over the past few months. He'd made excuses instead of visits. That was Ilya, she thought with a frown. He ignored the problems until he had no choice but to face them.

She said in a low voice, "You want to go grab a drink? Get some air? We're all here with her. You need a little break."

Ilya shook his head without opening his eyes. She sighed. He was so stubborn. Her fingernails scratched through the soft, faded fabric of his T-shirt, one he'd had for as long as she could remember. They'd argued over it once, when she'd tried to toss it, and he'd snagged it out of the donation pile. It had been one of their few true fights. She looked up to see Nikolai still staring. She stared back, like a challenge. He'd run off to live on the other side of the world, leaving them all behind. He didn't get to judge her.

"C'mon, man, let's go grab a couple of sodas and something to eat. You're fading." Nikolai stood.

His hand landed on his brother's shoulder, pinching the fabric of Ilya's shirt and coming perilously close to pushing hers away. Frowning, she refused to move it. Nikolai's fingers brushed hers, and that was when she finally let go.

"Ilya," Nikolai said, quieter. "C'mon. Talk a little walk with me. Grab a drink. You're going to make yourself sick if you don't take a break."

"I don't want to leave her."

Alicia let her eyes close for a moment at the sound of anguish in Ilya's voice. She believed it, and it still irritated her. She had to get away from Babulya's slow, rattling burble. Away from Ilya's rising stink and palpable anxiety. She had to get away from being her ex-husband's comfort simply because he had nobody else. All at once, it was everything Alicia could do not to scream. To run.

She needed to get out of there desperately, enough that she'd even deal with Nikolai.

"I'll go with you," she said, not looking to see if it surprised him. "We can bring back something for him."

She stood on shaky legs, swallowing hard against an uprush of both nausea and emotion. In the hallway, she didn't wait for Nikolai to follow her as she headed for the doors at the end. The home was built all on one floor, the residential wings like spokes leading to a central hub, with recreation and dining rooms beyond in another wing. She remembered a vending-machine area somewhere close to the lobby. She had not, however, remembered her purse or any money, something she only figured out when she got to the machine.

Alicia sagged against the soda machine with both hands flat on it. Shoulders hunched. Defeated.

"Here." Beside her, Nikolai slipped a dollar bill into the slot. "What do you want?"

"Water . . . no. Cola. Full strength." She needed the caffeine and the sugar. When the bottle fell into the slot at the bottom, she cracked the cap and took a long, grateful drag before offering it to him.

He shook his head. "No, thanks, I don't drink soda anymore."

"You used to guzzle it by the gallon. What happened?" Alicia took another long sip, feeling better.

"The color's coming back to your cheeks. You want a snack?" Nikolai put another couple of bucks into the snack machine and punched some buttons, then pulled out a bag of fried cheese crackers and a package of cake rolls.

Her favorites. How many nights had they spent gorging on treats like this, wrapped up in sleeping bags outside under the summer sky? Or in front of the television, sneaking movies their parents would've refused to let them see? Babulya knew about those late-night horror fests and had always shaken her head at them, but she never gave the kids away.

Her vision blurred as the tears she'd fought for hours finally broke free and burned trails down her cheeks. She'd escaped the room and the burden of having to support Ilya with her own strength, but it had been hours since she felt like she'd been able to take a breath. She put a hand on the wall, shoulders sagging.

"Hey."

One of Nikolai's arms went around her in an awkward squeeze until he embraced her fully. She fought the hug, not wanting to completely break down. Not here, and especially not with him. When his hand stroked down the length of her hair, she shook her head and forced herself to step back.

She wiped her face. "Sorry."

"Don't be sorry." Nikolai gave her a long, curious look, then bent to pick up the snacks from the ground. "Stuff like this is hard."

Before she could find the words to answer him, his gaze went beyond her. His eyes widened. Nikolai blinked.

"Holy . . . Theresa?"

CHAPTER FOUR

Niko's arms had been full of his former sister-in-law one moment and empty the next as Alicia stepped quickly out of his embrace. He barely had time to register that she'd been pressed against him before they both turned to face the tall, dark-haired woman who'd just come through the nursing home's front doors. Niko hadn't seen his former stepsister, Theresa, in . . . well, it had to be more than twenty years. Their parents had been together for about a year and a half, splitting as quickly and with as little fanfare as they'd gotten married. Theresa and her dad had moved out of the Sterns' house and ended up in the next town over. Theresa had gone to a different high school. They hadn't kept in touch.

It felt gross now, thinking of that—how once they'd been part of a family, and then it had ended, and they'd never even bothered to stay in contact. Heat prickled at the nape of his neck. Embarrassment. Theresa, on the other hand, didn't seem to be holding a grudge.

"Niko," she said warmly and hugged him.

Surprised, he returned the embrace. She'd grown taller. The last time he recalled being this close to her, he'd been giving her a knuckle rub on her head, arguing over what to watch on TV. Now she almost met him eye to eye.

Theresa turned from him to hug Allie. "Hey, you. It's been a long time. Thanks so much for letting me know about this. How is she?"

"Fading," Allie answered quietly. "They think it won't be long now. Thanks for coming."

Theresa gave them both a serious nod. "Of course. She was wonderful to me, and I've never forgotten it. I'm here if you need anything. I'm going to her room, if that's all right?"

Watching Theresa go, Niko waited until she'd disappeared through the doors to the corridor leading to his grandmother's room. He thought Allie would've followed, but when he turned, she was still there. She looked uncomfortable, her gaze going to the damp spot on the front of his shirt before cutting away.

"Ilya will be wondering where we are," she said.

"Wait." He snagged the sleeve of her lightweight sweater, not meaning to grab her but suddenly, strangely desperate to get her to stay. "How've you been?"

"All right." Slipping gently from his grip, she took another drink from the bottle of soda and then put the cap back on. She gestured at the bags of snacks he hadn't realized he was still gripping in one hand. "I'll take the cake rolls."

He handed them to her. "Your folks?"

"They're good. Loving Arizona." She tore open the plastic and offered him one of the pastries.

"No, thanks. I try to stay away from sugar."

Alicia burst into laughter, and the warmth of it hit him in the hollow of his throat and someplace lower, between his ribs. "God, Nikolai. What the hell? Don't tell me you've turned into some kind of . . . I don't know. Health nut?"

"I wouldn't say that. Just that when I'm traveling, it's too easy to fill up on junk food, and you get to craving it. Then a lot of times when I'm out in places where you can't find it . . . I didn't want to miss it, that's all. Easier to just give it up." He gave her a small smile.

There'd been a lot of things like that in his life. Better to abandon than risk longing for them. He shrugged.

Her laughter faded, her eyes still glistening with tears. "Easier to give up something so you don't have to miss it? That's pretty deep."

He hadn't meant it to be, but he supposed it was, if you wanted to analyze it. He didn't. He spent a lot of time trying to do the opposite of that sort of navel-gazing. It never did much good.

"Ilya never mentioned she was sick," he said, to turn the conversation. "If I'd known . . ."

He trailed off, not sure what he'd meant to say. If he'd known—what? He wouldn't have come home any sooner. He didn't plan to stay long, either.

Alicia shook her head and bit into the soft cake. She chewed solemnly, then tossed it into the nearby garbage can with a grimace. "Gross. Stuff like that always looks so good until you get it, but it's never as good as it looks."

"Talk about being pretty deep," Nikolai said.

She didn't answer, and he regarded her a moment. Sad eyes. Curved-down mouth. The last time he'd seen her had been a few months after she and Ilya divorced. Niko had run into her at the grocery store while on a brief visit home. Their exchange had been downright arctic. He hadn't been home for more than a day or two since then, and he hadn't seen her on any of those visits, not for years.

It might as well have been seconds; that's how different he felt when he looked at her.

"Sorry," Niko said quietly. "Trying to lighten the mood."

Allie's frown didn't smooth. "She wasn't sick for long. I try to see her at least once a week, and last week she was still doing great. Up and about, moving around. She'd complained about being tired, but she's ninety-three. That's to be expected. The staff said she took a downturn early Tuesday morning."

The call hadn't been a surprise, and he was grateful it hadn't been someone telling him his grandmother had passed. He'd had time to see her again; at least there was that. He'd applied for leave from the kibbutz board and had been approved at once. Booking the flight to Newark International, making the trip, and figuring out a way to get from New Jersey to Quarrytown had been a little more complicated. He'd arrived exhausted and jet-lagged. He still hadn't slept. He was sure he wouldn't for another few hours.

"I got here as soon as I could," Niko said, although she hadn't said a word about how long it had taken him.

"I didn't know they had your number. But it's good they did," Allie said with a pause that told him she knew as well as he did that *she* wouldn't have called him. "It's good for you to be here. Ilya's happy about it, I'm sure."

Niko noticed very particularly that she hadn't said *she* was happy he was there. It shouldn't have mattered, but it bothered him more than he wanted to admit.

He nodded. "Yeah. Me, too."

"I don't want to go back in there," she blurted, like a confession. She lifted her chin, meeting his gaze steadfastly. "I know I should, but I just . . . I can't. I don't want to see her like that. And I *really* don't want to hold Ilya's hand through this."

The last had been spoken with an undertone of biting venom that surprised him. He knew his brother's faults as well as she did, although maybe no longer better. She'd been married to the guy, after all, while Niko had left home at age eighteen and had spent very little time there since.

"He hasn't been here to see her in a couple months," Alicia continued, her voice low and bitter. "She asked about him all the time, but he was always too busy to show up. He had a million excuses, when the truth was he just didn't want to see her failing. Now he's in there moaning and mourning. He's going to let everything else fall to the side while he does this, Nikolai. I know him. He's going to focus entirely on himself, and I'm going to pick up the slack, and . . . I don't want to do it anymore."

She cut herself off, her lips pressed together. She shrugged, shaking her head as though words had failed her. Then she tossed the soda bottle into the trash and crossed her arms over her belly, hands cupping the opposite elbows. She scuffed her shoe on the tile floor.

"He can be kind of a dick," Niko agreed.

Alicia tilted her head to give him a sideways glance. "Yeah. Sorry. I shouldn't have said anything about it. It's not your problem."

"It's not like we don't all know it. Hell, Ilya would probably say the same thing about himself. I'm sorry he hasn't been better to you, Allie. You deserve better. You always have." Niko didn't mean to pull her close again, but there she was in his arms.

She felt good there.

She felt . . . right.

Nestled just beneath his chin, the soft fall of her strawberry-blonde hair against his cheek, Alicia sighed. One hand went flat to his chest, over his heart, which to Niko's embarrassment had started beating faster. Thump thump thump—no hiding his reaction to the way she felt against him.

She noticed. Of course she did. Alicia had always been the "smart" one of the two Harrison sisters, although Niko secretly had always thought she was just as pretty as Jennilynn. You couldn't put much over on Alicia.

He waited for her to pull away. Both of them would laugh a little nervously, not looking at each other. She'd make a caustic comment, or he'd try to joke, and they'd pretend there'd been no small but rising heat between them. She'd pull away and go back to ignoring him, and he would tell himself it was better that way.

She didn't pull away.

CHAPTER FIVE

Then

They were going to get caught; Alicia knew it.

"Did you get the beer?" Alicia paced nervously, repeatedly tucking her straight reddish hair behind her ears. She clamped the tip of her tongue between her teeth to keep them from chattering with anxiety.

Jennilynn tossed her blonde curls over her shoulders and gave Alicia a long, smug look. "Of course. I told you I would. A whole case."

"How did you get a whole case of beer?"

A six-pack—that's all they were supposed to get. Everyone was supposed to bring one. Alicia had also picked up some chips and dip, because you couldn't have a party without snacks, right? And the boys from across the street weren't going to think about it; maybe they'd grab some money from everyone later for a pizza or something, but they sure weren't thinking about party snacks . . .

"Allie!" Jennilynn snapped her fingers in front of Alicia's face. "Chill. You're making me nervous."

"How did you get a case of beer?" Alicia lowered her voice to a hissing whisper.

Mom and Dad were still here, getting ready in their room down the hall. They were going away for the weekend, leaving Jennilynn in charge for the first time. At seventeen, she was supposed to be old enough to handle things. She was supposed to be trustworthy, and what was the very first thing she did? Throw a party.

It's going to end up bad for everyone, and there's nothing I can do about it, because my sister is going to do whatever she wants. The way she always does. Jenni's going to get us all in so much trouble.

Jennilynn smiled. Mysterious and beautiful: that was Alicia's older sister. Jennilynn shrugged, her bare shoulders lifting and falling. It was October, but still warm. Jennilynn wore a halter dress, her collarbones exposed, and in the hollow of her throat rested the heart-shaped pendant Alicia had asked for, but had not received, for Christmas.

Two years apart in age, universes apart in coolness. It's not fair. And she doesn't even notice it.

"I know a guy." Jennilynn shrugged again as she looked in the mirror.

Black flecks speckled the glass where the silvering had come off on the back. This mirror was an antique, attached to an old dresser that had been their grandma's when she got married. When she died, their mom got it. It had been in their room forever, so both of them had gotten used to standing in weird poses in order to see all of themselves. Still, the way Jennilynn stood now, a hip cocked, her head tilting as she let her hands run up her sides until her fingertips rested on her chin, thumbs pressing downward on her throat . . .

Weird. And who's this random beer-buying guy? Something's going on with her, and she won't tell me what it is.

"Where did you meet a guy that old? The diner?"

Jennilynn had been working there since she got her driver's license, which was about the same time she started growing distant and irritable about things that never used to bother her. Now her dreamy, vacant expression went tight. She turned with another toss of her hair.

"What do you care? Ilya said bring beer. I'm bringing beer. What difference does it make to you what I had to do to get it?"

Asking *how* she got the beer and *where* she met the guy who was bringing it was totally different from asking *what* Jenni had to do to get it. "Jennilynn! What did you have to do?"

"Jesus, Alicia. Enough with the Spanish Inquisition. I met a guy, he's old enough to get beer, and he likes me enough to bring it to the party. Quit acting like this is some kind of big deal, because it's not." Jennilynn turned to the mirror again, pursing her lips and turning her face from side to side as though she was looking at something only she could see.

"What's going on with you lately?" Alicia demanded.

Jennilynn looked at her sister in the reflection, then once again turned to face her. Slowly, this time. Without the flounce. For a second or so, Alicia was sure her sister was going to come clean about all the secrets she'd been keeping lately, but then she shrugged and gave Alicia another vacant smile.

"Nothing." It was a lie, and Alicia knew it. Worse, her sister knew that Alicia didn't believe her, but she didn't seem to care. "It's going to be a slammin' party. Don't be such a loser."

Alicia ignored the *L* her sister made with her thumb and first finger pressed to her forehead. "We're going to get in trouble."

"Not unless someone narcs on us. Mom and Dad won't be back until late Sunday. Galina's working a double, or something. Ilya said she won't be home until morning. Barry went fishing for the weekend. And Babulya's staying with some friends in Camp Hill, some kind of quilting thing."

Galina worked a lot of nights and weekends. Her still-newish husband was also often away during the same times. Alicia's parents, however, went away for the weekend occasionally, and never before without having someone come to stay with them. Babulya was almost never gone. If there was ever a time to have a party, this weekend was it.

Alicia wasn't satisfied. This had all the makings of disaster. "What if someone calls the cops?"

"Who's going to call the cops?" Jennilynn rolled her eyes. "We're the only houses on this dead-end street."

◆ ◆ ◆

Four hours later, their parents barely two hours on the road, Jennilynn was wasted and dancing so hard in the center of the Sterns' living room that her halter dress could barely stay up. The guy who'd bought her the case of beer showed up to the party with a couple of bottles of rum. He was at least in his thirties, way too old to be at a high school party, but nobody seemed to care. Especially not Jennilynn. The Stern brothers pulled out a stash of vodka. Ilya was mixing some with red punch. Someone else spilled the chips all over the living-room floor, and kids danced on them, crushing them into the carpet.

"Of course it's vodka. Like water for Russians." Imitating his grandmother's thick accent, Nikolai lifted the bottle toward Alicia's nose until she recoiled from the stinging scent. "Water of life, come on, have a drink. It's Galina's."

"Won't she notice it's gone?" Alicia had to shout over the sound of the music getting louder, louder, louder, the bass thump pressing her in every place her heart beat.

Nikolai didn't hear her. He swigged right from the bottle, but she turned her head at his offer to drink. She already had a beer and didn't like the taste or how it made her feel. She needed to get outside, get some air, away from the now-hovering haze of marijuana. This party was getting out of control, just as she'd predicted.

The Sterns' backyard was rarely mowed. The flower beds went unweeded, unmulched, untended, and the flowers there grew wild and lush. Like a meadow. Alicia's mother tut-tutted about it under her breath, about how a woman alone raising two boys shouldn't need to hire a gardener to keep her yard in shape. That was what boys were for, Alicia's mother had said to her father in the kitchen after dinner one night. Or that new husband. To mow the lawn and take out the garbage. To fix the sagging shutters and the screen door that blew open every time there was a storm.

But what difference did it make? Out here at the very end of Quarry Street, with only two houses and nobody to even see the Sterns' backyard except them? It wasn't like they lived in one of those cookie-cutter neighborhoods, where all the houses looked the same, one on top of the other, every yard nudging up against the next so you couldn't be sure where one stopped or started except by the placement of the swing sets.

Sometimes she wished they lived closer to town, so she could walk to places the way her friends did, or so she didn't have to get up so early to catch the school bus, but most of the time, Alicia loved living out here on the end of Quarry Street with nobody but the Sterns. It was quiet, at least on nights when her sister and Ilya weren't throwing a party, and because there were no streetlights, there was never any problem seeing the stars.

Her feet whispered through the too-long grass, damp with night dew. There was a bench out near the dilapidated garden shed, and she sat on it to stare at the dark sky. The Quarrytown iron quarry was operated at one point in its history by a pair of brothers who preferred to live close to the site, so they'd built their houses directly across from each other outside the quarry's original entrance. The Sterns lived in what used to be the older brother's house, which was bigger and fancier because the older brother had never married and spent all his money on his property. The Harrison house across the street was smaller but kept in far better shape. Both houses were built from the same local limestone, but the Harrisons didn't have a shed. Their backyard edged up to a farmer's field that was usually planted with corn. The Sterns' backyard eased into the woods surrounding the quarry, which was abandoned in the early seventies after a hurricane flooded it. It had become a vast, clear lake fed by spring water that never got warm, not even in August.

When they were much smaller, the four of them used to build forts out of tree branches and the cast-off bits and pieces of machinery or other things the quarry workers had left behind. They used to hide junk food in the old equipment shed. Now, she'd be more likely to find a stash of weed and some empty beer cans and maybe even a used rubber or two rather than a box of Little Debbie Snack Cakes. They all still swam in the quarry, but Alicia couldn't remember the last time they'd hung out together in the woods. They were all growing up. Jennilynn and Ilya were high school seniors. Nikolai was a junior. Alicia and the Stern brothers' new stepsister, Theresa, were both sophomores. They all waited for the bus together at the end of their street, but that was about it.

Except for now, at this party. Cars lined the street. The music was way too loud. There wasn't anyone around to call the cops—Jennilynn was right about that—but in some way or another, by the end of the night, the cops were going to show up. The only time kids got away with mega parties like this without getting busted was in the movies.

For now, she sat on the old park bench nestled into the knee-high grass. The wood was splintered, so she was careful when she shifted. She looked up at the night sky. No moon. The stars were like bright pinpricks, diamonds on black velvet . . .

Shit. I'm actually drunk.

Or maybe she got a little contact high. Either way, her head buzzed, and the universe seemed vast and wild, but still so close she could reach up and grab it, if only she held out her hand.

"Hey."

Startled, she let out a small "meep."

"Nikolai."

He still had the bottle, though the amount of liquid sloshing in the bottom was a lot less than it had been inside the house. He sat next to her on the creaking bench and stretched out his legs. He'd grown taller over the summer.

Their shoulders touched. This time, when he passed her the bottle, Alicia took it. She sipped, choking, eyes burning. The vodka warmed her throat and belly. She hadn't noticed she was shivering.

"Got cold out here." Nikolai slung a companionable arm around her shoulders. "Trees will be changing soon."

From the house came a sudden flare of light and music and laughter. Dark silhouettes appeared in the doorway, then disappeared into the shadows. Nikolai laughed under his breath.

"Your sister," he said. "That guy."

Alicia tried to catch a glimpse of Jennilynn but could see nothing. "He's too old for her."

"Girls like older guys."

She looked at him. "He's *way* too old."

Nikolai shrugged. His eyes flashed, then his smile. "Great party, huh?"

"Your mom is going to kill you when she gets home." Alicia relaxed against the back of the bench and his arm.

"She'll blame Ilya." Nikolai drained the bottle and tossed it into the grass with a clink.

That was true. Galina and Ilya clashed all the time. Nikolai was Galina's favorite, but this was the first time Alicia ever heard him admit knowing that. She retrieved the bottle, setting it close to her side of the bench. "It will break and someone will step on it."

"You're always so in charge, huh?" Nikolai stretched.

She frowned. "I just don't want anyone to get hurt. That's all."

"Mother hen," Nikolai said.

"So what? What's wrong with wanting to make sure everyone is okay?" she demanded, suddenly angry, because Nikolai was always ragging on her. Always on her case. It wasn't fair.

Somehow they were both standing. She poked him in the chest, hard, because he was taller than she was now. Not by much—a couple of inches—but she still had to tilt her head to look up at him, and it annoyed her. She poked him again, but this time Nikolai's hand grabbed her wrist, holding her tight enough to hurt, if she struggled.

"I'm just teasing you," he said without letting her go, even though she tugged. "You get so mad all the time, Allie. Why you gotta get so mad?"

"Because . . . you . . . why do you always have to argue with me? Anything I say or do, you're always making it like some big deal!" She tried again to get her hand free but couldn't, so she smacked at him with the other.

Laughing, Nikolai grabbed that wrist, too. He took one of her hands and jabbed at her face. "Whattya hitting yourself for? Huh? Why are you hitting yourself?"

She wriggled, furious now. In addition to getting taller, Nikolai had gotten a lot stronger. Gone were the days when she could wrestle him to the ground and knuckle his head until he gave up. Being pressed up against him felt different now.

A lot different.

Alicia had kissed a couple of boys before, but nothing like this. Nikolai's mouth on hers was warm, sweet, and insistent. Her lips parted; his tongue slipped inside. Stroking hers. This kiss was inquisitive and also demanding. It left her weak-kneed.

It was over before she had time to even think about it, to protest or fight it, because of course she would have. Right? *Nikolai?*

"Shit," he said softly and took a few steps back. "Shit, I'm fucked up. Really fucked up."

She reached for him, but he was far enough away that her fingertips skated briefly down the front of his shirt, and then there was nothing but empty space between them. She should yell at him, she thought in a daze. Tell him off.

Instead, she pushed past him, toward the house. She didn't look back. Ignoring everyone else at the party, Alicia moved faster and faster through the dancing, hollering mass of kids. Out the front door. Across the street. In her own house, she slammed the front door hard enough to rattle the pictures on the wall. Alicia fled down the hall and into the bathroom, where she brushed her teeth over and over again, leaning over the sink, certain she was going to be sick.

It took a long, long time to scrub away the flavor of that kiss.

CHAPTER SIX

Nikolai smelled so damned good she wanted to eat him up.

Her brother-in-law, Alicia reminded herself sternly. Ilya's baby brother.

The boy who'd once kissed her in the backyard during a party, a kiss she'd never been able to forget.

The *man* whose arms felt like iron rods, but bendy. Bendy iron rods, she thought, a little dazed. Bendy, sexy iron rods. His chest, rock hard, firm, the steady thumping of his heart speeding up beneath the press of her palm against it. And lower, damn—not that she was going to assume anything, but there was a sudden rush of heat in her belly at the touch of his body on hers.

He moved away from her with an anxious snicker. Alicia's small, obnoxious titter was nothing like her normal laughter. Or her normal reaction to being embraced by a hard-bodied, gorgeous guy.

Then again, it had been a damned long time since she'd been held like that by anyone. No wonder her body had reacted that way. Hormones, she told herself sourly. Stupid.

"You don't have to go back in," Nikolai said quickly. "I can call you if she takes a worse turn. Really, if you need to get back home . . ."

If she had to go back to soothing Ilya, she was going to lose her shit. If she went home, she would simply fret and stew about what was going on at the nursing home. She cleared her throat. "I need to check in at the shop, for sure."

Nikolai nodded. "Right. I'll call your cell."

"Thanks." She hesitated, half hating herself for having a single second of concern about what Nikolai thought, but unable to stop herself from asking, "I'm not a terrible person, am I? If I leave? The doctor said he thought it could be any time. Or she could rally and linger on. They don't know."

"I don't think you're terrible."

She studied him. On impulse she hugged him again, harder this time. Arms around his neck. Cheek pressed to his. She clung to him with her eyes closed, wishing she could forget all the bad things that had ever happened between them, but that wasn't the way bad memories worked, in her experience. Those bitches stayed around.

"It's good to see you," she told him, and it felt like the truth.

The breaking off of the hug wasn't as awkward this time. Nikolai smiled. The small scar at the corner of his mouth made it crooked. She'd been there when a stray tree branch had caught him along the trail to the quarry, making him bleed. She'd been there with Nikolai through so much, and he with her.

And there'd been so much he'd missed.

"I'll call you," he said again. "If anything changes. You can be here in twenty minutes. Don't feel bad. Just go."

She did feel bad—there was no getting around that—but something in his off-kilter smile made it a little easier for her to leave. He would be there to take care of everything, to make sure his brother was all right. No matter what had happened between her and Nikolai, she knew she could trust him to do the right thing.

◆ ◆ ◆

In her office at the dive shop, she handled a few deliveries and rescheduled the classes she'd had to cancel so she and Ilya could make it to the nursing home. The classroom sessions were easiest—she could do those herself. The confined water classes that took place in the pool were a little trickier, since she had to go through the local VA hospital for the use of their facilities. The final certification classes were the hardest, though, because those students were the ones on a deadline. Ilya was supposed to be running a trip next month to Jamaica, but if the students didn't get their certification in time, the trip would have to be canceled. They'd be out a lot of money, nonrefundable, not to mention how disappointed everyone would be. Stuff like that turned customers to other places.

He was the one by Babulya's side at the end, when she'd been the one there with the old woman all along. A wave of irritation swept over her at all the paperwork in front of her. Ilya was the only one who could teach the water classes because, like the shoemaker's barefoot children, Alicia had never learned to dive. Everything would have fallen to her, anyway, though. She was the steadfast one who stayed behind. Ilya was the one who got to go to crystal waters and warm sands, hooking up with bronzed and bikini-clad hotties, while Alicia kept the proverbial trains running on time but never, ever left the station herself.

"Stop it," she told herself aloud. "There's no point."

And there wasn't, really. Ilya was the same as he'd ever been. His brother, on the other hand, had seemed to change quite a bit. Physically, obviously. Nikolai had been a short, skinny, geeky kid who'd always seemed to be all bony knees and elbows.

Now Nikolai Stern stood a few inches taller than she did, which put him at about five eleven. He wore his dark hair to his shoulders, shaggy and unkempt, though not hanging in his eyes. Greenish-gray eyes, clear and bright, not at all like Ilya's, which were a darker, greenish brown. And Nikolai's body, Alicia thought a little guiltily, letting herself remember it as she sat back in her chair to spin around with her eyes closed. Thinking of those hard arms, chest . . . his thighs—damn, they were like tree trunks. Nikolai felt like he'd been carved out of stone.

She couldn't name the cologne he wore, but the scent lingered in her memory. Something fresh. Clean, not overbearing. Like she could bury her face against his neck and breathe him in and in and in . . .

"Umm, Allie?"

With a small shriek, she stopped spinning in her chair and slapped her hands on the desk to bring herself to a stop. Her throat dried at the sight of her brother-in-law—former, she reminded herself. Her *former* brother-in-law.

"Nikolai. Hey. Is everything all right?" She coughed lightly into her fist, certain her sexy musings were shining right out of her eyes all over him. She lifted her chin and kept her expression neutral, pushing away anything remotely resembling a naughty fantasy about Nikolai. Because that was—no way—going to keep happening. Ever. No matter how his biceps bulged and flexed or how hard his body was . . .

"Yeah." He gave her a curious look and held up a six-pack of beer from the local craft brewery and a pizza box. "I thought you might want some dinner. I called your cell, but you didn't answer."

She looked at the clock, surprised to see how late it had gotten. She put a hand on her stomach, which let out an oddly convenient growl, and checked her phone. "I had the ringer off when we were in Babulya's room and forgot to turn it back on. How's she doing?"

"She perked up just after you left. They gave her some IV fluids, said she was a little dehydrated, but she was coherent. She was happy to see Theresa." Nikolai paused to put the pizza on the desk. "Crazy about her showing up, huh? I haven't seen her in years."

"We're friends on Connex, so I keep in touch with her now and again. I figured she'd want to know what was going on. Oh, God, you got anchovies? Nobody likes anchovies on their pizza!" Grinning, she looked up at him, surprised and touched that he'd remembered. "Other than you and me."

His slow smile matched hers, and for a moment they stared at each other. The tick of the clock became very loud in the silence. This was Nikolai, Alicia told herself.

Anythink Huron Street

9417 Huron Street
Thornton, CO 80260
303-452-7534
Mon-Thu 9:30 am-8:30 pm
Fri-Sat 9:30 am-5:30 pm

Date: 6/10/2019 Time: [illegible]:41:14 PM

Items checked out this session: 1

Title: All the lies we tell : a novel /
Barcode: 33021029240303
Due Date: 07/01/19

Page 1 of 1

... where anything is possible.

He only wants you because you remind him of your sister, and you'll never be able to take her place.

Damn, the memory of his words still hurt. Fierce and pointed. He'd always known just how and where to sting her.

"There are paper plates in the cupboard there." She pointed. Her voice had come out hard and cold; the grin vanished.

Nikolai shot her a glance over his shoulder. "Ilya went home. Said he was going to crash for a few hours, then head back tomorrow morning unless something happened overnight. I told him I'd be back at the house later. Figured I'd see if you were still working, since obviously he's not."

"Thanks. I'm starving." She lifted a greasy, dripping slice from the box and settled it onto one of the plates he handed her. Then another for herself. Watching him take the empty chair across from the desk, Alicia leaned back in hers. "Fox's still makes the best all around."

Nikolai bit into the gooey cheese with a sigh of bliss. He chewed, swallowed. Wiped his mouth like a grown-up, not a caveman. "I've dreamed about Fox's pizza. I mean, literally dreamed."

"Get out of here." She laughed, not easily but genuinely.

"It's the truth. You can't find American pizza like this in Israel. And when I was in Antarctica, I craved pizza like you wouldn't believe. Thick slices, greasy cheese, the salty anchovies . . ." He shivered with pleasure and took another slice. His tongue swiped along his lips as grease slipped over his sculpted chin and down his throat.

Mesmerized, Alicia watched the slow, glistening trickle move over his skin. How would that taste, to lick it away? He'd caught her staring. She covered it up by leaning over the desk to grab a beer.

When she looked up, she'd caught *him* staring.

"You look good without my brother's ring on your hand."

Heat rushed so fiercely up the column of her throat and into her cheeks that she swore she was about to burst into flames. She opened her mouth to castigate him, to really let it fly.

Every part of her tensed at his expression.

Narrowed eyes, slightly parted lips. Intensity in his gaze that had nothing to do with disapproval or lacking or anything but everything to do with pure, raw male appreciation. It wasn't the first time she'd had a guy look at her that way, but it had been a long, long time since any guy's look had made Alicia *feel* this way.

What was that old saying about keeping your enemies close? She wasn't sure she could call Nikolai an enemy, exactly. But all at once, keeping him close had become very appealing.

Still, there was that small and stubborn part of her that remembered how vocal he'd been about his disapproval when she and Ilya had announced they'd run off to Vegas and eloped. Looking back, she'd known as well as anyone—better, even—that she and Ilya had made a mistake, but you couldn't have made her admit that. Not at nineteen. Barely at twenty-nine, when at last she'd left him after one too many nights staring up at the ceiling wondering how she could spend the rest of her life being so miserable.

Based on her reaction to Nikolai's look, she seemed on the verge of making a brand-new mistake. A bigger one, this time. You'd think she'd have learned her lesson the hard way from Stern brother number one.

She drank some beer to cool herself down. "Well, I don't know if that's something to say thank you for. But thanks."

"It was meant as a compliment, but I sounded like a dick. Sorry." Nikolai grimaced, then grabbed his own beer and took a long swig. "I'll blame my lack of social skills on all the time I've spent alone in the wilderness, if you believe that story."

"I can tell you, being alone in the wilderness has nothing to do with why you're still such a colossal doofus."

It was easier after that. Less awkward, anyway. It wasn't that she forgot, exactly, that Nikolai had turned into the sort of guy who could turn her head so fast it gave her whiplash. It was more like she was forcing herself to remember to look past the arms, the thighs, the chest, the abs—oh, Lord, the abs. Rippling, rimmed ridges of delicious muscle she glimpsed when his shirt rode up as he stretched while regaling her with a tale of his adventures on a kibbutz in Israel.

She forced herself to remember him as the guy who'd made her feel like she was somehow lacking in comparison to her sister. That she hadn't been enough for his brother.

And there it was, she thought, watching Nikolai tip back in his chair and lift the bottle of beer to his lips. The real reason she'd been so angry at him for so long. All he'd done was reinforce the feelings she'd been pretending she'd gotten over. Hell, the ones she wanted to pretend she never had.

"You were right," she said quietly.

He'd been telling her about working in the kibbutz's apiary, taking care of dozens of hives and harvesting gallons of honey. Now Nikolai stopped, looking her over.

"About?" he asked.

"Me and Ilya." She didn't say the rest, but his expression told her he understood.

"Oh. That." He looked uncomfortable and scrubbed a hand through his hair, pushing it off his face. "I was a dick then, too. I thought we'd established that already."

"You were still right. You were the only one to say so out loud, though. That's why we fought." Alicia laughed ruefully and shook her head. "I was so furious with you."

"You and I always fought," Niko said. "We were constantly at each other. It was kind of the way we worked, I guess."

She nodded, thinking of all the insults and teasing. "This was different, though. What you said hurt so bad. That somehow I wasn't as good as Jennilynn—"

"Wait, what? No. No, Allie." Nikolai wiped a hand over his mouth and looked stunned. "That's not what I meant at all."

"It's what you *said*," she told him.

He shook his head. "It's not what I meant. When I said you'd never take her place, I didn't mean because you weren't good enough. I meant that my brother wasn't capable of giving you the relationship you needed or deserved. You weren't your sister. She might've put up with his bullshit and been satisfied with it."

Alicia swallowed a weakly bitter taste. "We won't ever know."

"No. We won't. But dammit, I'm so damned sorry if you thought back then I meant that somehow you weren't as good as she was. I never meant that. How could you ever have thought it? God, no wonder you haven't talked to me in years. What the hell must you have thought about me?"

The truth was, no matter how often she'd found herself thinking of him and what might have been, she'd always pushed those thoughts away so fiercely there'd been only one way to remember him at all.

"I thought you were a know-it-all jerk," Alicia admitted, certain he'd frown.

Nikolai smiled. "I thought *you* were smart and beautiful and amazing, and it made me nuts that you were with him, when he so clearly didn't deserve you."

Silence, a beat of it. Then another. The clock ticked, and so did her heart. She smiled.

"Maybe," she said, "we can get over all that crap and put it behind us. Be friends."

Nikolai leaned over the desk to offer her his hand. "It's a deal."

CHAPTER SEVEN

Then

Babulya and Galina were fighting again.

Dinner had been a disaster, with Galina leaving the table to go out back for a smoke and Babulya clattering pots and pans and slapping plates of food on the table before leaving the room without eating anything. Ilya didn't seemed to care. He shoveled his mouth full of food while he read some comics, ignoring everything around him. Niko wasn't able to eat, though. Too much tension. It left him with a sour stomach.

The women had always gone at each other, Babulya with her muttered, under-the-breath criticisms and her daughter with her too-loud defenses. Sniping and griping. It had been better when Barry and Theresa lived here, because Barry seemed to keep Galina in check, at least a little. Of course, that had gone tits up years ago. Niko had come home from school to find Barry's and Theresa's stuff moved out; their names had become persona non grata.

His mother hadn't said much about it, only that it wasn't working out, and that she and Barry would be getting a divorce. No counseling, no trial separation. Definitely no reconciliation. You didn't dare mention Barry or Theresa now, either, not unless you wanted Galina to totally lose her shit, which is what happened tonight when Babulya had made an offhanded comment about her daughter finding herself a new husband that she could toss aside after only a few months.

They were at it again by the time Ilya got home from work, and something about this set Galina into another rage. Something about doing his own laundry. Paying rent.

"Niko doesn't pay a damned cent," Ilya shouted, loud enough for Niko to hear him all the way upstairs. "If I'm going to pay, he better pay, too!"

Niko couldn't even be pissed off that his brother was throwing him under the bus. Three weeks past his high school graduation, Niko was already bored and tired of his job at the car wash. He'd quit two days ago. Hadn't told his mother yet. Not sure he planned to.

But Ilya knew. "Of course he's not going to be able to pay a damned thing without a job."

Niko groaned, wishing he hadn't told his brother about quitting. Things had been kind of messed up between them since Jennilynn died. It had been over a year, and Niko had started to think it was never going back to the way it was before. Nothing would. Across the street, the Harrisons functioned like a broken music box, playing a song that missed all the important notes. He'd hardly spoken to Allie since the night of the funeral and what happened between them. He wanted to, but he didn't know what to say.

Now he lay in bed and listened to the sound of his mother's screaming drifting up through the vents, and he turned to press his face deep into the pillow. He didn't want to hear her. He didn't want to worry about her. Didn't want to think about his brother, or Allie, or anything else about this place.

At the sound of breaking glass he went downstairs, expecting to find someone bleeding. Ilya was gone. Babulya was locked inside her bedroom with the music turned up high so she could pretend she hadn't heard anything. Niko found his mother on her hands and knees in the kitchen, weeping over a broken glass vase.

"This was a wedding present," she sobbed.

"Mom, get up. I'll clean that." He bent to help her up, thinking he might catch a whiff of alcohol on her, but she didn't seem to have been drinking. It might be easier if she was, he thought. She might be more predictable.

Still sobbing, Galina sagged against him. Her fingers clutched at the front of his shirt. Her breath stank, sour and stale. Snot bubbled in one nostril.

"Promise me, Kolya. Promise me you won't leave me."

Unsettled by her use of his grandmother's affectionate nickname for him, and more so by this demand, Niko put her in a chair and moved away to get the broom and dustpan. He cleaned up the glass, too aware of her staring and weeping behind him.

"They all leave me," she said.

He turned to dump the glass carefully into a paper bag that he would later take out to the trash. "Why don't you go to bed or something."

From behind him came a sound like rusted gears trying hard to move. A ratcheting, awful noise. He spun to see his mother's fingernails raking lines in the varnish of the kitchen table. She was no longer crying. Her eyes had gone wide, her mouth gaping.

"Go to bed. You're acting crazy." Niko put the broom and dustpan away. Sick of this shit. Done with it. Done with her—and this house and his brother being a constant dick to him.

"Don't you dare talk to me like that!"

Then, his mother began shrieking, wailing, flying at him with her fists and nails, and Ilya came through the back door to haul her off him, and Niko touched the place on his face where she scratched him.

There was blood, after all, but not from the broken glass.

He was gone by the next morning, taking only a duffel bag and the small amount of money from his savings account. First a bus. Then a night or two at the YMCA. He considered joining the military but saw a sign at the local Reform synagogue, a place he'd never been inside, although he knew Babulya was Jewish.

Heritage Trip

The rabbi was more understanding than Nikolai deserved, considering he lied through his teeth to get the guy to put him on that plane. Yes, he'd always wanted to visit the Holy Land and find his roots. Yes, he intended to become more observant in the ways of his ancestors. Yes, yes, he would gladly come back and volunteer with the synagogue youth group.

All of it was lies, but it got him out of Quarrytown. He regretted only one thing: that he left without saying good-bye to Allie.

CHAPTER EIGHT

Theresa had changed.

The gangly, awkward girl with braces who Ilya remembered torturing with scary stories had become a poised, voluptuous woman, whose dark hair hung in thick ringlets halfway down her back. When she smiled at him, the years of orthodontia proved well worthwhile. She wasn't smiling at him right now. She looked confused or concerned, or maybe amused. He couldn't tell, because there currently seemed to be two of her, neither of them quite clear.

"Hey," he said. "'Sup?"

"You're drunk." She shook her head and stepped inside the front door, closing it behind her.

"A little." He'd had three or four beers, then lost track. He moved aside so she could bustle past him and into the kitchen, where she set the reusable grocery bags on the table. "Just a little."

"What if you have to drive to the home?" she demanded, turning with a frown he could definitely see.

"I'll call Allie. She'll drive me. She lives across the street still. Right over there, where she always lived, except when she lived over here. Hey, *you* used to live here."

"I did."

He blinked, trying to focus. "Why are you here right now?"

"I brought food. It's what you do when someone's sick." Theresa paused to look him over. "You look like shit, Ilya. When's the last time you ate something? Or slept?"

It had been a rough few days; that was for sure. Learning that Babulya was failing had hit him hard. Hearing that his mother was on her way back to Quarrytown had been worse.

"Galina's coming home," he said by way of explanation.

Theresa nodded. "Ah. Well, I'd expect her to. Her mother's dying."

He didn't want to think about that. Ilya peeked into the grocery bags, then at her. "Lots of salad in there."

She laughed. "It wouldn't kill you to eat a vegetable or two. Isn't that what Babulya always said?"

"Eat some things green," Ilya said, imitating Babulya's Russian accent, and laughed.

Then all at once, he wasn't laughing anymore. He wasn't sure he was crying, but the world was blurring. Maybe spinning. He sat heavily in the chair and put his head in his hands.

Theresa's hands came to rest firmly on his shoulders. "It's hard, I know."

She couldn't possibly know. He shook his head without looking at her. "I don't want to talk about it right now."

"It's going to be okay, Ilya."

Nothing much had been okay for a long time. He could say it was because of the divorce, but that wasn't true. He missed being married to Allie when he tried hard to make himself wish he'd been a better husband, but truth was he *didn't* miss being with her for all the reasons he'd been such a shitty spouse.

"No." The word blurted out of him before he could stop it, and the pound of his fist on the table startled them both. "Everything's going to shit. Nothing sticks. I've been trying to make it all work, and it's not working. Couldn't keep a marriage, can't keep my business running . . ."

"Marriages end," she said. "Seems to me you're civil enough to keep working together, which says something, anyway."

"Sure, sure, we work together until Go Deep goes so deep it goes under." He tossed his hands in the air, thinking of the piles of bills, the dwindling number of students, the dip in the economy that had made the dive trips too much of a luxury to be a sure thing.

"What's the matter with Go Deep?"

Ilya shook his head. "Never mind. I don't want to talk about that, either."

Theresa squeezed his shoulders, then stepped away from him. "You should have some water and something to eat. You drank too much."

"So what if I did? That doesn't make anything less . . . true . . ." He thumped the table again but had run out of steam. "What do you know about it? What the hell problems do you have in *your* life?"

He peered at her, knowing he was poking hard but not seeing anything but blandness on her face. Not seeing much of anything. The world still blurred. He blinked, hard.

"Not a single problem," Theresa said as she shifted into focus. "My life is just perfect. I couldn't ask for a better life. Everything's peachy keen."

"Must be nice."

Theresa moved around the kitchen as easily as if she'd been there last week to empty the dishwasher instead of half a lifetime ago. She filled a glass of water from the tap and put it in front of him. "Drink this."

He half turned away, feeling the chair threatening to slip out from under him. Or no, that was just his body threatening to fall off it. He caught himself. Clearly, he wasn't drunk enough. "I'll have another beer."

"Drink that first," Theresa said firmly, and to his own surprise, Ilya did. "When is your mother going to get here?"

"Who knows? She said she's driving up from South Carolina. It could take her days. It could take her a month. She could be here tomorrow, for all I know. Maybe she's hitching a ride with a long-haul trucker. Maybe she's coming on a broom." Ilya shrugged. His mother's arrival was like a colonoscopy. He knew it had to happen, but he hoped he could be mostly unconscious when it did.

Theresa laughed and glanced at him over her shoulder from her place in front of the fridge, where she'd started putting away the groceries she'd brought in. "She hasn't changed, huh?"

No. His mother hadn't changed. That was the problem with Galina; she never did. She called him up every few months and casually asked him for money, or she didn't ask for money but kept him on the phone for an hour, spinning stories about her fantastic life, or she ranted about the alleged indignities she was suffering at the hands of whoever it was she'd decided was out to get her. Sometimes she threatened to come back to Pennsylvania, but this was the first time he believed she would.

He scowled. "She hasn't changed. Most people don't."

Theresa had once slept in the room next to his, back when their parents had decided they were in love and couldn't live without each other. That hadn't lasted long. Love never did. She tilted her head, looking him over. Or maybe he was leaning in his chair again; he couldn't be sure.

"Oh, I don't know about that." Theresa put her hands on her hips. "I think it's possible."

Ilya rubbed at his eyes against the burn from lack of sleep. His stomach churned. He brought his thumb to his mouth, chewing for a second before remembering the bitter taste of the liquid Babulya had put on his nails to keep him from biting them. He curled his fingers into his palm, making a fist and cutting into his skin with the nails that had grown long enough to leave marks.

He found his voice. "Thanks for coming. It was a surprise."

"I'm glad to be here." She paused. "Let me make you something to eat, at least."

He didn't want to eat. "Nah. I should just go to bed."

"I'm starving, and you'll be sorry if you go to bed without something in your stomach. I'll make grilled cheese." She was already looking in the cupboard for a frying pan. She glanced at him over her shoulder. "You want tomato on yours?"

"I don't have any tomatoes."

She laughed and twisted that mass of thick curling hair on top of her head in a messy bun. When she tucked a few stray tendrils behind one ear, he wondered what it would be like to touch it. Silky, he thought. Her hair would smell good.

She eyed him with a small smile and another of those curious head tilts. "I brought some. Drink the water."

The beers he'd shotgunned earlier were settling. He still felt buzzy, woozy, warm, but it was becoming easier to focus. Not quite as easy to walk, but he made it to the sink and drew another glass of tepid water from the tap. He didn't want to drink it, but he did while he watched her pull out the ancient cutting board and begin to slice the tomatoes.

"Babulya always used to put tomatoes on the grilled cheese." Ilya closed his eyes for a few seconds longer than a blink. When he opened them, she was staring.

Theresa's hand slowed for a second as she put down the knife. "I know. She's the one who taught me how to cook. I'd never had grilled cheese made that way until I moved in here. It's how I've made them ever since."

The food was ready in a few minutes, and she slid plates across the table with a gesture for him to sit. He hadn't been sure he wanted food, but once he took the first bite, his appetite roared, and he gobbled everything on the plate; then he went to the stove for another sandwich. She'd made extra, like she knew he'd want more.

"Will you be back tomorrow?" he asked, once he'd returned to the table.

Theresa wiped her mouth with a paper napkin. "I'd like to see her again. The nurse there told me they thought she didn't have much longer."

"Are you going to go all the way home?" He realized he wasn't sure where home was for her. For all he knew, she'd moved back to Quarrytown years ago, and they'd merely been missing sightings of each other. It was a small town, though. That didn't seem likely.

"I thought I'd find a cheap hotel room close to the home . . . crash there. I have some work to do in the area, too."

He also had no idea what Theresa did for a living, but despite the belly full of carbs and fat, he was still a little too hammered to figure out how to ask her without sounding like an idiot of the highest order. "There aren't any hotels close to the home. They were talking about putting in a business-suite-type place nearby, but it never happened. You can stay here if you want. Your old room. It hasn't changed much, if you want to know the truth. Galina made it into a sewing room after you and your dad left—"

"We didn't leave," Theresa said sharply. "She threw us out."

Ilya didn't say anything at first. His brain was still fuzzy at the moment—his memories faded even without the booze—but that had not been the way he'd heard the story. "Galina threw you out?"

"Yeah. She wanted to split up from my dad, so she told him we had three hours to pack our stuff and get out." She tilted her head to look at him. "You didn't know."

He should have. It was exactly the sort of thing his mother would have done and turned around later so she could make herself look like the victim. He frowned, heat tickling his throat with embarrassment. "No."

Theresa shook her head. "That was your mom, through and through. Anyway, I can get a hotel room. Don't worry about it."

Ilya knew he had his moments, but he'd never in his life been the kind of class-A bitch his mother could be. He wasn't going to be one now. Ilya stood on wobbly legs. This seemed important. Really important.

"Shit, no, you stay here. She threw you out? You should stay here, in your old room. Yeah."

"I don't have to—"

It wasn't going to make anything right, but he was so damned tired of everything being wrong. He shook his head and took her by the shoulders. "You lived here. This was your house—hell, it's too big and empty with just me in it, anyway. You stay here."

Theresa looked amused. "Okay. For tonight, anyway. In case . . . well. In case you need a ride."

From the kitchen doorway came the scuffle of feet. "What's up?"

Ilya and Theresa both turned to see Niko. Ilya greeted his brother with a clap on the shoulder and a chest bump. Niko looked past him at their former stepsister.

Ilya gestured. "I told Theresa she could stay here in the house, so she can be here when . . . well, she can be here for Babulya. I don't give a damn what Galina says."

Niko's brow furrowed. "Why would she say anything? Oh, shit, she's coming home? I mean, of course she is. When did you talk to her?"

"She left a voicemail. Yeah, she's coming. Sometime. I guess whenever she gets here." Ilya shrugged.

Niko looked confused. "Did Mom say Theresa couldn't stay here? Why?"

"Ilya, you should drink some more water," Theresa put in. "Niko, do you want something to eat?"

"Drunk?" Niko asked her.

Ilya waved them both away. "I'm fine. Theresa says she threw them out, her and her dad. Did you know that?"

Niko looked uncomfortable and embarrassed, the way Ilya had felt when Theresa told him the truth about what had happened. The way he'd often felt over the years when he'd discovered his mother had been untruthful about one thing or another. It should have stopped being a surprise but somehow never did.

"I didn't," Niko said. "She told us they left. She cried about it, remember?"

"She lied," Ilya said. "She lies all the time."

"I'm sorry, Theresa," Niko said. "You should definitely stay here if you want."

Theresa looked from one of them to the other, before her gaze settled on Ilya. "It wasn't your fault, either of you. It was our parents' business, anyway. Not ours. And it was a long time ago. I saw some ice cream in the freezer. Anyone want some?"

CHAPTER NINE

Back in Niko's adolescent bedroom, daylight cracked through the attic's twin narrow windows in pale-golden stripes, exactly as it had done for all the years he'd lived there. The house was so quiet he couldn't tell whether he was alone or whether Ilya and Theresa were still asleep, but he made sure not to make a lot of noise, anyway, when he went to the kitchen.

Someone had already been up. A plate of scrambled eggs covered in cheese, still warm, tempted him, and he noticed a stack of toast on a plate next to the toaster. He buttered some and made an egg sandwich, then took it into the living room to turn on the television. He didn't have one at the kibbutz, and although there was a communal one, he hadn't mindlessly watched anything stupid in a long time.

"The cable doesn't work." A low, husky voice came from the corner of the kitchen. "I guess your brother didn't pay the bill on time."

Nikolai had talked to his mother but hadn't seen her in close to eight years. She had some silver in her hair and a few more lines around her eyes, but the persona . . . that hadn't changed. Never would, as far as Nikolai was concerned—not unless she had a reason to become someone different, and why would she? Who she was had worked so well for her, all these years.

"Mom. Hi." Awkwardly, Niko hugged his mother while trying not to drop the egg sandwich. It was a familiar feeling—most interactions with his mother felt like he was performing a strange sort of dance while struggling not to break something. "When did you get in?"

"About half an hour ago. I went first to see Babulya at the home, but she was sleeping. They said I could visit her later. But I suppose that's good, yes? Means she's not actively dying anymore. But what do I know? I only took care of people who'd gone under the knife. If I wanted to understand geriatric medicine, I'd have gone to work in a nursing home."

He kept himself from flinching at the harshness of her words, a habit that hadn't changed no matter how long it had been since he'd seen her.

"Come close to me. Give your mother a hug." She opened her arms. Galina had never even visited Russia, but her own voice had always echoed Babulya's. Turns of phrases, some pronunciations. She sounded like her mother now, but Nikolai knew she was putting it on like she would have tried on a hat.

Despite this, obediently he went. Also an old habit. She smelled the same. Cigarettes, an undertone of cloying perfume, the mints she ate constantly to cover up the smell of smoker's breath. She felt smaller, though. More delicate. The bones of her shoulder blades jutted, sharp under his touch.

"Good, you found the food. I got here so early, but you weren't awake yet. I thought I'd surprise you with breakfast."

"Well, that's sure different, isn't it?" The words came out of him before he knew it but, once spoken, couldn't be taken back.

His mother shrugged and took a seat on the couch, tucking her feet beneath her. "So I wasn't there to make you breakfast before you went to school, the way Sally Harrison was. I worked, Nikolai. I had to work to support you and your brother. This is an old discussion, isn't it? Surely you're too old now to hold on to those resentments anymore."

His mother had done her share of twelve-step programs, of meditation, of meetings and assessments, and of making amends. She'd disappeared more than once to "communes" and had done a stint or two in both in- and outpatient mental-health facilities. Nikolai had never believed she was crazy, but she'd used it as an excuse for bad behavior more than once.

"Yeah. Sorry. It's good to see you." He bit into the sandwich, chewing quickly as he sat in the chair opposite her.

"You've grown so handsome. Such a handsome man. You look a lot like your father. Ilya, he's your Babulya all through, but I thought you favored me, at least when you were a little boy. But now I see your father in you." She shook a finger at him, but smiled. "He was a handsome man, too."

Steven Stern had died in a car accident when Galina was pregnant with Niko. He'd seen pictures of his father but had never thought there was much of a resemblance. It wasn't worth an argument, though.

With a sigh, Galina waved the remote and turned off the TV. "Nothing. Good eggs?"

"Yeah. Great." His stomach had stopped protesting.

"Next time, I'll have potatoes to make for the hash browns. Delicious for breakfast. Onions, garlic, the works."

"Where did you learn to cook like this?" He licked a smear of butter from his fingers.

His mother waved the remote again. "I learned how to make them at the diner."

"When did you work at a diner?" Niko asked, wary and aware of Galina's propensity for telling stories that weren't always true.

"Since last year." She tossed the remote onto the coffee table.

He'd thought she would say the job had been from her youth, but this revelation totally stumped him. "You're not working as an RN anymore?"

She looked up from fixing the stack of magazines that had gone askew when she hit them with the remote. "I lost my job at the hospital when they were bought out by another larger one and merged. They moved all the day-surgery patients to the other location. I didn't want to work that far away. I would have needed a car."

"Mom . . . what happened to your car?" Nikolai studied her, but her expression gave away nothing.

Galina stacked the magazines precisely, tapping the top of the pile before sitting back on the couch with a satisfied smile. "I didn't need a car when I could walk to work. And I didn't have my license anymore. So why have a car? It's just an expense I don't need. Upkeep, gas, the insurance. Too much."

"Why did you lose your license?" This had all the telltale signs of a typical Galina misadventure.

She gave him a long, steady look. "I didn't *lose* it. I just forgot to renew it, so it lapsed, and by the time I realized it, I didn't feel like going through all the hoops to get it back, when I didn't need it."

"But . . . you drove here," he pointed out.

Galina shrugged. "Borrowed the car from a friend."

His mother had always had her share of "friends." Nikolai didn't ask any more questions. The less he knew, the better.

"Well . . . thanks for breakfast."

She got up to ruffle his hair exactly as she'd done when he was a kid. "Too skinny. You don't eat enough. Too much time spent in the desert. Not enough time spent with a woman. Unless there is a girl? Oh, is there a nice Jewish girl, ready to make you a dozen babies?"

"Mom. Please." Nikolai made a face. It wasn't any more fun to have his mother quizzing him about his love life now than it had been when he was a teenager. There'd been women, of course. Nobody for a while. Nobody permanent.

"At least your brother, he got married. No babies." She frowned. "I'd be a wonderful grandmother, you know. If either of you gave me the chance. And your Babulya, she would love to have more babies to love. You should think about it, before she's gone."

This, coming from the woman who'd told both her sons that if they knocked up any girls, they'd better run away from home, because she wasn't going to take care of any bastards. Maybe the fact Niko had actually run away from home without getting anyone pregnant had changed her mind. Maybe time had mellowed her. Maybe she was just being Galina.

"Sorry, but I don't plan on having kids anytime soon. Maybe never."

Galina put a hand over her heart and shook her head, closing her eyes with a frown. She didn't say anything out loud. She didn't have to.

"Morning."

Both Galina and Niko turned to see Theresa, tousle-haired and wearing a pair of sleep pants emblazoned with cartoon characters that Nikolai didn't recognize. She yawned and gave Galina a small wave with her fingers half-curled. Galina let out a small, surprised laugh.

"Theresa? My God, it's you! Look at you. You're a woman."

The women embraced—Galina wholeheartedly. Theresa hung back, throwing Niko a look over his mother's shoulder. He understood her hesitance—there was history there, for sure. He had a bunch of his own.

"What are you doing here?" Galina asked.

"I came when I heard Babulya wasn't doing well." Theresa sat.

Galina waved a hand. "Of course you did. Everyone loved my mother, didn't they? Even the ones who barely knew her."

"I wouldn't say I barely knew her," Theresa replied evenly.

Galina laughed and put a delicate hand to her forehead. "Oh. Foolish of me. I'm sorry. Of course you did. I just had a moment."

"Don't worry about it." Theresa gave Niko a shrug and crossed her arms over her belly.

"I'm going outside for a smoke," Galina said abruptly and left the living room.

Theresa waited until the sound of the back door had clicked shut before she spoke. "Okay, then."

"Did you sleep all right?" Niko asked.

She laughed softly. "Yeah. But I woke up in the night to use the bathroom and forgot I wasn't in my old room, so I miscounted the doors and almost peed in the linen closet. How weird is that?"

"Not the weirdest thing that ever happened in the linen closet, probably," Niko said dryly.

"What's going on? Who's peeing in weird places? Did I miss the party?" Ilya padded into the living room in a pair of faded plaid boxers and nothing else. Saggy boxers, at that.

Niko grimaced. "Dude. Cover that shit up. Nobody needs to see your balls hanging out this early in the morning."

Theresa snorted laughter behind her hand. She covered her eyes with the other. "Agreed. Get a robe or something!"

Ilya turned, wiggling his ass at the pair of them, much the way he'd done when they were younger. "What? This? What's wrong with this? You got a problem?"

"Gross," Theresa said matter-of-factly.

For a moment, it was so much the way it had been during that brief year and a half when they'd all been a family that nostalgia washed over Niko in a rush, almost making him dizzy. If he closed his eyes, he could be sixteen again, just learning how to shave and figure out girls. Before everything had started to change.

A rap on the front door got him to his feet, though it was already opening before he could get to it. More nostalgia when he saw who it was—Allie letting herself in the way she always had when they were kids, running back and forth between their two houses. She'd lived in this house for a time, he reminded himself, watching her.

When she'd been married to his brother.

The house phone rang, distracting him before he could do more than wave a greeting. Yesterday it felt like he and Allie had made a peace of sorts, and he was glad of that. They weren't kids anymore, and it was stupid of them to hold on to any sort of old grudges. Plus, he felt terrible that she believed he'd ever thought she couldn't measure up to her sister.

"Oh. Okay, thanks." Ilya said into the receiver and settled the phone back into its cradle. He didn't move after that but put one hand on the wall, near the pad of paper with the pencil attached to it by a long piece of string—probably the same pencil that had been there for years. The end of it was bitten, teeth marks clear in the yellow wood.

Alicia had looked like she was ready to say something to Niko, but at the sound of Ilya's voice, she turned toward him instead. "Bad news? It's Babulya? Has she taken a turn for the worse?"

Ilya faced them, expression calm. Nothing much on his face at all, as a matter of fact. He barely even blinked when Galina came in through the back door from the yard.

"She's dead."

CHAPTER TEN

Then

Theresa heard her father's voice rising, rising, and he slammed the phone back into the cradle with enough force to send the pencil beneath it swinging hard against the wall. Turning, he caught sight of her standing in the hallway. It was her father there, for sure, but in that moment he wore a stranger's face.

"What?" Galina came in from the back door, the faint waft of smoke still clinging to her. "Barry, what's going on?"

He shook his head and jerked his chin toward Theresa, who only wanted to get a drink from the kitchen sink. "Not now."

She would never figure out what he thought he could do by keeping the news from her, but it didn't matter because Ilya burst in through the front door, screaming for his mother. Babulya shouted at him not to yell. Barry, who'd always butted heads with Galina's oldest son, also tried shouting at him, but Ilya ignored them both, stumbling across the kitchen floor toward his grandmother. He nearly knocked her over with the force of his sudden embrace.

"Slow down, slow down," Babulya said, trying to get him to make sense, but in the babble of words, all Theresa could make out was a name.

Jenni.

Jennilynn had been missing for the past two days. Nobody said it, but Theresa thought most everyone believed she'd run off with one of those older guys she'd been hanging around with. It was what Theresa thought, anyway.

"Go to your room, Theresa," her father commanded.

Barry tried to wrestle Ilya off his grandmother, who was trying to calm him, but Ilya fought them both. It was a huge, loud tangle of arms and legs and shouting. Theresa couldn't move, frozen in place, her stomach churning. Something had gone very, very wrong. All she could do was watch as Ilya hauled off and took a swing at her dad, who stepped out of the way without the punch landing. Galina moved in next, grabbing at his shirt, but Ilya wrenched himself from her grip.

Gentle hands and a murmured voice led Theresa away. Babulya sat her in the living room and patted her shoulder, leaning down to look into her face to reassure her that everything was going to be all right. From the kitchen came the sound of breaking glass. Then silence.

"They found Jennilynn." Babulya's fingers squeezed Theresa's shoulder.

Theresa found her voice. "Where is she?"

"She was in quarry." Babulya's eyes were bright with tears. She frowned and shook her head, closing her eyes for a moment before looking again at Theresa. "She is gone."

CHAPTER ELEVEN

Alicia balanced a pan of ravioli and a tuna-noodle casserole against her chest while she tried to open her front door. Food, so much food. Ilya's kitchen table had groaned with it, and his fridge had been packed to overflowing, the freezer in the garage stuffed full. That's what people did when you lost someone: they brought food. Babulya had been well loved in the community.

The service had been nice. Alicia had spent a few hours across the street, but too many people had turned to her to act as hostess for a house that was no longer hers. On the day they buried a woman who'd treated her like family, Alicia did not *want* to be irritated by anyone treating her like she was still Ilya's wife, but there it was. That niggling, burning annoyance at the number of people who'd asked her where to find the paper plates or plasticware. Or the trash bags when they were being helpful by emptying the garbage can, and she ought to have been grateful for their kindness.

The fact she still knew where to find everything had annoyed her, too. Hell, she'd found an old bottle of her hand lotion in the bottom drawer of the upstairs bathroom. Still half-full. She'd tossed that in the garbage and spent the next fifteen minutes trying hard not to burst into tears.

It wasn't that she wished she and Ilya were still together. It wasn't that she wished they'd never been married, either. It was that there was someone missing here today to mourn the old lady's passing.

Jennilynn's memorial service had been held in the same funeral home. People had also brought food, gathering in the Sterns' house because Alicia's mother had been laid so low with grief that she'd been incapable of hosting anyone in their house, and Babulya had insisted on doing it for her.

Jennilynn should've been here to weep and laugh with them over all the stories they'd gathered to share about Babulya. She would have hunted for extra garbage bags and accepted all the condolence hugs, but in Jenni's aching, endless absence, that duty had fallen to Alicia, and in that she had also stumbled and faltered, forever incapable of taking her sister's place.

Now back in her own house, Alicia filled her freezer with food she knew she was never going to eat. She sat down at her kitchen table. She poured herself a glass of iced tea. She checked items off a list one at a time. She moved with stiff joints—robotic—and focused on putting her efforts into action, not emotions, until finally she had no more things to distract her, and she gave herself permission to weep.

No tears came.

Instead, a deep and unsettling exhaustion settled into her with liquid and relentless ease. Filling her up from the inside, it weighted her bones. It scourged her.

Babulya had reached the end of a long and fruitful life; Jennilynn had never been given the chance. Her death colored nearly every decision Alicia had made after it happened. It had led her down the path to becoming Ilya's wife, for better or for worse, and though she couldn't bring herself to regret anything, in moments like this when she looked around at what her life had become, she couldn't remember what she'd once dreamed of having.

The knock on her back door startled her, but the sight of who'd done the knocking surprised her even more. A tendril of embarrassment at being caught in such a melancholy moment twisted inside her. It might've been anyone, but of course it was *him*.

"Hey, sorry to bother you. I brought . . ." Nikolai lifted the casserole in his hands as though in apology. "We didn't have room for this, either. Sorry."

"No, don't be. C'mon in." She stood aside, too aware of his warmth as he pushed past her. "You can see if there's any room in the freezer."

Nikolai fit the casserole into the freezer and closed it. Turned to her. They stared at each other.

What might she have done with herself had her sister not died?

What might any of them have done?

"I had to get out of there," she said quietly.

Nikolai scrubbed a hand over the top of his head and gave her a sideways glance. "Yeah. Me, too. I probably could've managed to find a place for that casserole over there somewhere. I really just wanted to get out of the house. I wanted to come over here."

"It's quieter here."

"You're here," he said abruptly, then stopped.

Slowly, slowly, something twisted and tangled between them.

Did she move? Did he? All Alicia knew was that she was in his arms. The chair she'd been sitting on got knocked over because it had been between them.

Nikolai's hands were in her hair.

His mouth was on her mouth.

His tongue, oh God, his tongue was sweeping inside with practiced strokes that drew a moan out of her from the very tips of her toes. He shook a little at the sound of it; she noticed that. Also the way his fingers dug deeper into the fall of her hair to tug her head back a little so he could plunder her mouth just a little harder. A little deeper.

She wasn't sure who'd started the kiss, but she was sure who ended it. With a short, sharp gasp, Alicia stepped backward. One step. She was still within reach, if he wanted to grab her, and oh, shit, oh, damn, did she want him to?

The answer, she discovered when she looked at his wet, open mouth, was yes.

The second kiss was softer. Lingering. His hands moved to her hips and settled there, drawing her closer so their bodies pressed against each other. There was no bumping of noses or clashing of teeth. He moved, and she moved with him, in perfect sync.

Both breathing hard, they let the kiss ease away at the same time. She didn't move out of his embrace this time. She looked up into his face.

"But you . . . you don't even like me," she said.

Nikolai smiled in the same lopsided, smart-ass way he always had. "I think it's pretty obvious, Allie. I do like you. At least a little."

"Maybe more than a little bit," she whispered, but when she moved to kiss him again, Nikolai turned his face away just enough to stop her.

"Right." Alicia cleared her throat. Awkward.

"It's been a long day. A long week," Nikolai added. "We're both tired."

She nodded and took a couple of steps back. "Yeah. Sure. We wouldn't want to do anything stupid."

They stared at each other again. His eyes gleamed, and she felt the answering burn in her own gaze. When she licked her bottom lip, she watched the way his eyes followed the motion of her tongue.

"Allie . . ." Her name slipped out of him on a little moan.

That's how he would sound if she took him into her mouth, she thought suddenly, stupidly, something like a fever rising within her. A scorching chill swept all the way through her, and Alicia crossed her arms to keep herself from shivering. She couldn't look away from his eyes.

"I should go," he said.

She nodded again, trying to keep her voice steady when she replied. She didn't quite manage to erase the tremor. "You should go."

With another groan, this one sounding more frustrated, Nikolai ran a hand through his hair again, scrubbing at his scalp as he turned away from her to pace. He threw out his hands, gesturing, speaking without looking at her. "This is crazy."

"Totally crazy," she agreed.

"Insane," he muttered. He touched the drips of water plinking steadily out of the faucet. "You need a new washer."

"Ilya promised to fix it, but . . ." She shrugged.

"He still takes care of things for you." It sounded like an accusation.

Allie frowned. "Sometimes. Sometimes he only promises to."

"Right." Niko opened her cupboard and pulled out a glass to fill with water.

The fact he knew without hesitation where she kept her glasses sent a pang of memory through her. Oh, to go back to the days of juice boxes and bags of chips parceled out during long summer days, when their parents were all working, and Babulya had shooed them all out of the house to find whatever amusements they could. She drew in a small, hitching breath.

"You never used to knock," she said.

Nikolai tipped the water glass to his lips and gulped, then put the glass on the counter. He put his hands on it, shoulders hunched, still not looking at her. "Huh?"

"You knocked," Alicia pointed out. "You never used to. None of us did. "

He twisted his head to show her his profile. "Yeah. I remember."

"You knocked this time," she continued. "Like we were strangers."

Nikolai turned, finally. The corners of his mouth turned down. "We're not strangers. We could never be strangers."

"You think so? I don't know, Nikolai. It feels like maybe we are." She lifted her chin and closed her mouth tight to keep her lips from trembling. For what felt like the hundredth time today, she felt very, very close to tears.

Something shifted and cracked in his expression; she hated the sight of him agreeing with her, but what could she expect? That he would stride across the room and take her in his arms and kiss her breathless again? That she would take him upstairs to her bedroom and let him undress her?

Is that what she really wanted?

"No. Never strangers. Family," Nikolai said after a moment. Then, in a lower voice: "I should get back over there. Ilya's probably shitfaced by now. And Galina . . ."

"Your mother hasn't changed." Those words came more easily. Lighter. Alicia shook off the lingering heat and gave him a smile. "It's good she's here, though."

It was Nikolai's turn to answer with a nod. He headed for the back door, and Alicia noted with a mixture of amusement and dismay that he took the long way around, keeping the kitchen table between them so he didn't come close to touching her. He paused in the doorway.

"Thanks. For everything. It means a lot," he said.

Alicia gave him a grim, polite smile. "She was my grandma, too, you know."

"Right, right." Nikolai's gaze slid away from hers, and he shut the door behind him.

When he'd gone, Alicia put her hand to her mouth, feeling the place where only minutes ago his lips had pressed hers. Then the tears came, burning and hateful and repulsive, knowing that she should cry over this when she'd been unable to weep for the true loss. Still, she shook with them until she was exhausted, spent, her eyes swollen and throat raw. When her grief eased, she was able to go upstairs to sleep.

CHAPTER TWELVE

Then

This was not real. It couldn't be. Just a few days ago, Jennilynn was yelling at Alicia about wearing her favorite sweater, the new one she'd gotten for Christmas, and now she was dead.

She would never come back.

Their parents were almost comatose with grief. Her father managed to get up and around, at least enough to make some arrangements, but her mother . . . she couldn't even get out of bed. Alicia had looked in on her this morning. The room stank of sour breath and sweat and something darker underlying all that.

Her mother made it to the funeral. There was that. It would've been easier if she hadn't. If Alicia could spend the rest of her life without ever again hearing sounds like the ones that had come from her mother's throat, she would be grateful. The rasping, keening wails had made Alicia want to clap her hands over her ears. Her mother had embarrassed her with the full-on force of her unmitigated grief.

Alicia would never forget it or get over it. Never be able to look at her mother the same way, not after seeing her as a person who could shatter into such tiny shards. Alicia didn't think she could ever forgive her mother for not being able to make all this disappear, the way she'd done with nightmares and scraped knees and fevers. For becoming so lost in her own sorrow that she couldn't help anyone else with theirs.

There should've been a meal at the church catering hall, but neither of Alicia's parents had arranged it. Babulya was hosting people across the street at the Sterns'. She was cooking, and everyone else was bringing potluck. Babulya sat with Alicia's mother for a long, long time that morning and probably was the reason she was able to get out of the room at all—Alicia thought she wouldn't be able to forgive her mother for that, either. That she could rally for the sake of the neighbor, but not her own child. The one who was still left.

Babulya hadn't been able to convince Alicia's mother to go across the street, though. Her father was there for an hour or so before he came home, hollow eyed but clean shaven, his tie still tight at his throat. He disappeared into the den, where he sat in front of the television, watching game shows with the volume turned down so low he couldn't possibly hear them.

Nobody had cooked a meal in the Harrison house since the news came that Jennilynn's body had been found on the rocks in the quarry, in the spot where they'd always done their swimming. The fridge was empty. Alicia was hungry.

She didn't want to be wearing the black corduroy dress with the stupid white Peter Pan collar and cuffs, the narrow red-velvet tie at the throat. It was the only black dress she had. She wanted to slip into jeans and her Converses and a sweatshirt and dive into a bowl of corn chips and sour-cream dip and another of ice cream with hot fudge, or a greasy burger and fries. She wanted to eat herself into oblivion and then roll herself into a cocoon of blankets and sleep until all of this went away.

Instead, she wore that black dress to go across the street and fill a plate with homemade lasagna, a turkey sandwich on a deli roll, a handful of chips. People looked at her, but most murmured as she passed and didn't actually stop to talk to her. Alicia was glad for that. She didn't want to talk to anyone. She wanted to stuff her face.

Too many people downstairs. She sought the refuge of the upper floor and found the attic, which was quiet and smelled faintly of burnt candles and old sweat socks. Her plate balanced in one hand, she gripped the rail with the other as she climbed the stairs. The last thing she needed was to fall down and break her neck.

Did she know she wouldn't be alone? She hadn't seen either Ilya or Nikolai downstairs with the adults, so it made sense that at least one of them would be up here.

"Hi," she said.

Nikolai looked up from the comic book he was flipping through. He put it down. Swung his legs over the side of the bed. "Hey."

"What's wrong with him?" Alicia pointed at a snoring Ilya, curled up on the army cot beneath the eaves.

"Drunk."

"Shit." She eyed him. "You'd better put a bucket by his head, unless you want to clean up after him."

She watched as Niko pulled the garbage can from beneath the small desk and settled it by his brother's head. She made a place for herself on the folding chair, plate balanced on her lap, and stared at the food she'd piled on it. She'd been starving. Now she didn't want it.

"I can't eat this." Her voice was hollow and distant. She sounded like someone pretending to be Alicia.

Nikolai took the plate from her and put it on the desk. "You don't have to."

They stared at each other for a few long minutes. Night was falling outside, an early dark that was more because of the storm clouds that had been hanging low and threatening all day rather than the hour. Alicia looked out the window. Maybe everything from now on would always seem too dark.

"How are your parents?" he asked.

She shrugged. "Shitty. What do you think?"

"We all are," Nikolai said.

"We aren't all getting drunk and punching someone in the eye," Alicia snapped with a wide-flung gesture at Ilya. "Yeah, I know what happened at the funeral parlor. Everyone knows. Everyone was talking about it."

"Just one more thing for them to talk about," Nikolai retorted. "Along with everything else about us, like they always do. Those fatherless Stern boys, the one with the crazy mother."

She was across the room with the front of his shirt in her fists before she could stop herself. She shook him. Tears slid in burning tracks down her cheeks.

"You think it's about you? It's not about you! Or him! It should be about her, about Jenni—"

He didn't try to wriggle out of her grip, but he put his hands on her wrists to hold her still. His lip curled. "Or about you, maybe? Is that why you're mad? That you're still not the one anyone talks about? Now that she's gone, what, you think you can step in and take over as the popular one?"

Alicia jerked her hand from his grip. The slap rocked him. The imprint of her hand on his cheek was first white, then pink and slowly red as he put his own hand up to cover it. His eyes narrowed. Nikolai grabbed her wrist again.

"Go ahead." She tipped her face up. Taunting. "Punch me in the face the way you did your brother at my sister's funeral, making asses of yourselves. Go ahead. You want to hit me, Nikolai? I'm right here. Go ahead! Do it!"

She tried to scream, but her breath came out in wispy, whistling gasps. She flailed and tried to smack him again, because why, why did Nikolai Stern always have to be such an asshole to her? He caught her wrist, holding both again. He didn't hit her.

He kissed her.

It was what she wanted, all along. It was what she'd been thinking about since the night of the party back in October, all these long months when they'd both pretended it never happened. It was all she ever thought about when she looked at him. The smell and taste of him, the pressure of his mouth on hers. The slide of his fingers in her hair.

Nikolai kissed her with an open mouth. Sliding tongues. Still holding her wrists, although she was no longer trying to hit him, he stepped back toward the bed until they both fell onto it, bouncing on the saggy, old mattress.

Alicia had thought about this, too. Of the sleekness of his skin. The weight of him on top of her. They moved together like they'd always known how. How easily she gave this up to him, this thing she'd imagined she would save for a night of candlelight and blowing curtains and someone who loved her.

But who else could it have ever been other than Nikolai? There was pain she'd been told to expect and fear, the sting that was hardly anything at all compared to the pleasure. Who other than him? Because it was love.

It might not be forever, but right then, it was love.

CHAPTER THIRTEEN

Niko and Allie?

Two shadowy silhouettes behind the sheer curtains of Allie's kitchen door, embracing. Theresa stepped back and away from the window, well aware that if she could see in, the pair of them could see out. And she didn't want them to see her watching them like she was some kind of voyeur, which she definitely was not, even though she'd taken another chance and peeked again to make sure she hadn't imagined what she'd seen. The curtain had blurred the details, but not enough that she could pretend they were doing anything else.

Without knocking, Theresa carefully took a backward step down off the porch and turned toward the house across the street. She'd momentarily allowed herself the luxury of the somewhat melancholy indulgence of memory. If she drew in a breath, closed her eyes, she could probably manage to convince herself she was fifteen again, just running next door to watch late-night TV and eat snacks with Allie and Jenni. The time she'd spent living with the Sterns was no more than a blink in the long, hard stare of her life. Why, then, did that period of time affect her so much to this day?

That was a question deeper than she wanted to go, at least today. With a backward glance at Allie's house, Theresa mentally tucked away the secret she'd stumbled across and headed across the street, where once inside she navigated the crowd of mourners in search of Ilya, who'd been looking for Niko.

"I didn't find him." She eyed him. His hand hadn't been empty of a bottle for the past few hours. "Have you eaten something?"

"Not hungry." He lifted the bottle to his lips and made a face when it was empty. "Where is he? He should be here, dammit. He needs to deal with *her*."

Theresa took the bottle from him and tossed it in the trash, then followed the lift of his chin across the room to where his mother sat in one of the dining-room chairs like it was a throne. "What's she doing?"

"She's talking to people." Ilya's mouth twisted. "Like she knows any damn thing about shit."

"Her mother died, Ilya." Theresa surprised herself with her defense of the other woman, who certainly had never done anything to earn Theresa's loyalty.

Ilya fixed her with a hard look. He wasn't as drunk as he was acting, she thought. Which made her wonder why, exactly, he was faking being hammered when he wasn't. What was it he meant to say that he could later pretend he hadn't meant?

"You're the last person I thought would take her side," he said.

Theresa looked again. Galina wasn't crying. Theresa hadn't seen a single tear out of her, as a matter of fact, but that didn't mean anything. People grieved in different ways.

"I don't hate your mother." It wasn't a lie, but that didn't quite make it the truth, either. She sealed her lips, thinking there was more to say. There always was. But now wasn't the time, and here wasn't the place.

"Ilya. Hi." A slight woman with pale-blonde hair pulled into a tight ponytail nudged Theresa to the side. "I'm so sorry about what happened."

"Dina." Ilya gave her a small nod but no smile. "Where are Bill and the kids?"

Dina coughed into her fist. "They're at home. I ran over to pay my respects, that's all. Maybe we can go somewhere and talk?"

"Sorry, can't. I promised Theresa I'd eat something." He reached for Theresa's sleeve, tugging her closer. "Thanks for coming, Dina."

With that, he pushed Theresa toward the dining room. Bemused, she shot a glance over her shoulder at the other woman, who was scowling, her arms crossed over her chest. Ilya went straight to the dining-room table, which was overloaded with platters and casseroles and a heaping basket of dinner rolls. He grabbed a paper plate from the stack and started loading it up.

Sloppy, not caring if he dripped sauces or splashed, Ilya layered his plate with slices of deli turkey, pasta salad, olives, and some horrifying concoction of Jell-O and fruit. He piled on enough food for three men twice his size. He balanced a thick sugar cookie laden with icing on top of everything else and swiped another from the plate. He shoved the second cookie in his mouth, chewing loudly.

People were starting to pay attention, and in that way Theresa had learned from painful experience would lead to whispers and the shaking of heads. Gossip grew quickly from seeds into vast, tangling jungles of strangling vines and carnivorous flowers. You could spend years trying to hack your way out of that poisoned garden.

Quietly, she went to the table herself and loaded up her plate in a similar fashion. She grabbed a couple of napkins and then hooked her arm through Ilya's, careful but not successful in keeping him from spilling a little. He resisted at first, but she looked him in the face.

"Come outside with me," she said. "You're kind of being a dick."

She hadn't known Ilya before their parents got together. She'd only met him as an arrogant teenage boy with an infectious sense of humor and a penchant for getting into trouble, as well as the talent to talk his way out of it. She'd heard stories about him over the years. Those small seeds of gossip had found a way to bear fruit even in the next town over. Still, it surprised her how readily he reacted to her murmured admonition.

"Sorry," Ilya said with his mouth still full.

Theresa shook her head and left the dining room, dodging the well-meaning, reaching hands of the women who'd gathered there to mourn Babulya, and avoiding Dina, who was still trying to catch Ilya's eye. The weather was still so unseasonably warm they didn't need their coats, but the day had been overcast, with a promise of more rain. There'd been no snow this year, a fact she was grateful for. Not having to deal with bad weather on top of everything else had made her life a lot easier over the past few months.

"Sit," she ordered.

He did. He dug his plastic fork into the slithering pile of macaroni salad, managing to stab a few noodles and get them into his mouth before pausing to swallow. He gave her a startled look. "Babulya's macaroni salad."

"I made it this morning."

He glanced up at her and took another bite before he answered. "I haven't had this in years."

"I haven't made it in a while. I thought it would be appropriate for today." She took a bite, savoring the flavors. Bits of green onion. Mustard. Small cubes of carrot. This macaroni salad was the perfect summer-picnic dish, as out of season as the warm weather, and yet somehow seemed perfectly right to also celebrate the life of a woman who'd been so loved.

"So, Dina," she said after a moment or so of silence, interrupted only by the sound of them both chewing.

"She lives next door to Allie. She's . . . nosy."

Theresa laughed softly, catching a glimpse of blonde hair at the kitchen's sliding door. "Ex-girlfriend?"

"She's married. Four kids. None of them mine," Ilya added sarcastically.

"I wasn't accusing you of fathering half the neighborhood," Theresa said after a pause. "Although the way she was looking at you, she might be looking for a daddy for number five."

Ilya grimaced with a shudder. "Shit, I need another beer."

"Do you? Need one? Or do you just want one?" Theresa asked.

He frowned and glanced at the house. "What difference does it make? Need or want?"

"It makes a big difference," Theresa answered quietly and focused on her plate. "But only you can figure out what it is. If you need one, go in and get one."

Ilya made as though to get up from the table, then settled back into the chair with a grumbling sigh. "Nah. I don't want to go back inside, watch my mother holding court like some kind of queen. You know she wants to sit shiva this week?"

"I heard her inviting people, yes. Not that most of them knew what it is." Theresa, baptized Catholic at her grandparents' insistence but raised without much of any organized religion, had toyed with practicing a few different faiths over the years. She'd never gone so far as to officially convert to anything, but she did know what shiva, the traditional Jewish practice of seven nights' grieving, was.

"It's ridiculous." Ilya rested his elbows on the table to let his hands make a cradle for his face for a few seconds. When he spoke, his voice was muffled. "Like what, she's Jewish now?"

"I thought you were always Jewish."

He peeked at her through his fingers. "Well . . . yeah. I mean, sure, but we never really did anything about it."

"Doesn't mean that your mom can't find comfort in the traditions of her faith," Theresa said mildly.

Ilya sat up and stared at her. "You're different."

She didn't think so, but then again, he didn't know her, did he? He'd hardly known her back then, this sudden younger sister forced on him by their screwed-up parents who'd thought they were in love until making it work got too hard. She didn't answer him.

"I mean . . ." Ilya shrugged, staring at her. "Hi."

Theresa's brows rose. "Hi."

"I'm a little fucked up."

"Too many beers," she said lightly.

Ilya shook his head. "That's not what I mean."

"I know," Theresa answered.

CHAPTER FOURTEEN

Then

School was a special level of hell, Niko thought. They put you in these small rooms and made you sit there for hours to do work you could learn in so much less time if they only bothered to figure out a way to teach that made sense. It didn't even have to be fun. His pencil tap-tapped on the notebook in front of him. Couldn't they just make it less freaking torturous?

It didn't help that all he could think about was Alicia Harrison.

All his friends had started panting after girls with their tongues hanging out like dogs since about the seventh grade, but he'd never seen much point in it. Why get all worked up over some flat-chested pimpleface who might or might not have to be pressured into opening her mouth when you kissed? Not to mention what you had to do in order to get her to touch your dick. Or to let you touch any of her parts. It hadn't made any sense to him—why did he ever have to fall in love? Or worse, have some clinging girlfriend claim she was in love with him?

Niko planned on getting the hell out of this piece-of-shit town the first second he had the chance, so why would he want to get tangled up with someone here? Why start something that was only going to end? If he got horny, he had his own two hands that could take care of business. He didn't need something else.

Except . . . now he couldn't stop thinking about the girl across the street. Allie was the last person in the world he'd have thought he would ever want to kiss. The party had been a bad idea from the beginning. He'd known it. But Ilya had a way of convincing everyone that even the worst ideas were going to be great, so Niko had gone along with it because he almost always did. He'd drunk his mother's vodka. And he'd kissed Allie in the garden. He'd done that, and neither of them had talked about it since. It had been almost a month, it had been a stupid thing, so why then couldn't he shake the memory of how she'd tasted?

Why couldn't he stop wanting to do it again?

Somehow he made it through the day, dodging a detention for not having his homework finished by arguing with Mrs. Haberstramm that straight As on his tests should prove that he understood the material.

"I can't give you credit for the work if you don't turn it in," she said with a sigh she reserved for all the students who tried to wiggle their way out of turning in their homework. "And it counts for half your grade, Niko. So, no matter how many tests you ace, if you don't turn in the homework, you're going to barely squeak by with a D, and that's only if I'm generous."

They agreed he could turn in all the missing homework he swore with an angel's face he really had finished and had just forgotten to bring in. Every day. For months. She gave him until Friday. Three days. He was never going to make it, not if he worked all night, every night, and had nothing else to do. The futility of the arrangement, the challenge, should've motivated him, but Niko headed home and tossed his backpack on the recliner in the living room the way he did every single day after school.

Babulya had snacks ready in the kitchen. She and Theresa had been baking again. Cookies, fresh from the oven, cooling on wire racks. He snagged one, knowing she'd scold him about ruining his dinner but not mean it. She wouldn't make cookies if she didn't want them to be eaten, right?

Gathering a couple of cookies in one fist, he crossed the street and went through the Harrisons' kitchen and into the den. Jenni was watching a soap opera while she painted her nails, and he tossed her a cookie. She squealed but managed to catch it.

"Jerk, you made me mess up my polish." She ate the cookie anyway.

"Bitch," Niko said, giving her the standard comeback they all used. "Where's your brother?"

Jenni and Ilya had been fooling around together for months, but they were acting like nobody knew it. Just to mess with her, Niko shrugged. "I think he went over to Kim Lee's house."

The way she flinched made him wish he hadn't tried to tease her. He flopped onto the couch beside her and propped his feet on the coffee table, but first snagged the remote to change the station. He laughed at her cry of protest and held the remote up and out of her reach.

"Jerk," Jenni muttered again, then fixed him with a sly look. "Allie isn't home, by the way. She stayed after to do something for the play."

Horrified and feeling caught, Niko forced himself to turn his burning face toward the TV screen. "Why do you think that matters to me?"

The pager on Jenni's hip beeped, and she grabbed for it with a small, secret grin, studying the number on the little black screen. She held the pager to her chest for a moment. Did a little seated dance. Ilya wasn't the one who'd paged her—he didn't have one.

Curiosity piqued, Niko turned toward her. "Got a boyfriend or something?"

"None of your business, buttstain," Jenni said, but she was distracted. Paying too much attention to the message on the pager to notice that Niko was close enough to snag it from her grip.

Getting under Jennilynn Harrison's skin, as well as her sister's, was a long-standing Stern-brother tradition. But what he saw spelled out on the pager's screen set him back a step. It was a string of numbers and asterisks, a coded message. Niko didn't have a pager, but he understood what it said because the list of codes and their meanings got passed around at school all the time.

I want to fuck you.

Niko'd seen porn. Randy Ebersole had found a whole stash of it under his dad's workbench, and they all got drunk and watched it. But somehow, seeing someone say that to Jenni, watching her blush and giggle over it, made it all too real. Too . . . adult. Lots of their friends were having sex, but something about that message felt creepy.

"Give me that, shithead!" Jenni swept the pager out of his hand and punched him on the arm for good measure.

Both Harrison girls knew how to land a punch; Niko was lucky she hadn't aimed for his face. He'd be sporting a black eye, for sure. Blushing now for a different reason, he avoided looking into Jenni's face.

"Sorry," he muttered. "You don't have to be such a bitch about it."

"Fuck you, Niko."

They swore at each other all the time. Ragged on each other. Something about this felt harsher, though. Angrier. Jenni cursed at him like she meant it, not like a joke, and Niko swallowed hard against a rush of something that felt like thorns in his throat. He wanted to apologize but couldn't make himself do it. He didn't want to have seen what he saw. He just wanted to get out of there.

So, he ran.

Out of the house, across the street. Past his own house and through his backyard, into the field and the woods beyond. He ran until he had to bend over, thinking he might puke. Not far beyond him was the fence that surrounded the quarry, but he was nowhere near the place where they usually hung out to swim and mess around. Even so, he pushed through the vines and bushes and found a spot in the fence that let him through. He wasn't the first to seek access, after all. Despite the signs warning people to stay away, nobody ever did.

Niko stood on the edge of the quarry, looking down to the water below. If he jumped from here, there was a good chance he would hit the water, legs and arms straight, making him a bullet. It was so deep there wasn't a chance he'd hit bottom. But he could mess up the angle, screw up the jump, hit a dozen places along the wall on the way down. Thinking of this, he shifted, and one foot slipped on a crumble of pebbles, which pattered downward and plink, plink, so far down he couldn't even hear them hitting the water.

Heart pounding, he stepped back, grabbing for the fence, for a moment certain he'd gone too far this time. He was going to end up a broken mess on the rocks below. It would be better to die if that happened, he thought, sort of incoherently, knowing it was smart to stay back from the edge, but somehow helpless to keep himself from leaning forward again, anyway. Better to be dead than hurt so bad you couldn't take care of yourself, or to be in a coma, or something like that.

He took in a deep breath when the ground beneath him didn't give way and send him hurtling toward the pit. He gripped the fence's rusty metal links with one hand and leaned forward with only that to hold him. Eyes closed, heart pounding, Niko considered letting go. Again and again he let his body swing forward, then back, with only his fingertips tethering him, until finally whatever was inside him that made him run had been appeased. Like a kind of dark demon, it ate something out of him and left him sort of shivering and empty, so that he stared at the marks of the metal fence gouged into his fingers, like he'd just woken from a dream. Shaking it off, Niko headed back to his house, which felt so different now that there was another man living there.

Barry wasn't home when he got there. Neither was Galina. Niko could hear the faint sound of music coming from upstairs, some boy band that Theresa favored. Babulya met him in the kitchen with crossed arms and a frown.

"You've been stealing cookies."

Niko was sweaty, with prickers and twigs scratching at him. Mud thick on his shoes that he'd tracked in on the clean kitchen floor. "I was hungry."

His grandmother nodded once, sharply, and fixed him with a look. "You'll always be hungry. You need to feed more than your stomach."

"I'll clean this up." He gestured at the skid marks of mud, hanging his head, ashamed of having made a mess when he should have known better.

"Kolya." Babulya put a hand on his shoulder and waited until he looked at her. She was so tiny he towered over her. "You don't have to stay here forever."

"Huh?"

Babulya shook her head. Her fingers squeezed for a moment, before she released him. "This house. This place. You don't have to stay here forever, Kolya, *moye solnishko*."

My little sun.

He'd only ever heard her call his brother that, and somehow even though he didn't want to, Niko was sitting at the kitchen table with his head in his hands. He didn't cry, although his throat closed and his eyes burned. All he could do was sit there. His grandmother put the plate of cookies in front of him, along with a glass of milk. She rubbed the spot between his shoulders in slow, steady circles for a minute or so, then patted his shoulder.

"I just hate everything," Niko said in a low voice, no longer hungry for cookies but taking one anyway.

Babulya laughed. "I know, you're like your mother in that way. She hated everything, too."

"I don't want to be like her," he muttered. The thought of it repelled him.

"We are what we are. That is the way it works." Babulya shrugged and went to the sink to fill the kettle with water so she could make some tea. "Ilya—he likes to fight when he knows he can't win. You like to win without fighting."

"Whatever that means."

He ducked away from her swat. When she hugged him, though, he closed his eyes and let her press his face to the front of her familiar scratchy sweater. Ilya was always her favorite, as Nikolai belonged to his mother. They wore the same lotion, Babulya and his mother, something the two of them shared, which they probably didn't realize. The faint scent of flowers made him think of how it had been when he was a little kid who'd had a bad dream, and Galina had let him climb into bed with her until he wasn't scared anymore. He was way too big for that now, too old for that comfort, though sometimes he believed his mother would gladly keep him that close to her forever.

Babulya hugged him tightly, then let him go. "It means that it will be all right when you run, Kolya. That's what it means. One day you will run toward something instead of away, and then you will understand."

◆ ◆ ◆

Run toward instead of away.

His grandmother had been full of stories, fairy tales, myths, and fables, but of all the advice she'd ever given him, those words had been the ones Niko carried with him. She'd seen something in him back then that he hadn't been able to see in himself, not until he was older and had started traveling the world, telling himself it was because he wanted to see and do and feel and live a life far beyond the tiny rural Pennsylvania town where everyone knew everyone else's business. That had been a part of it, but it hadn't been all of it.

He'd definitely been running away.

He wasn't so sure what he was doing now. He'd come back to Quarrytown without intending to stay longer than he had to, but a certain lethargy had overtaken him. If he wasn't running, it was because he'd started sinking back into the quagmire of this small town, this house, his mother and brother, and the girl next door.

Oh, her.

He shouldn't have kissed her. It was going to come back to bite him. Or haunt him, the way he'd been haunted forever already by the memories of her. He was supposed to be smarter, but it looked like he'd only gotten older.

Everyone was leaving by the time he got back from Allie's house, and since Ilya had disappeared, Niko was the one who shook their hands and accepted the condolences. With the front door closed behind the last of the guests, he took in a long, deep breath and thought about the mess of food in the dining room he was certain his mother wouldn't be doing much to clean up. To his surprise, he found her there packing away the leftovers into a pile of mismatched plastic and glass containers.

"Theresa and your brother went for a walk. She's trying to get him to sober up, but good luck with that." Galina shrugged and stuck a handful of dinner rolls into a plastic baggie, then sealed it. She straightened and shook her head so the fall of her long, dark hair skidded down her back. The silver in it glinted from the overhead light.

"Mom, let me take care of this. Why don't you go sit down?" Niko went to the table to start packing up the food.

"I've been sitting all night. It's good for me to be on my feet." She gave him a sideways glance. "Where were you?"

"I took some casseroles over to Allie's house. No room in the fridge here." When she didn't answer him, he glanced up.

Galina's expression was neutral, her faint smile not reaching her eyes. "I thought maybe you'd gone away already. So eager to leave again."

At least she hadn't said "so eager to leave *me* again," although he'd heard the whisper of it in her voice.

Niko put down the small box of cookies that had come from the local bakery. Nobody had even opened it. "I'm not leaving right away."

"So, you're staying here? For how long?" His mother tilted her head in a familiar mannerism.

He'd been given two weeks' bereavement leave, but the Beit Devorah council had also approved six weeks' sabbatical time. It was leave meant to be used for study and travel, accumulated over the years he'd been a *chaver*, a full member of the kibbutz. He hadn't made any plans yet; he only knew he wasn't going back to Israel right away. He'd booked only a one-way flight. He didn't feel like explaining any of this to his mother, though.

"I don't know," Niko said.

"It will be nice," Galina said, "to have us all here for a while. It's been a long time since we had any time together."

Niko wasn't entirely convinced it was going to be nice, but he nodded anyway. "Yeah. Sure."

"This is my house, now that my mother is dead." She said the words flatly, with little emotion, but Niko wasn't fooled. Galina could switch from hilarity to fury in a blink. He had no doubts she could just as easily erupt into grief. "We can all stay here together. You don't have to go away so soon, Kolya. That's all."

He paused at that. Babulya had often referred to him and his brother by the Russian diminutives of their names, but Galina hadn't made it much of a habit. If anything, she'd said more than once that the only reason she'd agreed to give her sons Russian names instead of American ones had been to please her mother.

"No, I guess I don't," he said.

His mother smiled then. It looked genuine. She looked at the table of food, then at him, and laughed. "Who else would help me eat all of this?"

"Mom."

She looked at him. "Hmmm?"

"I'm sorry about Babulya. I know losing her had to be hard."

Galina's smile faded. "We didn't get along very well, my mother and I. A lot like your brother and I don't always seem to get along very well. You and I were always so much closer."

"Mom—"

"She's dead, Nikolai, there's no point in telling lies to make it all better," his mother said firmly. "That serves nobody. If anything, we should take this as a chance to remember that we never know how much time we might have left in this life, and if we want to put the past behind us, we ought to start now."

He nodded, agreeing to keep the peace but knowing there was no way to leave the past behind. "Sure. Of course."

"Maybe you should run some more of this over to Allie's house." She held up a platter of brownies.

Especially when the past still lived across the street.

Niko hesitated. "Ah . . . it's late, Mom."

"Maybe tomorrow, then."

"Yeah, maybe."

They worked together in silence, clearing off the table and putting away the perishables. Galina paused at the back door, her cigarettes and lighter in hand. She said his name.

"Yeah?" Niko replied.

"Thank you. For what you said about my mother."

Before he could answer, Galina had ducked out the back door.

CHAPTER FIFTEEN

Then

Niko was watching her.

Alicia had her eyes closed behind the black-and-neon pink plastic sunglasses she'd bought at the dollar store along with the cheap plastic raft that got too hot in the sun and burned the backs of her legs. She didn't need to be able to see him from here to know it. He was plotting something, some kind of revenge for the prank she and Jennilynn had pulled two nights ago when they'd snuck out of their house and gone across the street to peek in the windows of the Sterns' den. Ilya and Nikolai had been watching some old scary movie, and they'd both screamed when the girls slapped at the windows and ran away. Now it was the boys' turn to do the scaring, and the anticipation was almost worse than whatever they were going to do.

Nobody was supposed to swim in the quarry, but that hadn't stopped anyone over the years. Most of the town kids got to it from the other side, on the old access road. There was a kind of beach there, mostly rocks and weeds, but at least it was at water level. The cops raided it sometimes, chasing away underage drinkers and pot smokers and the kids humping in their parked cars. The cops hadn't ever bothered the Harrison and Stern kids, who made their place here on the end of Quarry Street.

Nikolai was the one who found the long coil of rope in the abandoned equipment hut. Alicia had come up with the idea for the swing, but Ilya was the one who climbed up the tree to tie the rope to the branch. Jennilynn had been the first to try it out, pulling the length all the way up the hill as far as she could, then holding tight and jumping from the fork in the tree, over the hill's steep slope. Swinging out, out, making sure to let go so she wouldn't hit any of the rocks if she fell in the water. Their parents would have shit bricks if they knew what their kids were getting up to, but that was part of the fun, wasn't it? Doing the stuff you knew your parents would forbid because it was too dangerous?

They didn't have a beach on this side, and the hill was steep enough to make the climb a pain, but there was a trail down to an outcropping of rock that hung over the water. It was big enough for all of them to lie on. There was another trail down to the water. If you were too chicken to use the rope swing, you could still jump off the rock ledge, then swim over to the spot at the bottom and make your way back up the trail. They'd talked about building a dock or something down there to make it easier, but even though the equipment shed was filled with odds and ends of scrap wood, they'd never gotten around to it.

For now, it was awesome to float in the old quarry's chilly water. Baking on one side, freezing on the other. A can of cola and a peanut butter-and-jelly sandwich awaited her on the rock ledge, where they'd all spread their towels, and later she would eat her lunch while they played Uno or gin rummy. There was a blue sky overhead, and a popular new song they'd all hate by the end of summer blared out from Nikolai's radio.

"So . . . whattya think about Barry?" Jennilynn paddled over in her tube. She nudged Alicia until she opened her eyes. "He's pretty creepy, huh?"

Alicia gripped the sides of her raft, too aware of how easily she could tip. How deep the water was beneath her, and how cold. "Hey, watch out."

"He is, right?" Jennilynn nudged her sister again with a red-painted toe. "What are you afraid of? You'll melt or something?"

Alicia gripped the raft so hard it dented the soft rubber. "Stop it. I just don't want to get my hair wet."

"I know, you're afraid of Chester. You think he's gonna chomp you." Jennilynn grinned and disappeared for a moment inside the center of her tube, then resurfaced, ending up with her butt in the center with her legs dangling over the sides. She didn't give a damn about her hair getting wet, and why should she? It would dry in blonde ringlets and get even whiter in the sun.

Chester was the carnival goldfish Jennilynn had tossed in the water a couple of weeks ago. They'd been joking that he was out there, growing and growing like the sunfish in that movie they watched a few months ago about a mountain where all the animals had mutated because of mercury poisoning or something from a mine.

"Answer my question, Allie."

Alicia settled back on the raft, though she hooked a foot against her sister's to keep them from floating away from each other. "About Chester?"

"No-o-o-o. About Galina's new husband."

"I dunno. He seemed okay at the wedding. He's been nice to us so far." Alicia shrugged. Barry Malone was one more adult in their lives they all did their best to avoid.

"Theresa's okay, I guess." Jennilynn, for once, kept her voice down so it didn't carry across the water and alert the other girl that they were gossiping about her. "Can you imagine, though? Having to actually *live* with those guys?"

"At least she doesn't have to share a room," Alicia said. Nikolai had taken over the attic so Theresa could have his old room.

"No shit," Jennilynn agreed. "Sharing a room totally sucks."

Alicia laughed and shoved Jennilynn's tube with her toes, but her sister was too fast and grabbed Alicia's ankle so she wouldn't tip. Also, so the force of Alicia's shove didn't force them apart. She dug her nails in a little too deep, though.

"Ouch!"

"Sorry." Jennilynn didn't sound sorry at all, but then she hardly ever did.

They floated in silence for a few minutes. Alicia thought to put on more sunscreen so she wouldn't burn, but that would have meant paddling back to the rocky shore, securing her raft, hauling her ass up the steep slope and onto the ledge . . . it was a lot of effort. Maybe she would tan, she thought, drifting, drifting . . .

"I don't know what I want to be when I grow up," Jennilynn said.

Alicia didn't open her eyes. "Who says you have to?"

"Everyone has to decide at some point, Allie. You can't just screw around forever. You have to decide."

"But not right now." Alicia wasn't sleeping, not really. Dozing a little. Aware of the hot sun, the cold water, and her sister's voice. "It's not like the world will end if you don't."

"Easy for you to say. Nobody's counting on you to make them proud."

Alicia's eyes opened at that as her heart clenched like a fist. The words hadn't sounded hateful, only resigned, but they cut deep. She couldn't even dispute them, because they both knew it was the truth.

The sudden splash swamped them both, nearly tipping them. Nikolai had swung out on the rope and dive-bombed them. Shrieking, both girls kicked at him as he tried to swim closer. Laughing, Nikolai shook his dark hair as he treaded water.

"Nice going, jerk!" Alicia said as he splashed at her, but she couldn't be too angry. It was payback, after all.

"Bitch," Nikolai said around a long spurt of water.

Jennilynn laughed, but Alicia flipped him the bird. For a second he made as though he was going to swim closer and tip her off the raft; she squealed and kicked at him. He gave up too easily. That was suspicious. He would finish his revenge soon, but she didn't know when . . . and her skin crawled with delicious anticipation.

"He must have a big dick," Jenni said suddenly.

Alicia choked a little. "What? Who? Nikolai? Ew, Jennilynn!"

"No, not Niko. Gawd, Allie, don't be stupid." Jennilynn used her hands to paddle in the water, turning her in the tube so she could get her head closer to her sister's. "I meant Barry."

How could her sister even think such a thing, much less say it out loud? "Gross, Jenni."

"I bet they screw like rabbits," Jennilynn said in a tone of secret glee.

There was something dark in her voice. Something secret and strange, and Alicia didn't like it. She grimaced. "Yuck."

Jennilynn spun, kicking gently. "I bet they do. I bet they do it every night. They're newlyweds, right? Isn't that what they do? I'm going to ask Ilya if he ever hears them. You know his room is right next to theirs."

"Jenni, no. That's . . ." There was something so off about that, so disturbing, that she couldn't even finish her thought out loud.

Laughing, Jennilynn started to float away, and although Alicia reached for her, she was too far to grab. That was when Nikolai jumped off the rope swing again, this time landing much closer to them. The water swelled, tossing Alicia off the raft. She took in a huge gulp of water and flailed, forcing her way to the surface, where she choked and splashed. Blinded by the water in her eyes, her hair in her face, she grabbed for her raft, for anything, but found only more cold water. She went under again.

And again.

There, glittering in the water, was something orange. Fins tipped with black. It fluttered around her face, and she screamed, taking in water.

Strong hands grabbed her around the waist and pulled her upward. They were on the shore in a minute or so after that. Alicia heaved up a gush of water but managed not to puke. She swung and punched Nikolai just below the eye, making him fall back.

"Where's Jenni?" She demanded.

"I'm right here. Hey. It's okay. You're okay, right?" Jennilynn gave Nikolai a worried look.

Alicia fell back onto the dirt and weeds, ignoring how they poked into her. She closed her eyes, letting her sister and Nikolai worry. Screw them both, but especially Nikolai for overturning the raft and scaring her so bad. But it wasn't the way the water closed over her head that lingered, or the chill of it that made her shake, and it wasn't the glimpse of that carnival goldfish that somehow was still alive. It was how she'd reached for her sister and couldn't find her; it was thinking Jennilynn had also gone under but hadn't come up.

"I'm sorry, Allie." Nikolai sounded anxious. "I was just getting you back for scaring me the other night. Hey, Allie, look at me. I'm sorry."

His apology didn't stop her from being pissed off, even if it sounded sincere. She sat. "You're such a giant asshole, Nikolai!"

"I said I was sorry." He grinned, knowing that her anger meant she was all right. That it would be her turn next to get back at him.

Because that was how it worked with all of them. Playing pranks on one another. Giving one another a hard time. Yet watching her sister climb the slope toward the rocks above where she would lay out on her towel and bake in the late summer sun, all Alicia could think of was how it felt in those few terrifying moments to think she was so alone, and how it had been Nikolai who'd saved her.

CHAPTER SIXTEEN

Ilya stretched the corner of a flowered sheet from one end of the hall mirror to the other and secured it with blue painter's tape until it completely covered the glass. An Internet search had told him that was the tradition during shiva, along with tearing a hole in his sleeve. Where his mother had gotten the crazy idea that Babulya would've wanted this sort of honor, Ilya had no idea, but it was typical of her. If Galina thought she was going to one-up him in the grieving department, though, she was going to be disappointed. She didn't get to come back around and act like she was better than any of them. Not better than he was.

"Hey."

Ilya jumped, turning to see Theresa in the kitchen doorway. She still wore her coat, though she was tugging off the silky scarf around her throat. She hung her shoulder bag on the back of one of the kitchen chairs.

Ilya straightened, self-conscious suddenly that he hadn't showered in the past three days. Or shaved. He ran a hand over his chin, wincing at the scratch, wondering why in the hell it mattered if he looked like he'd been sleeping under a bridge. This was Theresa, not a woman he had to impress or anything. Yet at the way she wrinkled her nose, he wished he'd taken the time to clean up.

"You're back?" he asked instead.

She glanced at him over her shoulder as she went to the fridge to grab a drink. "I am. Your mother asked me to come. She said it's okay if I stay here for the week, for shiva, but if it's a problem . . ."

"Apparently it's not my house," he told her with a shrug. "So it's not like I could kick you out, even if I wanted to."

She eyed him over the top of her cola can, sipping, then let out a sigh. "Do you want to kick me out?"

"No," he said after a second or so. "Of course not. You're welcome to stay here as long as you need to, although why you'd want to, I have no idea."

"I want to be here to celebrate Babulya's life and help to mourn her death. Isn't that what shiva is?"

Ilya made a face. "You sound like you know more about it than I do."

"I dated a Jewish guy a couple years ago," Theresa said with a shrug. "I picked up a few things."

Time had passed—a lot of it—Ilya reminded himself. Theresa had lived a whole other life, just like he had. He imagined, briefly, Theresa kissing some faceless guy. Laughing, walking hand in hand. Weirded out, he shook away the thoughts.

"Besides," she said lightly before he could reply, "my landlord decided he was going to finally replace the furnace and all the ductwork. So I need a place to crash, anyway."

"A hotel would be better than this house," Ilya said. "The shower's a nightmare."

"Oh, I know, believe me. I thought it was going to flay me alive." She grinned.

"Grab me one?" Ilya gestured for her to get him a cola, and she did, which he opened and drank from before asking, "So, what've you been up to the past few decades?"

"That covers a lot of ground." She took another long drink and shook the can to judge how much was left. Leaning against the counter, she crossed one arm over her belly to prop her opposite elbow on it.

"Well . . . you have a job?"

"Of course I have a job," she said.

Ilya laughed. "What do you do?"

"I make connections," Theresa answered. She drained the can, then tossed it into the recycling bin.

Ilya shook his head. "What do you connect?"

"Mostly real estate. I find properties that are in foreclosure or other financial difficulty and connect buyers that have the finances and desire and abilities to turn those opportunities into successful projects."

"You lost me," Ilya said.

Theresa laughed. "I spend a lot of time on the Internet looking up properties for sale or the places that have liens and back taxes, or are in an underserved location, or are somehow unique. Then I get in touch with people who like to invest in that sort of thing and try to connect them."

Ilya chuffed somewhat amazed laughter. "And this works out for you?"

"Oh, yeah," Theresa said airily, with a wave of her hand. "It's been terrific. Best job ever."

Something in her tone sounded a little off. Her smile, a little dim. Ilya tossed his cola can in the trash and went to the fridge to pull out a couple of beers. He handed her one. "How'd you get started with that?"

Theresa waved away the beer. "Not for me, thanks."

He put it back in the fridge and cracked the top of his. "You don't drink?"

"Nope."

Ilya frowned. "Since when?"

"Since . . . forever," she said. "For a long time, anyway."

"You used to."

She laughed and shook her head. "Maybe once. Here. That party you guys had."

“That was a long time ago, Theresa. You’re telling me you haven’t had a beer since then?”

She shrugged. “Yep. It happens, you know.”

“But . . .” He shook his head. A life without booze? “Why?”

She brushed past him to grab a glass from the cupboard. Her perfume, something fresh, wafted over him. Her hair, long and thick and dark, tumbling over her shoulders and down her back, brushed his shoulder. He took a step back as she drew a glass of water from the tap and turned to face him, sipping.

“I don’t like it, that’s all. Where’s your mother and Niko?”

“She’s upstairs. I don’t know about him. People should start arriving soon, though. I think Galina told them around seven.” Ilya tipped the bottle to his mouth and drank, savoring the tang of hops and the underlying flavor of honey. His brother had picked this up. It was fancier than what Ilya usually drank. “You don’t drink at all? Not even a glass of wine with your girlfriends? Not ever? That’s weird.”

She looked him over. “It’s not weird. I need to get changed before everyone gets here. You didn’t go in to work today?”

“Nah.” He’d thought about it, but Alicia would take care of things better than he ever could.

“Are you planning to go tomorrow?” Brow furrowed, Theresa looked him over with that same wrinkled nose from earlier.

“Look, you can get off my case, okay? All of you can get off it.” He drained the beer and tossed the empty bottle into the garbage with a clatter of glass. He took the second—the one she didn’t want—from the fridge, and popped the top without looking at her.

“Sorry.” Her voice was cool. Theresa glanced at the teapot clock that had hung over the sink forever. “You’re right. It’s not really any of my business. I need to go get changed before people get here.”

“And you want to know what else is weird? You.”

She turned back to look at him with narrowed eyes. “Me?”

"Yeah. You showing up here after all this time, and you're staying in the house? That's *weird*." Ilya tipped the bottle at her, enjoying the way the word clearly needled at her. Getting a rise out of her.

"Your mother offered," Theresa said after a pause. "It was nice of her."

"In this house with a shitty shower and drafty windows? And that bed's hard as a rock. Don't tell me it's not." He laughed harshly. "You'd be better off in a hotel."

Theresa frowned. "Why are you always such a colossal dick, Ilya? Really. I haven't seen you in a long time, we have nothing to be angry at each other for, and I haven't done a damned thing to you. Ever. I mean, are you holding a grudge against me because I used your toothpaste a couple decades ago, or what?"

The truth was, he had no idea why he was so bent on being such an asshole to her. In reply, he set the bottle on the counter and crossed his arms. Theresa rolled her eyes.

"Fine. I'll pack up my things and be out of here tonight, then. I'm sure I can get a room somewhere, even this late. I'll leave after the shiva is over." Theresa went to the table and rustled around in her bag for a moment, glaring. She stopped to look up at him. "Or maybe I should just go now? Since obviously I'm causing such a problem for you."

Now Ilya felt exactly like the giant dick she'd accused him of being. It was a stupidly familiar feeling, only this time instead of keeping up with it, he sighed. "Ah, shit. Theresa . . ."

"What?" She stood and put her hands on her hips.

"Sorry." He attempted what was meant to be a charming smile, the one that usually worked on the women he'd pissed off. He'd had a lot of practice using it.

Theresa didn't seem charmed. "Does that usually work for you? The 'Aw shucks' look?"

There didn't seem to be much point in denying it. Ilya grinned. "Yes. Usually."

"You are your mother's son, Ilya."

This set him back a step, a hard one. He frowned. "Harsh."

"Look . . ." Theresa sighed, then gathered the thickness of her hair in one hand to tie it on top of her head with the elastic band she tugged from her wrist. She gestured. "Do you want to talk about it?"

"About what?" Ilya reached for his beer, surprised to find it had somehow emptied faster than he could remember drinking it. He bent to open the cabinet and pulled out a bottle of whiskey. He poured himself a glass, neat. Offered her the bottle just to see what she'd do.

Theresa gave him a hard look and made no move to take the bottle. "About anything. Or maybe you'd rather let the liquor listen."

"Hey." Ilya sipped, grimacing at the kick of whiskey against the back of his throat. "Now who's being a dick?"

She laughed, just a little. "Touché."

They stared at each other for a few seconds. Ilya sipped more whiskey. It was smooth going down, but he put the glass on the counter without finishing it. He didn't have a problem drinking alone, but it looked like he had one drinking while being judged. He scrubbed a hand through his hair.

"Shit," he said.

Theresa pulled out the kitchen chairs, one for him and one for her. She gestured until he sat, then went to the fridge to pull out the fixings for sandwiches. Deli meat, cheese, pickles, mustard, mayo. Rolls from the back he hadn't noticed, along with a container of macaroni salad. She laid it all out along with a couple of plates while he watched.

"Eat," she said.

"You sound like Babulya."

Theresa smiled. "She was a smart lady. I'm starving. If you don't want to eat, fine, but I'm going to murder a roast beef with cheddar."

"You eat a lot," Ilya said.

Theresa snorted soft laughter and shook her head, giving him an amused glance. "Yeah? And?"

"No *and*," he said. "Just an observation."

She was quiet for a moment. "Your grandmother spent a lot of time with me in this kitchen, making sure I was fed. It feels like the thing to do when someone needs taken care of."

If that was what she thought of him, she was going to be in for a sad surprise, but that she might think it of him had Ilya swallowing the smart-ass comment he'd been prepared to make. Instead, they both made towering sandwiches mostly in silence, broken only by requests to pass the mustard or hand over the pickles. He had to admit, it was the right idea. He didn't need to be taken care of, but it felt kind of nice to let someone try.

She took her first bite and let out a low, breathy moan that sent a shiver through him, one that Ilya cursed himself for feeling. It had been weeks since the last woman he'd brought home. And he hadn't been doing any self-maintenance in that respect, either, not with a houseful of people and feeling the way he'd been. That was all it was, he told himself, uncomfortable at the way he couldn't stop staring at the swipe of her tongue along her bottom lip to capture the slick of mustard that had dripped from her sandwich. He was thinking with his dick, the way he usually did.

"So good. What?" she asked, quieter this time. Less confrontational.

"You have . . . umm . . ." He passed her a paper napkin from the basket in the middle of the table. "Something on your . . . yeah."

Theresa wiped her mouth. Her gaze on him was constant. Steady. Before this moment he wouldn't have been able to say what color her eyes were, but he could see they were a deep and liquid amber. The color of the whiskey in his glass, actually. The one he'd left on the countertop, still mostly full.

"Thanks." She dragged a fork through the macaroni salad and ate a bite, watching him. "So. You want to talk about it, or what?"

"I don't have anything to say." Ilya eyed the sloppy sandwich on his plate. His stomach rumbled, so he took a big bite, not giving one damn about how the condiments squirted out all over his face.

Theresa handed him a napkin without a word. He used it. Set the sandwich down. Gave her a long and steady glare, challenging her to say anything more.

"It's okay to miss your grandma, Ilya," she said finally. "It's okay to have mixed feelings about your mother coming back around. And your brother . . ."

He stabbed his fork into some macaroni salad but didn't eat it. "What about my brother?"

"Look, all I'm saying is that it's okay to miss Babulya. It's okay to feel uneasy about your mother being here, or feel a little competitive with your brother—"

"Why would I feel competitive with him?" Ilya broke in.

Theresa's mouth twisted for a second, before she gave an exaggerated shrug. "He's been gone a long time, but now he's back. It must be strange, that's all. But it's not cool to let yourself get stuck in some kind of depressive lethargy. It's not going to help you in the long run, you know? You need to get up, get back to work."

"I wasn't there for her," Ilya spit out, uncertain why he was saying it but unable to stop himself.

Theresa nodded as though she understood what he meant, even though he hadn't been totally clear. "Babulya?"

"Yeah. I wasn't there for her. I was too busy to see her. I didn't like the home, I didn't like seeing her that way, so I put it off. I wasn't there for her, even though I knew . . . shit, I knew . . ." He drew in a hitching breath, horrified that tears were clogging his throat and threatening to slide out of his eyes. He covered them with his hand, fingers squeezing his temples to keep from weeping. He couldn't do that, couldn't break down. Not in front of her.

The scrape of the chair alerted him to her getting up. She put a hand on his shoulder. The weight of it was more of a comfort than he'd expected. Way more than he wanted.

"It's okay to be upset, Ilya."

"I'm fine! You don't know a damned thing about me or how I feel!" He stood, pushing against her before he could get some distance between them.

That perfume teased him again, along with the cloud of her hair. He grabbed her wrist, turning her, not sure why. More to say, maybe, or at least that was what he thought. The motion pulled her close against him. Too close. Theresa drew in a breath, her eyes going wide. Lips parting. He let her go when she yanked her arm from his grip.

"You might not believe that I cared for your grandmother and that I'm very, very sorry that she's gone, but you don't have to believe me," Theresa said. "I don't really care if you do or not. I don't care what you think about me, or my reasons for coming back here or anything else."

"What *do* you care about?" Ilya shot back. "Me?"

Theresa's gaze searched his. "I barely know you anymore. But yes. I guess I do. Why wouldn't I?"

"Why would you?" he muttered.

"Good question. I have no idea." She stepped back, out of his reach. "You certainly aren't giving me any reason to."

He waited until she'd left the kitchen before he went to the counter where he'd left his glass of whiskey and tossed it back. Anything to get rid of the scent of her. She was his . . . well, she'd been his sister. Sort of.

A long time ago.

CHAPTER SEVENTEEN

Alicia was never going to untangle herself. She was stuck, wrapped up, trapped in the Stern-family web. The question was, which of the Stern brothers was the spider, and how long was the venom going to take to kill her?

She could've made an excuse about not going over there tonight. She no longer cared much what Galina thought or said, and she was used to dealing with Ilya. It was Nikolai causing the twisting in her stomach. Seeing him, not seeing him, pretending they hadn't kissed in her kitchen, hoping he would look at her. Wondering what she'd do if he did not. She could have stayed home, but then she wouldn't know, would she, whether he was going to look at her, and what he might see if he did.

She'd had to Google what *shiva* meant and how to observe it. Wikipedia had said to bring food, so here she was on the front porch of the Sterns' house with an angel-food cake and a pan of brownies she'd baked herself, realizing too late that she could neither ring the bell nor open the door without dropping something. She was saved when Theresa opened the front door.

"Galina told me to wait for people to come, then open the door," Theresa said as she stepped aside to let Alicia pass. "She said you're not supposed to knock at a shiva house? I don't know, exactly."

Alicia gratefully handed the other woman the heavier plate and caught sight of the mirror that had always hung in the front entry. It had been covered with a familiar sheet, pale blue with patterned pink flowers. It was part of a set she and Ilya had received as a belated wedding gift from a distant relative she'd barely known. The gift had been a surprise, but seeing the sheet hanging over the mirror was another.

"Oh," she said.

Theresa looked at the covered mirror. "Yeah. It's tradition, I guess. Ilya did it."

"Ilya . . . did that?" Once more, Alicia paused in surprise.

She'd always known the Sterns were Jewish, of course. In a town this small, that had been an anomaly. She and Ilya had been married in a Vegas wedding chapel in a nondenominational ceremony. They'd put up a Christmas tree every year because she'd made the effort, and he'd never argued against it. She would never have guessed he knew the first thing about religious observances.

Theresa looked uncomfortable for a second or so before she shrugged. "Yes. He's . . . he's taking this hard, I guess."

"He *was* her favorite." Alicia waited for Theresa to move ahead of her down the hallway and into the kitchen. "Where are they?"

"In the living room. He and Galina aren't really talking to each other, but they're both in there. He got drunk last night, and I guess they got into it a little bit." Theresa gave Alicia a wry grin over her shoulder as she set the plate of brownies on the table among all the other platters and trays. She gestured at the oven. "I put in a few of the casseroles from after the service. So many came to the house after that, I don't know how many people will be stopping by. Galina sent out a bunch of e-mails and texts, she said."

It looked like Theresa had wasted no time in making herself useful, Alicia thought, then cringed at her own—what was it, exactly? Jealousy at how easily the other woman seemed to have slipped into the role of hostess? A place Alicia herself had disdained and wished she didn't have to fill, right? Theresa was family, too, after all. The other woman gave Alicia a lingering, contemplative look, but if she sensed Alicia's stupid flare of emotion, she didn't say anything about it.

"Niko's upstairs," Theresa said. "If you wanted to know."

Alicia kept her focus carefully on the angel-food cake she was trying to find room for on the table, careful not to give away any hint of interest. "Oh?"

When the other woman didn't answer right away, Alicia looked up. Theresa couldn't possibly know. Could she?

Theresa said nothing after that, because a shuffle of feet and a murmur of voices came from the front hallway, and with a small shrug, she headed out of the kitchen to greet the new guests. Alicia let herself grip the back of one of the kitchen chairs for a moment, her eyes closed. Breathing in, then out.

Kissing Nikolai had been one of the dumber things she'd ever done, but it wasn't like they had to act like the strangers she'd told him they seemed to be. They could keep their distance from each other if they both wanted to. They didn't have to act stupid about it. They were adults. She didn't need any kind of reassurances from him about what had happened, she told herself as she slipped out of the kitchen before anyone could come in that she'd have to talk to. She didn't need him to make her feel better.

She crept up the narrow back stairs, each step only about half the width of a normal one. As kids they'd made a game of running up and down this back staircase without falling, at least until Babulya had gotten tired of the thunderous noise and the multitude of bumps and tumbles. She'd locked both the bottom and the top doors to keep them out, and the stairway itself had become more like a storage closet than anything else. She inched her way past ski boots, mop handles missing their heads, stacks of magazines. At the top she paused, certain she'd find the door locked and her attempts at stealth all for naught, but the door creaked open on cantankerous hinges, and she stepped out into the house's upper hallway.

She drew in a long, slow breath. Funny how it felt to be here on whisper-toed feet, sneaking. She put an unsteady hand on the plaster wall, feeling the roughness. Refusing to give in to the desire to close her eyes and lose herself in memories—she was here right now. In this moment. In this place.

Making this choice.

Both houses on the end of Quarry Street had been built of the same local rock, but unlike the house in which she'd grown up, with its central stairway and the rooms surrounding it, the Stern house's layout was of a long hallway lined with doors, with a staircase and windows at each end to let in the light. At the end farthest from her, another set of stairs led to the attic. It had been volcanically hot in the summers and brutally frigid in the winters, yet the space with its slanting ceiling and tiny windows had been coveted by the brothers, who'd fought over who got to make it their room. She and Ilya had talked about finishing it into a more usable space, but as with everything else in their marriage, time, money, and ultimately a lack of desire had squelched the project.

She knew, somehow, that's where she'd find Nikolai. The wonky latch on the attic door hung loose as she opened it. She then put a foot on the bare wooden stair and listened. She could warn him that she was coming up, but she didn't. Her breath caught in her throat as she ascended, her hand on the wooden railing worn smooth by years of palms passing over it. As her head cleared the floor level and she could look into the attic space, she saw him.

He wore a pair of black dress pants and a pale-blue button-down open at the throat to reveal the first few curling dark hairs on his chest. He'd slicked his hair back from his face, the comb marks defined. The style revealed his profile to her—the high forehead and strong black brows, very much like his brother's. The high cheekbones and full mouth, very different.

He twisted in his place at the end of the bed to look at her as she came all the way up the stairs. He didn't look surprised, which amused her. He didn't look annoyed, which relieved her.

"Hey," Nikolai said.

"Hey."

"Mom and Ilya are—"

"In the living room. I know. Theresa told me. I heard someone else arriving just after I did, but I'm not sure who it was." Alicia looked around the space. Same sagging double bed with the brass headboard wedged into the only space that allowed you to stand upright. Same battered dresser and shelves built in against the walls.

How many hours had they spent up here, she thought in a bit of a daze as her feet moved of their own accord. No hesitation in her step, no matter what she might be feeling or thinking. Or not thinking, as the case might be.

There was the stack of board games and puzzles missing pieces. In the back corner, where the ceiling almost met the floor, she'd find the outline of their hands, traced in Magic Marker, if she looked. Memories of things they'd already done.

She was here to make some new ones.

"It's hard to believe she's gone." Nikolai leaned forward so that his elbows rested on his knees. His shoulders hunched. He shook his head once, twice, looking at the floor. "I shouldn't have stayed away so long, especially when I knew she wasn't doing so well."

"You came back. That's what matters." Standing in front of him, Alicia put her fingertips on the top of his head. His thick, dark hair, so much softer than Ilya's, brushed her knuckles. She tightened her fingers in it, tipping his face up.

"I wasn't here . . ."

"You were here when it counted," she told him.

Moments later she was on his lap with her mouth full of the taste of him. His hands clung to her hips while hers cupped his face. Her skirt tangled around her knees, making it difficult to straddle him, and he rolled them both onto the bed in a twist of arms and legs.

"Allie—"

She shut him up with another kiss. She didn't want to hear him talk about how this was wrong, or how they shouldn't. Later they could talk this to death, if they had to. Or they could ignore it and live with the guilt. Right now, all she cared about was touching him.

With a low groan, Nikolai opened his mouth to her. At the nip of her teeth on his bottom lip, his moan became a small growl. He opened his eyes to look into hers, his brow furrowed. Deliberately, his gaze never wavering, he pushed his hand between them, beneath her skirt. Up, up, pushing her thighs apart to get his fingers against the front of her panties.

When he rubbed his thumb slowly over the front of the silky fabric, Alicia bit back a moan of her own. Her hand slid from his face to grip his shoulder. Her nails dug deep enough to make him wince but did nothing to deter him from circling his thumb against her again, all without ever looking away from her.

She should've known better than to think she could ever be in control of this. With Nikolai, it was always, and would always be, a matter of one-upping the other. Winning had been so important to both of them as kids—but could there be a loser in this? She nudged his chin upward so she could get her teeth at the sensitive flesh of his throat. She nipped him, urging Nikolai to arch and grind against her, as his fingertips skidded a little higher and then dipped inside the waistband of her panties.

He covered her mouth with his hand when she moaned again. The salt taste of his skin sent a shudder of pleasure all through her, even as the urge to bite him so he would take his hand away made her bare her teeth. Instead, she reached between them to yank at his belt buckle and find the zipper beneath. Her hand was in the front of his pants a few seconds after that, her fingers curling over the hot, hard bulge in the front of his briefs.

The headboard squeaked as they rocked the creaking bed frame, shifting and moving against each other. Frantic. Furtive. She couldn't touch enough of him—she couldn't open herself to him fast enough.

Yet there was the barrier of clothes and the necessity for silence, even though she doubted anyone would hear them from downstairs unless they started shrieking. Nikolai rolled them again, and her hair came down from the loose knot. His elbow landed on it, pulling hard enough to bring tears to her eyes. Her low cry of protest was still muffled by his covering hand. It became a different sort of cry when he replaced his palm with his mouth. His tongue swept inside her mouth, and she no longer minded the ache in her neck from the angle it was being bent into by the weight of him on her hair.

They shifted again, this time ending with her on top of him. Her knees gripped his sides. Her hands moved over his belly, pushing his shirt up to reveal the taut muscles beneath. With shaking hands, she traced the line of thick black hair curling below his belly button and disappearing into his briefs. His erection pressed the soft fabric, a hint of his flesh peeking out from the waistband; when she drew her fingertips along it, Nikolai bucked his hips upward and grabbed her wrist to stop her.

Alicia gave him a challenging stare. She wasn't strong enough to force him to let her touch him, of course, and she didn't want to force him, anyway. She kept up the pressure of her grasp just enough that he had to make the effort at keeping her from touching him. It lasted only a moment before Nikolai bit his lower lip, and, brow furrowed, he took her hand and put it on the thick ridge of him. He moved her hand up and down, his briefs sliding between her grip and his bare skin.

He pushed his other hand between them to find the front of her panties again. With a curl of his fingers, he pushed aside the damp, silky fabric and found her heat inside. The tight knot of flesh, the slickness—the angle was wrong for him to push deeply inside her, but it was enough. Oh, it was more than enough.

Alicia pushed herself up just a bit to give him more room. She used the motion to release him from the confines of his briefs—nowhere near enough for her to have full access, but in the heat of the moment, it was working. They moved together as she leaned to kiss him again.

Incredibly, she felt the rise of climax twisting inside her. Sex was something Alicia had always needed to work at, pleasure a goal she'd had to strive for. It had never come easy for her. Yet here, dry humping on this ancient mattress in a chilly attic room with her childhood archenemy, all her body wanted to do was fill itself up with the sweet electricity of ecstasy.

All she could do was let it.

Nikolai was the one who kept her hand moving on him, matching the pace to his own fingers now sliding inside her, then, coated in her arousal, over the place where she most needed him to touch her. Nikolai kept the rhythm. Nikolai was the one now murmuring encouragement into her ear while Alicia rode the waves of desire beginning to consume her.

"C'mon, girl," he whispered into her ear, his voice thick and rough with need. "I want you to feel good . . ."

She felt better than good. Alicia sat up, arching her back, letting her body move to some inner pulse Nikolai had so skillfully initiated. She moved her hands up her body and beneath the fall of her hair, letting it slide through and tangle between her fingers. Her vision had gone a little hazy, red tinged around the edges.

Pleasure cascaded through her, and she shuddered. Her fingers dug into Nikolai's bare sides below the hem of his shirt. He gasped, thrusting harder into her curled fingers. At the very last second, as she looked into his eyes and gave him the full sight of her climax coursing all through her, his fingers bore down on hers, and he stopped her from moving.

"Someone's at the door," he whispered hoarsely. "Get off me."

They rolled, shifted, moved. Alicia was up and off the bed, standing by the shelving unit laden with old photo albums and board games, with swift fingers twisting her hair back into the semblance of a knot rather than a sex-tangled mess. Her clothes were easy to rearrange, she thought with a horrified laugh she bit back—they'd barely come off. She could do nothing about the slickness between her legs or her still-throbbing center, but fortunately all she had to do was force herself to catch her breath. Nobody could see she'd just come hard enough to bring tears to her eyes.

"What's going on?" Ilya spoke from the stairs, only his head visible. "We're waiting for you."

She risked turning, half expecting to see Nikolai in a compromising position, but it seemed he'd been as fast as she was at hiding any evidence of what had been going on. She caught his gaze across the room. His eyes flashed. His mouth thinned. He gave her the tiniest shake of his head.

Like she was going to tell Ilya anything, Alicia thought sourly. "I'm looking for some old pictures. Nikolai said there were some here in the dresser."

"I'm just getting my tie," Nikolai said. "I know I packed one."

"You don't need a tie," Ilya said. "We're supposed to be mourning. You think anyone's going to give a shit if you're not wearing a tie?"

Nikolai cleared his throat. "People talk."

"You think I give a shit what people say?" Ilya took another couple of steps higher into the room, his hand on the railing.

"You're a business owner. You should." Nikolai flipped open the lid of his suitcase and rifled around inside it, keeping his back to them both.

"You think I—"

"I found some." Alicia held out a handful of loose photos she'd pulled at random from one of the albums in the top drawer. "Let him wear a tie if he wants to, Ilya. It's not a big deal."

Ilya frowned. "It's a big enough deal when I'm down there with her, and you're all off doing whatever it is you're doing and I have to deal with it."

"Galina? What's she doing?" Alicia knew she shouldn't be glad for the distraction her semicrazy ex-mother-in-law provided, but it had already been established she was of the morally gray persuasion by the simple fact she'd just been getting a hand job from her ex-husband's brother.

"She's not doing anything. She's just being herself."

"Say no more." Alicia shook her head and glanced at Nikolai, who seemed to have found his tie and was busy putting it on with the help of an age-spotted mirror hung at an angle on the slanted wall. Ilya must have missed that one. Nikolai caught her gaze in the reflection, but she looked away. "I'll come down."

"Yeah. Me, too. In a minute." His back still facing them, Nikolai fussed with his tie.

It was probably wrong for her to hold back a smug grin, because the reason why he had to keep himself turned away was the raging hard-on she'd given him, right? Wrong to feel now that she had somehow one-upped him the way they used to. Alicia did her best to keep her expression neutral as she started down the stairs behind Ilya. Still, at the bottom, she had to hold on tight to the railing and give her weak knees a moment before she could step out into the hallway.

"What's wrong with you?" Another man might've asked it suspiciously, or maybe solicitously. Concerned for her well-being. But Ilya, being Ilya, barely waited for an answer before he pulled her into an embrace she didn't fend off only because he'd taken her by surprise. "Shit, Allie, all of this feels like shit."

What could she do but put her arms around him and squeeze him? To rub his back as he buried his face against the side of her neck? All she could do was pray he didn't smell his brother on her skin. Alicia sighed as Ilya clung to her.

"I know, honey. It's all terrible and sad," she said.

He grunted against her and pulled away. No tears, but red eyes. He hadn't shaven, nor showered, by the smell of it. Not for days. "How could you know? You have no idea how I feel."

Alicia blinked. "I guess nobody else can ever really know, but—"

"You have no clue," Ilya muttered, and stabbed a finger directly at her. "You couldn't possibly begin to imagine what this is like for me. She wasn't *your* grandmother."

"She wasn't . . . ?" Stunned, Alicia cut herself off midsentence.

Ilya had always been capable of using words to slice and tear, just like he'd been able to use them to seduce and charm and woo. If you loved him, you learned to forgive him, and Alicia had loved him, in several different ways, for a very long time. But this cut deep. Cruelly so.

"I loved her, too, Ilya." From behind her, the attic door creaked, but she didn't turn. She didn't want to look at Nikolai right now.

"It's not the same," Ilya said, then delivered the final, burning wound. "You have no idea what it's really like, to lose someone so close."

"You're drunk, right? You have to be. Because surely you did not just accuse me of being incapable of compassion and empathy, and certainly," she spat out, "that I don't understand. Did you?"

"Shit. Allie." Nikolai stepped through the doorway, but she shrugged off his touch.

"You did not just tell me," she repeated softly as she advanced on Ilya, stabbing him in the chest with her fingertip, "that I've never lost someone close to me."

"I—" he began, but she poked him again, and wisely, for maybe the first time in his life, Ilya was smart enough to shut up.

"Yeah, I didn't think so." She was too angry even to cry. "Don't you ever try to tell me I don't understand what it's like to lose someone. Don't you ever fucking dare."

He might have said more to her after that, but she was already pushing past him and heading down the back stairs. Her breath came fast and hard, burning in her throat as she fought against the urge to scream. Dodging the junk lining the stairs, she made a misstep at the last moment and tripped. She fell against the door at the bottom, which wasn't locked. It flew open so hard it banged against the wall with a hollow thud. Alicia stumbled down the final two steps, certain she was going to face-plant on the kitchen's faded linoleum.

A strong hand caught her. Held her up. Struggling to get herself settled, Alicia didn't at first see who'd saved her from falling.

"Jenni . . . Jennilynn?"

The big hands gripped Alicia's arms harder, then released so she could stand on her own. She pushed her hair out of her face. The man who stood in front of her looking so stunned wore a dark-gray suit and the shadow of a beard. She hadn't seen him in a couple of decades.

"No, Mr. Malone, I'm Alicia."

"Jenni's sister. My God." Barry wiped a hand over his mouth, clearly shaken. "You looked so much like her for a second there . . ."

She'd heard that before, although not for years. She supposed it was meant as a compliment. She stepped away from him.

"I guess I haven't seen you in a long time." Barry gave her a weak smile. "I'm sorry. How are you, Allie?"

She wasn't much in the mood for small talk, but she managed to force her lips into the semblance of a smile. "Under the circumstances, I'm as good as I can be, I guess."

"Right. Of course." He cleared his throat and shifted on the balls of his feet, looking uncomfortable. "I'm here to sit shiva. Umm . . . Galina invited me. I hope that's okay."

"She's allowed to ask whoever she wants," Alicia said. "If you'll excuse me."

She left the kitchen without waiting for him to answer her, not caring whether it was rude. Only once she was across the street again, safe behind her own locked door, did she allow herself to let out the strangled breaths she'd been holding. But then, no matter how hard she tried to scream, all she could do was whisper.

"Don't you ever tell me that I don't know what it's like to lose someone."

CHAPTER EIGHTEEN

"No matter what I do, I always screw it up." Ilya waved a hand toward the back stairs, down which Alicia had disappeared, then grimaced. "Shit."

Niko rubbed his forehead, where a faint, throbbing ache was rising, with the back of his hand. "Yeah, man. What the hell was that all about?"

"I don't know. Shit," his brother repeated, then looked over at Niko. "I didn't think."

It wasn't the time to point out that not thinking about other people's feelings was one of Ilya's bad habits. "It's a tough time for everyone, Ilya. She's upset, too."

"She'll get over it." Ilya's confident dismissal set Niko's jaw on edge, but what could he do, argue? Ilya knew Allie better than Niko did.

Niko didn't want to think about that.

Ilya shrugged. "We should get downstairs."

"We could stay up here," Niko said with a small, tight grin. "Until they all go."

Ilya didn't return the smile. His red eyes and disheveled appearance hinted at another bender, but Niko didn't think his brother was drunk. He would've been more charming if he was.

"You avoid it however you want. I'm going downstairs," Ilya said.

Niko rubbed again at his head. He could still taste Allie. Still hear the soft, breathy moans she made when he touched her. Looking at his brother, he waited to feel some kind of guilt about what had happened, but if it was going to hit him, it was taking its sweet time. That was the thing about water under a bridge. It could get caught up in a bunch of debris, or it could sweep everything away, leaving nothing behind; it all depended on the ferocity of the storm.

Without answering, Niko followed Ilya down the front stairs, back into the formal living room, where the small group of friends who'd come to honor Babulya had thinned to one or two. Theresa was still there, along with another familiar face he hadn't seen in a long time.

"Barry?"

Theresa's father turned from his conversation with Galina. "Niko. Hey. Ilya. Hi, good to see you. Wish it was under better circumstances."

They shook hands briefly. Niko gave his mother a look, trying to gauge how she felt about the sight of her ex-husband, but she appeared serenely unmoved. Theresa, on the other hand, looked as though she'd eaten something that wasn't sitting very well.

"It was nice of you to come, Barry." Galina smiled. "You know, my mother never liked you."

Barry didn't seem put off by this, but then he'd been married to Niko's mother, and it would hardly be a surprise if he knew exactly the sort of woman she was. "I didn't come here for your mother."

That little exchange seemed like the cue for everyone else to start leaving. Ilya took on the role of handshaker and gratitude giver, accepting hugs and putting on his most sincere face to listen to everyone's condolences. Niko and Theresa exchanged a look. She shrugged. Niko stood by his mother. At least she wasn't crying.

Later, when the house had cleared out and Theresa had started to clean up while Galina and Barry were still talking in muttered whispers in the corner, Niko found his brother standing on the back step. Ilya tipped his head back to look up at the cloudless night sky littered with stars. They stood in silence together for a few minutes.

"You should put on a coat or come inside," Niko said finally. "It's cold out here."

Ilya slanted him a look. "Thanks, mother hen."

"Okay, then, forget it. Freeze your ass off. See if I care." Niko shrugged and leaned against the door frame, drawing in a few frosty breaths. He'd endured worse weather than this, of course. A hundred times. But there was nothing quite like how it felt to be back home on this back porch, looking out across the yard to the straggly patch of trees beyond.

He'd kissed Allie for the first time in that backyard, right over there. Under a sky something like this. He should have kissed her a hundred times back then. If he had, they wouldn't be groping each other in the attic, praying nobody caught them.

"Never expected to see Barry," Ilya said after another minute had ticked by.

"Nope."

Behind Niko, the door opened. Theresa poked her head out, saw them, then came out the rest of the way. She let the door hang open for a moment so they could hear Galina's rising voice.

"Hey," Theresa said with a grimace. "Brrr, it's cold out here. Finally."

Before she pulled the door closed, another shout pierced the night air.

"Man, she's really letting him have it," Ilya said with a glance at Theresa, who shrugged.

"He shouldn't be here," she said.

Behind her, Niko nudged the door open again, cocking his head to listen as his mother's tirade grew louder. The tone of it changed, something more desperate in her voice, and he was moving before he thought of it. Ilya behind him. Theresa, too.

"Don't you blame me for that!" came Galina's shout from the other room.

Niko moved forward, thinking to intervene, but Theresa snagged his sleeve. She shook her head. He gave her a look.

"He deserves to get his ass handed to him," Theresa said. "Your mom can handle herself."

"Don't you blame me for your bad choices!" Galina continued, getting louder. She was heading for the kitchen, and there was nothing they could do but stand there and pretend they hadn't been eavesdropping. Not that Galina seemed to care as she flew into the kitchen with Barry on her heels. She whirled, facing him as he tried to grab her wrist. "Don't you dare touch me. You come here, to this house and try to put your hands on me? My mother died!"

"That's why I'm here!" Barry looked like he meant to reach for her again, but at the menacing way both Ilya and Nikolai stepped forward, he stopped. Barry looked uncomfortable, avoiding their eyes. "I came out of respect, Galina. And because you asked me to."

The brothers shared a glance. Galina had put herself in this situation. Not a shocker. Ilya rolled his eyes. Theresa saw the look and sighed, rubbing at her arms against the chill coming in from the outside.

"Barry, you'd better go," Niko said.

Barry, whose cheeks had gone high with a hectic crimson flush, kept his eyes on Galina. "We aren't done."

"Oh, yeah. You're done." Ilya stepped up to grab at Barry's sleeve, but the older man moved easily aside.

Barry held up his hands. "Fine. I get it. You still hate me. But you're the one who invited me here, Galina. You don't get to play the martyr now."

"I'm uninviting you," she said coldly, her gaze bright and piercing. Nobody crossed Galina when she looked like that. Nobody who was smart, anyway.

Niko had never thought Barry was particularly smart, but he took two steps back.

"Fine. I'm going." Barry looked at Theresa, who very carefully did not return the gaze. He held out a hand to Niko, who took it automatically to shake, then Ilya, who didn't. "Sorry about the ruckus."

"Just go," Ilya said.

Niko started toward the front door. "I'll walk you out."

"We all will," Ilya said with a subtle clench of his fists.

If there was going to be any trouble with Barry, Niko and Ilya were going to take care of it. Galina might be an instigator, a pain in the ass, but she was their mother. At the front door, Barry grabbed his coat from the closet and put it on. He turned to face them, making a move as though he meant to hug his daughter. She casually and with grace stepped away, not making a big deal out of her avoidance—making it seem like a coincidence, even—but Ilya must've also noticed, because he moved between her and her father.

"Good night, Barry," Ilya said. Barry left without another word. Ilya shut the door behind him, then turned to Theresa. "What the hell?"

She shrugged, crossing her arms. "I have no idea. He said she invited him."

"She probably did," Niko said.

Theresa shook her head. "Whatever. He's gone. I should go, too. It could be awkward now."

"You're welcome to stay," Ilya put in, surprising Niko, who wouldn't have thought his brother gave half a damn what Theresa or anyone else did tonight. "It's late."

She hesitated, her glance going back and forth between them. "I'll help clean up. If your mom seems weird about it, I'll go. Okay?"

Galina had moved from the dining room into the living room, where she had a bottle of beer in one hand and was flipping through a photo album with the other. She looked up as they came in, her eyes bright, cheeks flushed.

"Look, Theresa, here are the pictures from the day I married your father." Galina patted the sofa beside her, and Theresa, with a look at

Ilya, sat next to her. Galina took a pull on the bottle. Like Ilya, she was more charming when she was drinking, and Niko felt a small rush of relief that at least she was no longer shrieking. "It was nice of him to come, wasn't it? He doesn't look very good, though. He hasn't aged very well."

"Mom," Ilya said. "What the hell?"

"He doesn't take good care of himself," Theresa agreed, not sounding annoyed. "I'm surprised you invited him, though."

"When someone dies, you do what's right." Galina flipped another page, leaning forward to look at the pictures. "You hated that dress I bought you. Remember?"

Theresa laughed, low. "Yes. I remember."

"Why *did* you invite him?" Niko asked quietly.

His mother shrugged, not looking up. "I thought it was the right thing to do at the time. I guess I'm not allowed to make mistakes?"

"That's not what I meant," Niko said, but stopped himself from apologizing. He tried to catch his brother's eye, but Ilya wasn't looking at him. He'd gone to stand behind the sofa to look over their shoulders. With a sigh, so did Niko. It was clear she wanted them to see the pictures, and with his mother, there was hardly ever a point in resisting. She would make her point or get her way.

"So handsome. My sons." Galina tapped the photo of the two of them each wearing suits. The wedding had been in the early summer. Those suits had been ill fitting and hot. Niko couldn't even remember ever seeing those pictures. With a snap, Galina shut the album and tossed it onto the coffee table. "I have something I need to talk to you both about."

Theresa coughed. "Should I go? Is it private?"

"It's a family matter," Galina answered, "but I suppose you can stay."

She looked around at all of them, fixing each with a few seconds' worth of a steady, unblinking gaze before she looked down at her hands folded in her lap. Niko and his brother exchanged looks again. Waiting for the drama, because with their mother, there was always drama.

Galina looked up. "I've spent too much time away from my family. Losing my mother showed me how important it is that I be close to my boys. You never know how much time you have left, and I want to spend it with you."

Niko coughed and tried to catch Ilya's eye again, but his brother had turned away. "Mom—"

"What exactly do you mean," Ilya broke in without facing them. "More time? Like a long visit, or what?"

"Oh, no," Galina smiled. "I'm not going back to South Carolina. I'm staying here."

CHAPTER NINETEEN

"What do you mean, she's not going home?" Alicia put aside the pile of envelopes and mail that had been piling up over the past couple of weeks and gave Nikolai her full attention. "She's planning to, what, move right back into the house like she'd never been gone?"

Nikolai nodded, leaning in her office doorway as though it would kill him to come all the way inside. Like she might jump over the desk and wrestle him to the ground to seduce him. Alicia's mouth twisted, sour, and she smoothed it at once, not wanting him to see her giving him one bare second's worth of her emotions. She hadn't heard one damned word from him in just over a week—not a text or a phone call or a random visit with a casserole as an excuse. Let him stand in her office doorway forever. There was no way she was ever going to invite him in.

"Yeah. A bunch of her stuff was delivered yesterday."

Alicia swiveled in her desk chair and frowned. That was serious. "Wow."

"Yeah."

"What's she going to live on? Retirement? Does she even have any?" Alicia's parents had both taken early retirements so they could leave the cold winters of Pennsylvania for the snowbird climate of Arizona, but they'd both had full-time, consistent work histories and enough savings to allow it.

"Maybe she'll get another job? I don't know." Nikolai shrugged. "Who ever really knows with her?"

Alicia sighed. "Why didn't your brother tell me any of this? I just talked to him yesterday."

When she'd called to ask him whether he was going to bother coming in to work at all, Ilya had told her only that he was still taking care of things at home, leaving her to deal with everything at the shop. He'd been quiet, but not snappish or irritable. They hadn't fought. She'd been too nice, probably, but the effort of arguing with him about responsibility and picking up his share of the load had been too much for her. She could spend a lifetime juggling her resentments toward Ilya.

"Who ever really knows with *him*?" Nikolai said with a grin she figured he meant to be conspiratorial.

Alicia didn't return it. "Don't do that."

"What?" He frowned and stood up straight, even going so far as to take a single step over the threshold so he actually stood inside her office instead of just beyond it.

"Don't try to get me to talk shit about him," she said.

Nikolai let out a short bark of a laugh. "I wasn't trying to get you to talk shit about him . . . I just meant . . . wow, Allie. Wow."

The abbreviation of her name, as it always did, scraped at her. A snagging thorn. She was done ignoring it, especially for him.

"Alicia," she said tightly. Everything was coiling inside her, twisting and twisting.

"Huh?"

"I don't like to be called Allie. My name's Alicia."

His brow furrowed. "We always called you Allie."

"I never liked it," she told him in a clipped, biting tone.

"Ilya calls you Allie," Nikolai said, like a challenge, his voice dipping low. His gaze flared.

Alicia met his eyes without looking away, both of them pressing hard the way they'd always done, neither willing to give an inch. "Yes. He does."

"Did you ever tell *him* not to call you Allie?"

"All the time," she said. "But he still does it."

She did not want this heat between them. She didn't want to remember his hands on her, his mouth, the huff of his breath in her ear. She didn't want to think about how easy it had been, every shift and move and touch, everything effortless and perfect, at least physically. Everything else between them still seemed as difficult as it had always been.

"I'm sorry. *Alicia.*" Nikolai hadn't taken another step toward her, but the distance between them that had seemed so vast a few minutes ago had become far too close.

Her heart throbbed so hard it hurt, a flare of pain in her chest that faded when she remembered to take a breath. He'd said the right words to defuse this impending argument but had done nothing to relieve the tension.

"Thank you," she bit out.

She hadn't invited him in; he'd entered anyway. Another creeping flush of heat touched her throat and cheeks as she remembered the way she'd seduced him in the attic bedroom. She'd made such a fool of herself, for what? Asking for what she wanted? Why should she ever feel embarrassed about that?

Yet she did, and she couldn't bear to do it again. The thought of it sent a wash of ice all over her that cut through the heat and made her teeth want to chatter. She settled for crossing her arms over her stomach and clenching her jaw.

"So, anyway, I just stopped by to tell you about Galina," he said when she didn't speak.

She nodded. "Okay."

"I thought you'd like to know."

"Okay," she repeated with as little inflection as possible, giving him nothing.

Nothing.

Nikolai's eyes narrowed. "Thought you might like to know that I'm not heading out for a while, either. The house needs a lot of work, and my mother is asking me to do it."

"And you're the one who fixes things. Right?" she said in the same flat tone.

"Doesn't someone have to?"

"Don't look at me because things fell apart," Alicia said coolly, deliberately ignoring the double meaning of his comment.

"Hey, you. Fancy meeting you here." The feminine voice from behind him made Nikolai turn, revealing Theresa standing in the doorway. "Hey, Allie."

"She likes to be called *Alicia*," he said.

Alicia kept her mouth in a thin line, refusing to smile or rise to his taunt. "Hey, Theresa. What's up?"

"Everything okay at home?" Nikolai asked his former stepsister.

Theresa gave him a small smile and a shrug. "Your brother was still sleeping when I left, and Galina was on the computer looking up laminate flooring."

Nikolai sighed. "Great."

"I came to see if you wanted to grab some lunch, Alicia." Theresa hitched her shoulder bag a little higher and waited until he'd moved out of the way so she could come into Alicia's office. She glanced at Nikolai.

"Sure," Alicia said. "I have nothing better going on."

Nikolai made a noise low in his throat, not quite a word, and said aloud, "I'm out of here. Theresa, are you coming back to the house later?"

"I wasn't going to," she said with a shake of her head and a wry grin. "But your mother insisted. She said as long as I had business in town, I should stay at the house. Of course, she also made a big point of telling me that she plans to turn the room I'm using into a library, something about custom-made shelves. So I'm not sure she really wants to me to hang around."

Nikolai groaned and rubbed at his eyes. "Great, custom shelves. Guess who gets to build those. I'm pretty sure fixing that shower is the first priority, though. Well, I guess I'd better call and find out what else she needs me to pick up from the hardware store. All . . . icia, can I bring you back anything? New hammer? Some nails? Doggy door?"

"I don't have a dog."

Nikolai snapped his fingers. "Right. Want me to grab you one while I'm out? How about a nice little shitzapoo, or something like that? A poodoodle? A cockashitz!"

"Get out of here," she said, breaking, wishing she could maintain her anger with him the way she wanted to, but helpless not to laugh. She stifled it behind her hand, but the flash of Nikolai's grin and a totally cocky wink told her he'd heard the giggle in her voice.

He saluted them both. "Good day, *ladies*."

He added an ominous emphasis to the word, and with a flourish, exited the room. Theresa watched him go, then threw Alicia a curious look. She pretended not to notice.

"I have to finish up a couple things, and then we can go." Alicia said with a wave toward the chair across from her desk. She waited for the sound of the bell at the front door to jingle, announcing Nikolai's exit. "What a crazy couple of weeks."

Theresa took a seat, her bag on her lap. "Yeah. Totally."

"Nikolai said his mother isn't going back to South Carolina." Alicia closed out of the multiple browser tabs she'd had open. Travel blogs, mostly. Just because she'd never gone anywhere exotic didn't mean she didn't like to read about the trips other people took.

"She mentioned that to me, too," Theresa answered. "I guess I hadn't realized that she'd been down there so long."

"Since before Ilya and I got married." Alicia talked to her parents weekly, sometimes on the phone or via video chat, and while they never came back to Pennsylvania, she visited them several times a year. Galina had often contacted Ilya over the phone or e-mail, but had also gone long stretches of time without a word. Alicia hadn't thought it was right to have such sporadic contact, but Galina wasn't her mother, and therefore it hadn't been up to her.

"Why do you think she's staying up here this time?"

Alicia thought about it for a second. "Is it wrong of me to feel suspicious? Like she has an ulterior motive?"

"No," Theresa laughed. "When someone behaves the same way for as long as you've known them, it's natural to expect they'll keep behaving the same way. It has that feeling about it, doesn't it? Like an accident waiting to happen."

"That's a good way to describe it." It wasn't Galina who made her feel that way, it was Nikolai, but she wasn't going to let herself think about him anymore. Alicia stood. "Ready for lunch? Where do you want to go?"

"You pick. Do you mind driving separately? I have some appointments on the other side of town this afternoon."

They agreed to meet at a local pizza shop, not yet crowded since it wasn't quite lunchtime. They ordered slices and drinks and took them to a back booth. Alicia looked up at the sound of a cough to see a woman who looked semifamiliar, but whose face she couldn't place.

"I'm Mimi Zook," the older woman said. "I work at the home where your grandmother lived. I'm sorry to hear of her passing. She was one of the loveliest residents."

"Thank you, I appreciate that so much," Alicia said.

When the woman had moved away to her own table, Theresa said, "Everyone loved Babulya. Do you know that she sent me a birthday card every single year?"

Alicia's eyebrows rose. "She did? Even . . ."

"Yeah, even after. I mean, I only had one birthday when I lived there, but she remembered. Sent me a card every single year, with two—"

"Two brand-new dollar bills!" Alicia clapped her hands. "Yes. Wow."

Theresa's eyes glittered a little, and she smiled. "Exactly. There were times when my father didn't even remember, but Babulya did."

"I'm going to miss her."

"We all are." Theresa pulled a napkin from the holder and wiped her eyes. "But hey, listen, I came here for something totally unrelated to any of the craziness going on at the Sterns'. Talk about an ulterior motive."

Alicia grabbed a napkin, too, her own voice thick with tears. "Yeah?"

"Yep." Theresa pulled a thick white envelope from her bag and passed it across the table.

"What's this?"

"It's an offer from the company I work with. Diamond Development." Theresa cleared her throat and inched forward to sit on the edge of her seat. "They want to buy the quarry."

CHAPTER TWENTY

"Hey." Niko nudged his sleeping brother. Ilya hadn't been off the couch for the past couple of days except to use the bathroom and go back to bed. "Are you ever getting your ass up? Going back to work? I'm sure Alicia would appreciate it if you'd at least let her know what's going on."

Ilya cracked open an eye and gave his brother the finger. "I have the flu."

"You don't have the flu." This came from Galina, who'd just come in from outside. The tang of smoke clung to her clothes. "You have the laziness. Get up. Take a shower. You stink."

Ilya muttered something and flopped back onto the couch, facing the back cushions. This was all getting out of hand. He should've left a week ago, yet here he still was, dealing with everyone else's bullshit.

Irritated, Niko poked him again. "Get up. Or I'm going to make you get up, and I'll throw you in the shower myself. Mom's right. You do stink. It's been two weeks, man. You need to get up and get back to work, starting tomorrow."

"Bite me," Ilya said.

Niko grabbed his brother by the back of the shirt and hauled him upright, ducking out of the way when Ilya tried to swing at him. "You want to hit me? G'head and try."

"Boys." Galina tut-tutted, shaking her head. "Take it outside."

It was what she'd always said when they were young. They were too old now to be scrapping, but Niko put up his fists anyway. Like a dare. Watching his brother's expression for any sign that he meant to take another swing.

"I don't *want* to fight you," Niko warned.

Ilya snorted laughter. "Yeah. Sure you don't. You've been aching to punch me in the face since you got here."

The only person Niko had ever punched in his life was his brother, and most often then only at Ilya's instigation. He uncurled his fingers and held out his hands. Not a target. He'd gone away and come home again, but that didn't mean he had to keep falling into *all* the same stupid patterns.

"Boys!"

Both of them turned to look at their mother. She'd put her hands on her hips. Today she wore her hair in a braid that swung over one shoulder. The lines around her eyes and creases at the corners of her mouth were a little deeper, but not by much. She didn't so much look older as smaller, Niko thought. Galina had always been built tiny but strong. She looked frail now.

"I'm making dinner. It will be ready in an hour." She poked a finger at Ilya. "You. Shower and change your clothes. Niko, clear off the table in the dining room. We're going to eat in there like civilized people. And set a place for Allie. I invited her to come over."

Both brothers stopped their posturing to face their mother. Ilya laughed. Niko didn't.

"What? Why?" Ilya asked with a shake of his head. "Jesus, Mother."

Galina waved a languid hand. "Because that girl used to be my daughter-in-law, and, so sue me, I always liked her. She was good to your Babulya and, frankly, Ilya, to you. So why shouldn't I invite her over to spend some time with us? She's family. We're all a family. I told you, it's time we started acting like one."

There wasn't much to say when she put it like that, not without sounding like a dick or making too much of it and calling attention to a situation Niko really didn't want to overthink more than he already had. He studied his mother's expression, trying to see if she had any idea about Alicia and him, but Galina had always been difficult to read. Whatever her reasons for including Alicia in the "family" dinner, he convinced himself it probably had nothing to do with what had happened between them.

"Go. Do as you're told," Galina said now with an imperious wave of her fingers that brought back flashes of memory from when they were kids. First she commanded, and if she wasn't obeyed, she screamed. Even as an adult, Niko discovered he didn't want to tempt his mother into a meltdown.

To Niko's surprise, Ilya didn't argue. Maybe he also didn't want to deal with Galina's temper. Niko waited a beat or two longer before he went into the dining room to clear the table from the remnants of last week's shiva. From the kitchen he heard the rattle of pots and pans. He smelled the tinge of smoke different from Galina's cigarettes, and the underlying aroma of garlic and wine.

He looked up when she followed him into the dining room. She went to the antique china cabinet in the corner and opened the door. She ran a hand along the interior, leaning forward to look deep.

"Use these dishes, the good ones." She glanced over her shoulder with a smile. "There's no point in saving them for something special if we never make anything special, yes?"

"Sure. Okay." He went to the cabinet while Galina bent to pull out a tablecloth from the lower drawer. "If that's what you want."

"It's good to have nice things, don't you think?" She spread the cloth on the table, smoothing it.

Niko pulled out a couple of plates, gold rimmed and edged with flowers. He could not recall ever once using them. "Yeah, I guess so. Or it's good not to have things you're tied down to."

"Hmm, is that how you feel? Is that because you don't have anything of your own?"

He looked up to see her staring at him with a slightly twisted smile. "I have things of my own. Just not the same way you do. I don't need fancy china I never use, because I eat in a cafeteria. I don't spend my time or money accumulating stuff for the sake of it."

"You know, I always liked the letters you sent from the kibbutz. I envied you that experience. I thought about going over there myself. I could be a socialist, sure, why not?" Galina gestured for him to put the plates on the table.

Niko settled two of them, then pulled out a few more, handing them over for her to place at each chair. "Oh, you think so?"

"Oh, yes. It seems like it would be good, you know? You work hard, you contribute, you don't have to worry about where you're going to live or how you'll eat. That sounds very nice, to me. Very comfortable." Galina shrugged and stepped back to look at the table, then gestured for more plates.

"It was all right for a time, but you wouldn't like it long term," he told her. "Not when you have to take what someone else determines you deserve to have."

She looked at him thoughtfully as she finished setting all the places with dinner plates. "That's what you think of your mother?"

"*I* don't always like it, how about that." Niko shrugged and looked in the cabinet for glasses or bread plates or whatever other fancy things might be in there that she wanted to use.

"Well, I've always wanted to visit Israel. Do you know that when Babulya came here to America from Russia, she almost went there, instead? But they weren't letting anyone in. They'd get on the ships and be turned away—or worse, they put them in camps. It was near the end of the war, and, still, they wouldn't let them in," she said lightly. "She always told me she'd barely escaped the Germans putting her in a camp. She wasn't going to let the British put her in one just so she could find a place in the homeland. You have to remember she wasn't even allowed to be Jewish growing up in Russia."

Niko pulled out a stack of smaller dishes and handed them over. "I never heard that story."

"She didn't talk about it much, not to you boys, anyway. She didn't like to think about it. She came here instead, to America. And she met my father, and she had me. And I had Ilya," Galina said. "And then you. And here we are now. But I always did envy you spending time there. I think how different my life would've been if my mother had made a different choice."

"If she'd made a different choice, you probably wouldn't have been born." Niko waved toward the kitchen. "What are you making?"

"Smart-ass stew," his mother quipped, and fixed him with a look he remembered well from his childhood. "An old family recipe."

They finished setting the table together without a lot of small talk after that. It seemed she'd learned how to prepare more than breakfast at her diner job. It was a simple meal—roast chicken, salad, couscous with onions and garlic, and wine. Yet Galina plated it expertly and had it on the table with Niko's help by the time Ilya finished with the shower.

"Just about blasted my balls off," Ilya grumbled as he took his place at the head of the table, where Galina had told him to sit. "I thought you were fixing it. Hey. Fancy dishes?"

"It's time we used them," Galina put in.

"The shower's on the list," Niko said. "Sorry I'm not working around the clock to fix everything that's been broken around here. Maybe instead of sleeping on the couch all day long you could pitch in, since you've apparently decided that you're not going back to work."

"I didn't say I was never going back," Ilya replied. "I just needed some downtime."

"Downtime doesn't pay the bills," their mother said.

Ilya shrugged. "What's the point of being your own boss if you can't make your own hours?"

"It just seems like a shitty thing to do to Alicia, that's all." Niko took the bottle of wine his mother was handing him, along with the corkscrew.

"Since when do you care about my business *or* Allie?" Ilya jerked his chin in his brother's direction. "What's she been saying about me? Has she been bitching to you?"

Niko didn't answer that, not trusting himself to talk too much about Alicia. He focused on opening the bottle of Malbec. He was saved from further interrogation when the doorbell rang as a warning, and, moments later, Theresa came into the kitchen.

She held up a large boxed chocolate cake. "I brought dessert."

"A working woman," Galina said with a pointed look at her older son. "With responsibilities. And a paycheck. Someone raised her with a good work ethic."

"Well, it wasn't you," Ilya said. "So I wouldn't get all proud about it, like you can take credit."

Oh, shit, Niko thought. *Here we go.* The tension that had been brewing since Galina had returned home was about to get ugly.

"Let me get an opener," he said to soothe them both. "Mom, dinner smells fantastic. Let's eat."

Theresa set the box she'd brought on the counter. "Ilya, don't be a jerk. What can I do to help?"

For a moment it still felt as though Ilya and Galina were going to launch themselves at each other like Godzilla versus Mothra, or something, but at Theresa's admonition, Ilya quieted.

"Good job," Niko said under his breath as they were both dispensed by Galina into the dining room with handfuls of food.

Theresa gave him a small smile and shrugged as she put down a basket of rolls. She cocked her head at the sound of Galina's laughter from the kitchen. "I'm good at peacemaking."

"Part of your job?" Niko had a vague idea about what Theresa did for a living—something to do with real estate development and property management.

"You could say that." Theresa hesitated, looking as though she meant to say more, but looked toward the dining-room doorway that connected with the hall, not the kitchen. "Hey, Allie."

Niko turned. Alicia stood with a pie in her hands. She looked him right in the eye and held it up.

"I brought dessert. It's cherry."

"My favorite," Niko said.

Alicia didn't smile. "I know."

Then Ilya came in with a steaming platter of chicken, Galina on his heels, and whatever Niko had thought he might say to Alicia was lost in the bustle of everyone taking places at the table. Once they'd all been seated, Galina raised her glass of wine and waited for everyone to quiet. She cleared her throat.

"It's nice to sit down with family at the beginning of the week. Talk about what we're doing. Be involved with each other's lives. Thank you all for coming to Sunday dinner. I'm happy to have you here. My sons . . . and both my daughters."

Niko saw Theresa and Alicia sharing a look. Alicia's lips thinned, though he couldn't tell if it was to hide a laugh or a cough of surprise. Theresa rallied first, lifting her glass of water.

"To family," Theresa said firmly.

There wasn't anything to do but join the toast, so Niko raised his glass, too. He tried catching Alicia's eye, but she wasn't looking at him. "Family."

"Family," Alicia agreed, her own glass raised, but her gaze averted from his and everyone else's.

"Fine," Ilya said at last, and clinked his glass against each of theirs. "To family."

◆ ◆ ◆

"It wasn't the weirdest dinner we've ever had," Alicia said quietly with a glance over her shoulder to make sure they were alone in the kitchen.

Galina had declared that since she'd cooked, it would be someone else's job to clean up. With the fancy china, that meant handwashing, not the dishwasher. She'd disappeared upstairs to the master bedroom she'd commandeered from Ilya. Theresa had apologized but excused herself to take a conference call in her room—the fact she was actually staying in the house while she was in town still made Niko shake his head. Ilya had claimed exhaustion and gone up to his old bedroom.

That left Niko and Alicia to handle the dishes and put away the food. It hadn't taken them long. They worked together like they'd planned out every move ahead of time.

"No," he agreed. "Not like when she was into tarot, and we had to get a reading just to see if she was going to serve cold cereal or tacos."

Alicia laughed. "Oh, wow. I guess I must've missed that."

"I was in about fifth grade, I guess. It didn't last long. Babulya was very against it. Said tarot were the devil's cards." Niko laughed, too.

"I think it's kind of nice, actually. That she wants to spend family time together. Losing her mother must've had her thinking about things." Alicia ran her hands under the faucet and dried them on a towel, then leaned against the counter. "Having everyone here is different, huh? Feels weird. It's been a long time."

He nodded. "Yeah. Totally weird. And Theresa. How about that?"

Alicia gave him a sideways glance. "She's got some business in town. I'm not sure I'd want to stay here instead of in a hotel, though. I guess it's only for a few days more. Then she'll be leaving. And you?"

"What about me?" He leaned on the counter.

"You'll be leaving again soon, won't you?"

Run away.

Run toward.

Make a decision; you can't just stand still.

"Actually, no," Niko said. "It looks like I'm going to be hanging out here for at least the next few weeks."

"Oh. Really? That's a surprise." She gave him a steady, thoughtful look, her eyes a little narrowed. "I would have thought you'd be out of here as soon as you possibly could. How come you're staying?"

Because he hadn't been able to stop thinking about the taste of her and the feel of her and the sound of her saying his name, and now faced with the reality of her, there was no way he could go back to the kibbutz. All he had to do was tell the council that he was going to cash out his contract and move back home, because the thought of being away from her again was unbearable. All he had to do was run toward and not away.

The heat he'd been trying to ignore all evening flared between them. Neither of them moved, but they didn't have to. He could feel the tension from all the way across the room. He swept his tongue over his bottom lip, remembering the flavor of her. Wishing he could forget, but knowing he wasn't going to. Not tonight, anyway. Maybe not ever.

"Why are you staying, Nikolai?" She gave him that head tilt, that up-and-down look that drove him crazy.

Niko took a step closer, getting off on the way she drew in a breath. At the darkness growing in her eyes as the pupils dilated. "Unfinished business."

"Funny thing, that unfinished business," she murmured. Her lips parted. She shifted, her fingers gripping the countertop as she settled her feet wider apart.

By the time he got to her, they were both reaching for the other. He couldn't hold back the groan when he kissed her. Laughing, she covered his mouth with her hand.

"Shhh." She did let him pull her closer, his hands cupping her ass cheeks. "You don't want anyone to hear."

"Definitely not." He nuzzled at her neck, nipping. It was his turn, then, to cover her mouth with his fingers to stifle a noise, but only for a few seconds because he had to get his mouth on hers again. "I'm starving."

Alicia let her head fall back so he could mouth her throat again. "We just ate."

"Not for dinner. For you."

She looked at him. "Careful, Nikolai. You're going to make me think you like me a little."

He palmed her ass again, kneading. Then slipped his hand between her legs to press her there. "I think we've already established that I like you more than just a little."

She rocked against him, her fingers curling in the front of his shirt. Her back arched as she offered him her neck again. Whatever she meant to say eased into a mumbled moan.

"I want you," Niko said. "I want you so fucking much . . ."

The fall of footsteps above them pushed them apart. Alicia turned to the sink to fake rinsing a dish. Niko put the lid on a plasticware container of leftovers. Nobody came downstairs, and after a minute or so, both of them started laughing.

"It's worse than in high school, waiting to get caught making out on the couch," Alicia said.

"I never worried about getting caught. I never had a girlfriend."

She made a face. "Not one you brought over here, anyway. Don't tell me you and Deb Smith never got hot and heavy in her rumpus room."

"What about you and Mike Taylor?" Niko took her by the hips and pulled them together again, one ear cocked for sounds from upstairs.

"What about him?" Alicia gave him a coy smile. "What makes you think he and I were an item?"

"Because he used to brag about it in gym class." Niko frowned at the memory. "Used to piss me off."

Her jaw dropped. "Ew, gross, no! He did? Oh, yuck. What did he say?"

"Just that he was taking you out." Niko's lip curled.

Alicia swatted at him. "And what . . . you were jealous?"

"Maybe." He gave her a steady look, watching the way her smile softened. "I did think he should have kept his mouth shut about you. I remember that."

"We never did more than kiss," she told him. "And only then a couple of times. If I'd known you cared—"

"What? What would you have done?" he asked when she broke off.

Alicia shrugged and linked her fingers behind his neck. "I don't know, to be honest. It wasn't like I thought you and I would date or something. Back then. We just had a *thing*."

"A thing. Like we have a thing now?"

Her smile didn't quite all the way reach to her eyes. "Yeah."

"This thing," he said in a low voice. "This unfinished business."

"What happens, do you think, when it's finished?"

Niko had a feeling it would never be finished between them. It had been more than twenty years in the making. What would he do without this desire that, once sated, would surely disappear? What would he do without the thoughts of her that he turned to when he needed to remember he *was* capable of feeling? Where would he run to then?

"I think that's a much longer conversation," he said finally.

She bit her lower lip for a second. "Why can't we have it, then?"

He said her name, meaning for it to push her away, but it only pulled her close to him again. The kiss went on and on, and he lost himself in it and her, trying hard not to be that guy, the guy who took advantage of someone who wanted something from him he knew he couldn't possibly provide . . . but he failed. Of course he did.

"We can't do this, Alicia."

When they were younger, it had always been her older sister who'd pushed the boundaries and crossed the lines. Alicia had been the one to hold back. To follow the rules.

Obviously, she'd changed.

"Why not?" she challenged. "Why can't we do this?"

Niko sighed. His fingers tightened on her hips. He wanted to let her go, to step away and put some distance between them to make it easier to deny the heat still palpable between them.

"Because we can't."

"You're not going to stick around. You're going to fix some things around here for your mother until you can't stand it here anymore, and then you'll be back off into the world, having your adventures." She sounded only the tiniest bit bitter. "So why can't we do this thing we both want to do, at least for the time you're here?"

"You were married to my brother."

Alicia snorted soft laughter. "Who was in love with my sister."

"It doesn't matter," Niko said. "It doesn't make this right."

"You had me first," Alicia told him boldly. Bluntly. She stood on her tiptoes to offer him her mouth, brushing her lips over his before pulling away when he tried to kiss her back. "Everything about this is messed up, Nikolai, believe me. I get it. But you can't tell me that you want me and then not follow through. It's not fair. More than that, it's cruel. Is that what you want? To be cruel to me?"

He shook his head, then pressed his face to the side of her neck. Holding her close. Breathing against her skin. "No. That's not what I want."

"What *do* you want?"

It should've been easier to tell her. He'd thought about it so much over the years, after all. Yet words failed him, as they almost always did. All he could do was scrape his teeth along her throat to make her moan again. He pushed his hand between her legs, pressing against the heat there.

"This."

"Then take it," Alicia whispered into his ear. "Take all of it."

Footsteps overhead pushed them apart again as they both breathed hard. The sight of her nipples outlined against the thin fabric of her shirt made his mouth go so dry he had to swallow hard. His cock ached, confined in the denim.

"Niko?" Galina called down the back stairs, her voice getting closer. "Is Allie still here?"

"Just leaving," Alicia called. "We finished the dishes."

The door at the bottom of the stairs creaked. Galina peered out. She'd wrapped herself in a silk kimono, her hair piled on top of her head. She had her pack of cigarettes in one hand.

"The hinges need to be oiled," she said.

Niko frowned. "Okay, I'll get right on that."

Galina shrugged and moved past them to go out the back door, where the brief flare of her lighter lit her shadow through the glass. Alicia turned her head to look where Galina had gone.

The line of Alicia's neck and the curve of her shoulder made Niko turn away so he could get himself under some kind of control.

"I should go," Alicia said.

Niko nodded. "Yeah. I guess you should."

She made no move to leave, though her gaze cut again to the back door. The soft mutter of Galina's voice talking on the phone meant her attention was on that, not them, but even so, Niko wasn't going to risk another embrace. He walked her to the front door, though, where he did pull her close when it looked as though she meant to leave without another kiss.

"This is crazy. You know that," he said against her mouth.

"Maybe we can't help it," she whispered. Her eyes flashed in the dim light of the front hallway. "Would that make you feel better? Thinking that you can't stop yourself? Would it give you an excuse?"

He could stop himself. He didn't want to. He was saved from answering, though, at the sound of his mother's shout.

"Niko!"

They both turned at the sound of his mother's voice. He sighed. Alicia laughed.

"I'll see you," she told him, and let herself out the front door.

CHAPTER TWENTY-ONE

Theresa had spent a good portion of the past few days putting this deal together, and she had to admit, it was one of the best she'd ever come up with. Making connections was a skill, one she'd had to rely on more than ever since . . . well, if this all worked out, none of that other stuff would matter. She pushed aside all that to look over the packet she'd printed up. The lists of agreements and concessions for each party, the responsibilities and, most important, the payout. She grinned. This was going to work. It was all going to be okay.

"Ilya?" She knocked lightly on his door and stepped through, looking around the room. "Oh. Wow."

"Galina insisted on taking back the master," he said from his place on the sagging double bed.

Theresa looked over the yellowed posters of sports figures and cartoon cats and racing cars. "Uh-huh. Okay."

Ilya sat up, looking irritated, but then he laughed. "Okay, you caught me. I'm still a really, really big fan of Garfield."

She moved farther into the room, looking for a chair and finding only the bed to sit on. She took a spot at the foot, laughing self-consciously at the bed's sudden creaking protest. "Yikes."

"Right?" He bounced, making it squeak. "What a pain in the ass."

"Listen, I brought you something. I was going to talk to you and Allie at the same time after dinner, but she's busy." Theresa had overheard the soft murmurs of conversation between Allie and Niko in the kitchen but hadn't wanted to risk walking in on them if they were doing something they didn't want anyone to see. She slid the thick white envelope, his copy of the offer, across the bed to him. "So I brought this for you. The two of you can talk about it together and get back to me."

He shifted closer to take the envelope. "What is it?"

"It's an offer. To buy the quarry. And Go Deep." Theresa cleared her throat. "I work with Diamond Development Corporation. They want to put in a hotel with a water park and make some improvements—"

"Allie knew about this?"

"I gave her the official offer a couple days ago. Yes." Theresa nodded. "That's part of what I've been doing here in town—"

"Talking to Allie behind my back?" Ilya stood and tossed the envelope onto the bed toward her. "What are you doing, ganging up on me? What the hell, Theresa?"

She frowned and gathered the loose papers that had started to come out of the envelope. "Of course not. Don't be ridiculous."

"My grandmother died," Ilya said through clenched jaws. "She's dead, Theresa. And you're using that as a way to get me to agree to get bought out by some bunch of corporate pricks who want to rip apart everything I've built and turn it into some . . . what, some kind of amusement park?"

"It wasn't like that!"

His fists clenched at his sides. "No? Pretty convenient that you showed up just in time, huh?"

"I came to pay my respects, and I would have done that, anyway," Theresa said. "I told you, I make connections—"

"And you just happened to be making this one?"

She paused to swallow hard, keeping her voice neutral so it didn't shake. The truth was she hadn't planned any of this to take advantage of his grief, but of course she *had* taken advantage of the information he'd given her when he didn't realize what, exactly, he was revealing. He'd told her Go Deep was struggling. It hadn't been hard at all to look up the records to find out how much.

"It was . . . it just worked out that way."

"They sent you after me? Figured you had an in or something, because you knew me?"

For a moment, the truth rose to her lips. That she'd put this together on her own because it had looked like the way out of a very deep and very dark pit she was in. What came out instead was not the truth.

"I'm only doing my job, Ilya."

"I'm not interested in selling. I told the last guy that."

"I'm not aware of any previous offers, and this doesn't have anything to do with that."

"I'm not interested."

Theresa's chin went up. Her shoulders straightened. "It's not only your decision, is it? Allie has a say, too."

"So," he said in a cold, flat voice, "why don't you go on and talk to her about it? For now, get the hell out of my room. Go enjoy sleeping down the hall, unless now that you've figured out I'm not going to give you what you want, you have no reason to hang around here anymore."

He would not be sympathetic to her situation; she was not going to tell him that she had no other place to go right now. Instead, she gathered up the papers and left, closing the door behind her.

In the room that had been Babulya's, she looked at the small weekend bag holding her clothes, some toiletries, a few other odds and ends. Her phone lit up from where she had set it to charge on the nightstand. The message was from Wayne.

Figures, she thought as she thumbed the phone screen to read what her ex-boyfriend had to say. It was a deadline for her to get her stuff out of his garage. Terrific.

She was so screwed.

CHAPTER TWENTY-TWO

Then

Jennilynn hadn't come home last night.

She was supposed to be home by eleven, but Mom and Dad had gone to bed around ten. Alicia was the only one who'd waited up, listening for the sound of a car in the drive or the front door opening. Jennilynn had been out after curfew before. Sneaking in through the window, giggling and hissing at Alicia to be quiet even though she was the one making all the noise. The stink of beer and smoke on her clothes. She'd come home late, but at least she'd always come home.

"Girls!" her mother hollered down the hall. "C'mon, you need to get up or you're going to be late for school!"

The very last thing in the world Alicia felt like doing was getting out of bed. She'd stayed up for hours last night, first angry because she knew, just knew, that the second she fell asleep, her sister would be stumbling into the room, waking her up. Then later, about three in the morning, the anger had turned to anxiety. Alicia had tossed and turned, sleeping fitfully.

Something was going on with her sister, and Alicia didn't know what to do about it.

She should do something about it, right? Jennilynn might be a pain in the ass, but she was still Alicia's sister. If she was in some kind of trouble, something she couldn't get out of on her own, then Alicia had to help her. When Alicia was failing math two years ago and didn't want to tell their parents, Jennilynn was the one who convinced her to get a tutor from the school, so that by the time their parents found out how poorly she was doing, Alicia already had the solution in place.

This felt like something so much worse than a bad grade. Alicia wanted to blame Ilya for it. In the past year or so, the friendships between all of them had changed and shifted, and it had a lot to do with the fact that he and Jennilynn had this on-again, off-again weird thing going on between them that neither of them would admit to. Alicia wanted to make this Ilya's fault, that her sister started drinking and smoking dope and staying out all night and coming home with love bites on her in places that Alicia could barely imagine getting kissed. She knew, though, that whomever Jennilynn was staying out late with, it was not Ilya.

It could be the guy from the party, the one who brought the beer. It could be any number of guys, Alicia thought with a sudden, fiercely painful throb of anxiety and jealousy. The ones Jennilynn met at the diner. The ones who drove trucks and smoked cigarettes and paged her weird messages. Her sister had become the sort of girl that all the guys liked, and Alicia . . . was not.

She thought of Nikolai.

Kissing him was one of the worst things she'd ever done, and she couldn't stop thinking about it. Months had passed with neither of them speaking of it. Worse, though, was how it seemed they were no longer even friends. No more joking, no more teasing, no more pranks. If they had to be near each other, he looked right through her as though he'd never met her instead of knowing her for most of his life, even instead of a girl he'd kissed at a party when they were both a little drunk. There were times when Nikolai made Alicia feel like she might lose her mind with fury, but the loss of this friendship had sunk deep and aching all the way to her bones, and it wouldn't go away.

If she'd known kissing him was going to change everything, would she still have done it? She couldn't be sure. All she knew was that now everything was going wrong, and she couldn't seem to stop it.

She didn't want to get out of bed, but if she didn't get up, their mom would come in and see that Jennilynn wasn't there.

Maybe for once they'd see that she's not perfect.

No matter how mad she was, Alicia wouldn't rat Jennilynn out, not on purpose. It was an unspoken pact that they'd always have each other's backs. Jennilynn had been taking too much of an advantage of it lately, but there was a small good point to that.

Jenni is so going to owe me.

After grabbing her robe, Alicia headed into the bathroom to take a shower. There was something else good about her sister not being there—Alicia got all the hot water. Her parents had been up for hours already. There was no fighting for the shower or the sink or the mirror. She took her time, soaping and conditioning and shaving her legs, until her mother pounded on the door with another command to hurry up or she'd be late.

Jennilynn was in bed when Alicia went back into the bedroom. There was nothing but a glimpse of pale-blonde hair peeking out from beneath the faded quilt made from blocks of fabric cut up from her old baby clothes and blankies. Alicia was supposed to have one, too, but her mother never got around to finishing it.

Alicia put her hands on her hips. "Hey. Get up. You're going to be late for school."

"I'm sick."

"You're *not* sick," Alicia said. The sister pact was only about them against the adults. It didn't count for them against each other. "You're *hungover*."

"Not." Jennilynn didn't so much as twitch back the covers. Her voice was husky and low.

She did sound like she might be sick, at least a little. Alicia tried to pull on the blanket, but Jennilynn had a death grip on it from underneath. They struggled for a few seconds before Alicia won.

"Shit," Alicia said, stepping back at the sight of her sister. "What happened to you?"

"Nothing." Jennilynn sat up, clutching the blankets to her chest.

Her hair was tangled, sections of it dark with dirt, like she hadn't washed it in a few days. Bits of crumbled leaves were scattered throughout. Beneath the protection of her robe, Alicia shivered with a sudden, inexplicable chill.

"You look like crap," she said. "What happened to you? Jenni, what happened to your neck?"

Dark bruises impressed her sister's pale flesh. There was even a small but angry red scratch just below her chin. Jennilynn pulled the blankets up higher, hiding herself from view.

"It's just a hickey or two."

It didn't look like a hickey at all. "Gross. Mom will kill you—"

At the words, Jennilynn let out a low, snorting laugh that cut off, strangled. "She won't. Kill me. She wouldn't actually *kill* me."

Alicia grabbed clean panties and a bra from the dresser and slipped into them with her back turned, self-conscious in front of her sister, even though Jennilynn had no such issues with modesty and wouldn't notice or care if Alicia did the hokey pokey buck naked right in front of her. Alicia pulled on a pair of jeans and one of her favorite T-shirts.

"It's just a saying," Alicia replied, trying to keep her voice down so their mother didn't overhear. "And if she or Dad see those hickeys all over your neck, you'll be in such bad trouble you'll maybe wish they'd kill you, instead."

"I would never *wish* to be dead."

The words were so quiet, so bleakly bland and without any remnant of her sister's usual sassy attitude that Alicia turned, certain she heard wrong. "What?"

"Nothing. Never mind. Forget it, you're right, I'm hungover. Shit, maybe still drunk." Jennilynn mumbled her answer, words slurring a little, and cut her gaze from Alicia's. She dove beneath the blankets again. "Leave me alone now. Tell Mom I'm sick, please? She'll believe you."

Alicia was quiet for a second. Her own stomach began to hurt. "Where were you last night?"

"Out in the woods."

"Yeah. I can tell. With who? A boyfriend?"

Last year, before Jennilynn and Ilya started up whatever it was they thought nobody knew they were doing, she'd gone out with Franco Dalton for a few months. It hadn't lasted long. Before that, she'd dated Brad Kennedy, who went to a rival high school. There'd been others. Jennilynn'd had half a dozen boyfriends while Alicia was still waiting to have *one*.

She carefully didn't let herself think about Nikolai. Or that party in October. Or the kiss. Definitely anything but that kiss.

Jennilynn was silent for a few seconds before letting out a giggle that finally sounded at least a little bit more like her usual self. "What if I was?"

"Since when do you have a boyfriend?" Alicia asked, deliberately casual, while she found a matching pair of knee socks in Jennilynn's drawer. All of her own socks usually ended up there, anyway.

"I didn't say he was a boyfriend."

Alicia turned, socks in hand. "You're out with him often enough, whoever it is. Just tell me, Jenni. Who is it? Is it someone I know?"

Jennilynn was silent beneath the blankets for a moment, before she mumbled. "Yes. You know him."

"Ilya."

"Who? What about Ilya?" Jennilynn flipped the blanket back just far enough to reveal one mascara-smeared eye.

"He's your boyfriend?"

"Why? Did he say he was?" Jennilynn sounded weirdly . . . hopeful. She pulled the blanket back over her face. "Was he talking about me?"

"I haven't asked him. I asked you." With an eye on the clock, Alicia ran a comb through her hair, still damp from the shower. She had just enough time to swipe on some mascara and lip gloss and grab a toaster tart on the way out the door to the bus. She hesitated, though, staring hard at her sister, at the mysteries she was concealing beneath the cover of the comforter. "If it's not Ilya . . . who is it?"

The only answer was a soft snore that had to be fake. If she went over to her sister's bed and yanked off the quilt, that would force Jennilynn to get up. She'd have to go to school instead of getting to lie around all day watching TV. Alicia wanted to force her sister to stop lying about where she'd been and what she was doing, and with whom, but though Alicia wanted to do this, she couldn't quite make herself. Because then she'd know, she thought as she left their bedroom with a click of the door behind her. And if she knew exactly what her sister had been up to, she wouldn't be able to keep pretending that nothing was wrong with her.

"Jenni's sick," she told her mother, who was already wearing her coat and putting the lid on her travel coffee mug.

"Again?" For a moment, her mother looked concerned, the crease between her eyes deepening in a way that Alicia realized made her mother look . . . old.

"It's her period, I think." The lie slipped out easily enough.

Her mother wrinkled her nose. "Does she need anything?"

"She's sleeping," Alicia said. "I gave her some aspirin for the cramps."

"Thanks, honey." Her mother gave an absentminded look upward, as though she could see through the floors and into her daughters' bedroom. "I'm going to be late for work, and I don't have time to take you if you miss the bus. You'd better run."

Alicia grabbed a toaster tart and allowed her mother to hurry her out the back door. She walked down the long lane toward the bus stop, where she could already see the Stern brothers and their still-newish stepsister waiting. Just once, she paused to look up to the window of her bedroom, but not even a shadow hinted at the sight of Jennilynn looking back.

CHAPTER TWENTY-THREE

It felt good to be fixing something, to have a concrete task he could put his mind to and complete. Niko had always liked working with his hands for that reason. It took his mind off everything else that was going on.

Everything except Alicia, anyway, and since she was the main thing taking up all the room in his brain lately, he'd set out this morning to plan a day of tasks that would fill his time so he wouldn't have to . . . what? Decide? Choose? And what had he done but go to see her—like that would help him forget the sound of her soft moans when he'd touched her.

"Yuck," Niko muttered as he pressed the perpetually damp spot on the wall surrounding the tub. He poked a little harder, making a hole.

"It's bad." Galina said from the bathroom doorway. "But you can fix it?"

Niko shrugged, turning. "I'm not sure. I mean, yeah. I think so. I should be able to. The plumbing part of it, sure. The wall, I dunno. It's going to depend on what kind of mess we're looking at behind it. This might be a bigger job."

Galina pursed her lips, studying the damage. "You can do it."

"Nice that you have such faith in me, Mom," Nikolai said with a grin.

"You'll come through for me, Kolya." His mother went to the sink and opened the medicine cabinet, then closed it with a creak. She smiled at him in her reflection. "This next. I'd like a nice mirror in here. Maybe a pedestal sink instead of this useless thing. New, fresh paint. We'll get rid of the wallpaper."

Niko brushed the crumbles of plaster dust off his hands. "Sure. We can do all that. Why not pull up the linoleum while we're at it? See if there's a real wood floor under here?"

"Ooh!" Galina clapped her hands and grinned at him. "Yes. That would be great. You can do that, too?"

He could, but that wasn't so much the point he'd been trying to make. "Look, I know you want to get this place in better shape, and it certainly needs a bunch of work done to it, but . . . where are you getting the money for it?"

Money had always been a sensitive topic with her. He knew she'd often asked Ilya for loans she'd never paid back, or flat out asked his brother to cover her expenses. Ilya had bitched about it, but he'd done it. Galina had never come to Niko for money. She'd always relied on him for other things. Sometimes, he wished he'd been able to simply write her a check, instead.

"Don't you worry about that. It's my problem." Galina shrugged. "And it's not so much, is it? When you're doing the work for me? If I had to pay someone, it would be much more."

It would not have been the first time his mother had come up with some grand plan or scheme that she'd been unable to see all the way through. Not even the first time she'd put herself in debt chasing some crazy idea. One of the reasons Niko had gone so far from home, stayed away so long, was to distance himself from this very thing. The mania and the inevitable crash that came after.

"It's a lot, that's all. This house, it's a big project."

Galina laughed and shook her head. "It's my house. My responsibility. Is it so wrong for me to want to make it nice for you boys? It's all I have to give you, really."

Niko frowned. "I don't need you to give me anything."

"That doesn't mean I don't want to. I'm your mother, and I know I haven't been the best one." She studied him. "Besides, the more you have to do here, the longer you can stay."

"If I can. I have some things coming up I won't be able to get out of."

That was a lie. He'd already started talking to the council about cashing out his contract. He wanted to stay here, and not so he could fix up his childhood home for his mother. He wanted to stay because the thought of leaving and not seeing Alicia again had woken him more than once in the night, his mouth dry and tasting sour, his heart pounding painfully. He wasn't sure what he was going to do about that. He was still running, but not sure in which direction.

He did not want his mother to know this. Her decision not to go back to South Carolina wasn't trustworthy. Unless maybe she knew he wasn't leaving, but he absolutely didn't want to be the reason Galina stayed.

She tilted her head to look him over. "Surely you can find work around here that won't take you away."

"You don't understand how the kibbutz works. I signed a contract with them. It's not so easy to simply walk away. "

"Really? You seem to walk away so easily from everything else." Galina shook her head. "But I let you go because I thought it was important for you to have a chance to see the world, if you wanted to."

All this time, and she so obviously was still telling herself some kind of fairy tale. Living in her own reality. Niko shook his head.

"You didn't let me go, Mom. I just went."

CHAPTER TWENTY-FOUR

Alicia had asked Theresa to meet her at a new coffee shop on the edge of town, where they each picked up a mug from the rack to take advantage of the "bottomless cup," along with a couple of pastries. They took seats at one of the tables in the front window. The warmer-than-usual winter meant there'd been little snow, but there had been some ice. It was melting now, pattering like a mini waterfall down the glass, streaking it. Alicia liked this reminder that winter was on its way out.

"So," Theresa said before Alicia could start the conversation, "I'm sure you have a lot of questions."

Alicia sipped her coffee for a second. Too hot. She blew on it, then nodded. "A few, sure. Mostly like, how much of a coincidence is it that you're the one assigned to this project?"

Theresa laughed and wrapped her hands around her mug. "Not much. The people I know with Diamond have been talking about acquiring a new property and expanding for a number of years. I was the one who suggested they look at the quarry."

That wasn't the answer Alicia had been expecting. "You were?"

"Yep. It's the perfect spot. There's nothing else like it in the area. With a new hotel and the proposed indoor water park, along with access to the water for swimming, boating, fishing—"

"Scuba diving?" Alicia asked.

"That, too. Of course. They'd be crazy not to take advantage of the work you and Ilya have already put into the spot. They'd want to expand it, of course. With some real money behind it, imagine what it could become." Theresa pulled apart the brownie she'd ordered, then tucked one of the pieces in her mouth.

Alicia had ordered an apple pastry, but she didn't much feel like eating it at the moment. She'd agreed to meet with Theresa to talk because the idea of selling the business had put other ideas into her head, but now faced with the reality of it, she wasn't so sure she wanted to even consider it. "Ilya and I have put a lot of work into building our business. And money. Lots of it."

Just about everything either of them had ever made, as a matter of fact.

"I know you have." Theresa hesitated, looking as though she meant to say something, but didn't.

"And?"

Theresa sat back in her chair, holding her mug in both hands. "Have you spoken to him about any of this?"

"About the offer? The plans? Not yet. With everything that happened lately, I haven't had the chance. Ilya handles the classes and the trips. He's the one who scouts out the new things to sink. He plans out that stuff. I'm the one who handles the numbers. I'm the one who keeps it all working." Alicia cleared her throat, aware she'd gotten a little too loud for a public place. She softened her voice so she wouldn't draw attention to herself.

Theresa nodded. "You'll have to talk to him about it, though, of course. You can't make a decision like this without him."

Alicia focused on the coffee, sipping. She looked outside at the gray sky. The people passing by. She could not look at Theresa, who was one of the people who should've known exactly the reasons why she and Ilya could not—would not ever—sell the quarry.

"Of course not," Alicia said finally. "I wanted to get more details about it before I talked to him. In case you hadn't noticed, Ilya's been having kind of a rough time with things."

"Oh, I've noticed." Theresa toyed with the crumbs of her brownie.

Something in her voice snagged Alicia's attention, but nothing in the other woman's expression gave a clue about what it might be.

Alicia sighed. "The truth is, we paid a lot of money for the quarry. Too much. We've put even more into it over the years, nearly every penny of what we've ever profited. All those things we sunk in it, the school bus, the helicopter. Those things weren't cheap to acquire or to transport or to sink. We're operating with a very, very low profit margin, Theresa. And this offer . . ."

This offer would open doors Alicia had always believed would be closed. Opportunities she'd never allowed herself to imagine or consider. Getting out from under the debt, the work, her failed marriage . . . this life . . .

This life, the one you chose. Remember? You made your choices. You've lived with them.

She *had* lived with them, but did that mean she always had to?

Theresa leaned forward a little. "It's a very generous offer, considering the property values and what they'd need to put into the site in order to upgrade it for the intended use. Allie . . . I know it's a tough decision, and I wish I could give you all the time in the world to think about it, but I have to tell you that the clock is ticking on this one. They're looking at a number of properties and options, so they want to move on this. This isn't official, and I'm not supposed to know about it. But they're talking about bringing the zoning board into it."

Alicia had already had her share of battles with the zoning board over the years. "Ugh. Of course they are, right? Bully the little guy out of business?"

Theresa looked solemn. "I'm sorry. Believe me, I know how hard this decision has to be. So, please. Talk to Ilya about it. And get back to me, okay? I have to get back to work. But call me if you want to talk more. Or if you want me to talk to Ilya—"

"No, thanks. This has to be something I talk to him about." Alicia pulled out her purse, frowning when Theresa waved her away. "No, I got this."

"Thanks. I wasn't expecting that, but thank you." Theresa's voice sounded rough, and she cleared her throat.

Alicia gave her a curious glance. "Everything okay?"

Theresa hesitated, then nodded. "Oh, yeah. Absolutely. Just . . . well, it's been good seeing you again. All of you, I mean, believe it or not."

"Even Galina?"

Theresa laughed. "Yeah, even Galina. I have mostly fond memories of that time, to be honest. After my dad and Galina split up, things got . . . well, they weren't so good."

Alicia's brow furrowed. "I'm sorry."

"Not your problem." Theresa shrugged. "We all had our stuff to deal with. For what it's worth, I've thought of Jennilynn often over the years. And all of you."

"Thanks. I mean, I did, too, of course. It all ended so weird." The words sounded hollow, probably because she didn't mean it. Alicia pulled her mug closer to her to warm her fingers on it. The truth was that she'd rarely thought of Theresa after she'd left their lives. There'd been a lot going on. If not for the Internet, she doubted they would ever have reconnected.

"It was not an easy time," Theresa said. "But my dad and Galina splitting up couldn't possibly compare to what you and your family had to deal with. I can't really even imagine it."

Alicia didn't want to imagine it, either. Years later, and the memories of that time were still strong enough to turn her stomach. Some of that must've shown on her face, because Theresa's expression twisted.

"I'm sorry. If you don't want to talk about it, I understand."

Alicia had spent her life not talking about it. She'd not talked about it so much there didn't seem anything to say about it. She stood. "I should get going. I have a bunch of things I need to do at the shop, including running some numbers so I can get a better handle on this offer."

"Sounds good. If you need something else from me, just let me know. I mean about anything," Theresa added.

"Will you be going back to the house?"

The other woman shook her head. "No. I don't think so. But Ilya . . ."

Alicia frowned. "Yeah? What about him?"

"I'm a little worried about him. That's all." Theresa coughed uncomfortably. "We had kind of an argument a few nights ago. If you see him, could you tell him that I'd like to talk to him?"

"I can give you his phone number—"

Theresa shook her head quickly. "I have it. He's not answering my texts or calls."

Alicia sighed. "Yeah. He can be like that."

"I know. I just . . ." Theresa cleared her throat again. "If you could tell him I said I was sorry. That's all. I'd appreciate it."

"Sure." Alicia nodded and stood to give Theresa a hug. It wasn't the other woman's fault she and Ilya hadn't made Go Deep into what it might've been. It wasn't Theresa's problem that they were tied to each other and that place by what had happened to Jennilynn. And it wasn't her fault Alicia had made the choices she had. "It was good to see you. I'll be in touch."

"It's a good offer," Theresa said. "I know it might not seem like it, but I promise you I've worked with them to make it as fair as possible."

Alicia knew better than to think that any big real estate company was going to put anyone's interests before its own, but she smiled anyway. "I'm sure. Thanks. I'll talk to Ilya about it. I can't make any promises . . ."

"Of course not," Theresa said. "But think about it. Okay?"

"Sure. Okay." Alicia nodded and watched the other woman leave the coffee shop.

It wasn't about money. It had never been. It was about the quarry.

◆ ◆ ◆

Then

Alicia didn't tell her parents she still went out to the quarry. She wasn't sure they'd forbid her to go, not that they could, really. She was almost twenty years old. Yeah, she still lived in their house, ate their food, didn't pay rent, but if they didn't expect her to be home by any sort of curfew, she didn't think they'd tell her they didn't want her wandering around in her childhood stomping grounds, either. When they asked her where she'd been, she told them work. Out with friends. Shopping. She lied to her parents not because she didn't want them to worry, but because she was more afraid they wouldn't. That there wouldn't be any comments about how morbid it was for her to go to the old equipment shed, where she sat as though the beat-up, old wooden shack with the light streaming through the cracks in the roof and walls was some kind of church. When she sat there, prayer was the furthest thing from her mind.

Jennilynn had died three years ago.

Alicia never brought flowers, but there was almost always a bouquet there. Sometimes more than one, in various stages of rottenness.

In the summer, the stink inside the shed was enough to turn her stomach, but in the crisp autumn air, there was nothing but the lingering hint of cigarette smoke and the faint perfume of flowers only recently dead.

They used to keep candles here, and matches, thinking it made them big shots to have access to fire. She was surprised they never burned the shed to the ground, filled as it was with various bits of old papers and junked office furniture, with dried leaves that blew in through the cracks and never blew out. She looked around now to see if there was a candle to burn, but no kids seemed to hang out in there anymore, not even the few who lived in the new houses being built all along Quarry Street. She couldn't blame them. If there was a haunted place in Quarrytown, this shed would've been it.

Jennilynn's body had been discovered in the water. She hadn't drowned. She'd stripped out of her clothes in the shed and left them there, then tried to go swimming, but had fallen off the rocks and broken her neck. When they were looking for her, the shed was the place where they'd finally found a clue about where to find her. It brought Alicia a sort of peace to sit there, in the silence unbroken but for the occasional cry of the crows outside or the scamper of squirrels in the leaves. She liked to sit with her eyes closed. Thinking.

Once, her sister had said she didn't know what she wanted to be when she grew up. She didn't have to decide now, not ever. Sometimes, though, Alicia tried to think about what Jennilynn might have done with her life. It was easier than trying to figure out what she should do with her own.

The crunch of feet in the leaves outside turned her head. From something much bigger than a squirrel. Not a dog . . . or a deer. It was the distinct sound of human feet pushing through the branches, and Alicia drew into herself. She put herself in shadows to keep hidden from some random glimpse from a stranger's eyes through the old shed's cracks, because surely whoever it was would keep on hiking by.

When the door, hanging by one hinge, creaked open, her heart pounded so fast and hard that for a moment she saw the red-and-gray throb of a faint coming on in the corners of her vision. She had no weapon but the jagged, broken leg of a wooden chair she found in a corner. She gripped it, white-knuckled, not sure what she meant to do with it, only that she would do whatever she had to.

The man in the doorway wore a slouchy knit cap over rumpled dark hair. An unbuttoned red-and-black flannel shirt over a mismatched green T and a pair of faded jeans with holes in the knees and ragged hems hanging over battered work boots. She was ready to hit him with the broken chair leg but held back at the last second when she recognized him.

"Ilya," she said on a gasp of relief as she lowered the leg. "What the hell are you doing?"

"What are *you* doing?" He looked at the impromptu weapon, then at her face. Beyond her to the scattered remains of all the flowers. "I didn't know you came here."

"I didn't know you did." Shaking, she put down the chair leg and dusted her hands off on the seat of her jeans. She thought about sitting—her knees were knocking enough to make her unsteady—but she didn't want to with him there. What she did there in the equipment shed was private. She didn't want to share.

"I was just passing. I don't always stop in here. But I like to go look out at the water on days like this." Ilya cleared his throat.

Alicia had always known she was not the only person who'd lost Jennilynn. Her parents didn't talk about it, but here was someone who might understand at least the smallest part of what she felt. Ilya loved her sister, too.

"I'll go with you," she said. "If that's all right."

He hesitated, then nodded. "Sure. Okay."

"Haven't seen you around." She let him lead so he could bend the branches out of the way to clear a path. "I heard Niko was working in Antarctica."

She hadn't heard it from Niko. Galina had told her one day when Alicia came out to get the mail. Waiting for a letter that never came.

Ilya glanced over his shoulder. "Yeah, yeah."

"How's Galina taking that?"

He laughed. "She's fine. Babulya is worried he's going to freeze to death. We all tried to tell her they don't live in igloos or whatever, but you know her."

"Right." They crunched along without talking for a few more minutes until the trees and brush began to thin and they reached the chain-link fence.

"How's school?" He gave her a sideways glance.

"Fine." Two years, business degree. She hadn't had to leave home and, better than that, hadn't needed to think hard about what she wanted to do or be. She would graduate in a few months, though. Then she'd have to figure out what she wanted to do. "Are you still working at the warehouse?"

"Yeah. Good money. Shitty hours."

On the other side of the fence, they both headed in the same direction. Not toward the old rope swing and the outcropping of rocks where they'd spent so many summer days swimming. The other way, toward the quarry's steep drop-off.

Together, they walked toward the place where Jennilynn's body had been found.

There was no marker or memorial, nothing even like people sometimes put at spots along the highway to show where a fatal accident had occurred. The bushes that had been broken to show the place where Jenni had fallen had long ago grown back. The rocks beneath covered with water after the last few weeks of rain.

"I always think there will be . . . blood." Ilya looked out, out, across the water to the high stone walls on the other side of the quarry.

Alicia shivered. "There wasn't any blood, not even when they found her. It had all washed away."

Ilya scuffed the dirt, kicking pebbles over the edge. Alicia listened but couldn't hear the splash. She didn't want to get any closer. Didn't want to take the risk of slipping over and falling. She'd dreamed, a few times, of jumping. But she didn't want to fall.

"Hey, look." Ilya pointed at the broad white sign with red letters set up on the quarry's other, higher, side. It was the size of a billboard. "It's for sale."

CHAPTER TWENTY-FIVE

Ilya had finally made it in to work.

He'd shown up in ample time to handle the in-water classes at the VA, which was where he would spend his morning and most of the afternoon. He'd also given Alicia all the updates about the trip to Jamaica that was due to leave the following week—a trip she'd been on the verge of canceling, even though it would've meant losing all their deposits.

She had not yet spoken to him about the offer from Theresa. The thick packet of papers was on her desk in the plain white envelope. She hadn't looked at it again since the meeting with Theresa earlier. She didn't need to. The numbers inside it were burned into her mind enough so that all she had to do was go to her computer files and run some reports on what Go Deep owed and had earned over the past few years, and was likely to earn in the next few.

The truth was, no matter what she and Ilya might want, no matter how hard—or not—each of them worked, the shop wasn't making money. It wasn't going to make money. It was always going to hover on the bare brink of bankruptcy, especially if Ilya, as he was certainly wont to do, intended to keep seeking out bigger and more extravagant items to sink into the quarry's chilly, spring-fed depths so that the few people who did visit it for local dives could be entertained.

Maybe, she thought, it was time to let it go.

All of it.

And then what? For the first time in a couple of decades, she allowed herself to contemplate what she could do or where she could go. What did she even want? What had she ever wanted?

She didn't know and really never had. Oh, in high school she'd thought here and there about being a teacher or a nurse or working in human resources, idle considerations based on the results of standardized career-placement tests. None of that appealed to her now.

She'd spent her life doing nothing because her sister had never had the chance to do anything, and the realization twitched her hand so hard she knocked Theresa's envelope onto the floor.

"F-f-f-f-f," Alicia muttered, biting off the curse before she could finish it. She picked up the scattered papers and shuffled them back together.

"Trying to keep yourself from putting money in the swear jar?"

She looked up at the sound of a familiar voice. Her heart leaped, catching in her throat at the sight of him; she thought it always would. A dozen more years could pass without seeing him, and she would still find it hard to breathe the first moment she saw him.

"You caught me. I'm trying to be more ladylike."

Nikolai laughed. "Good luck with *that*."

She tossed a crumpled piece of paper at him. "Bitch."

"Jerk." He grinned and ducked out of the way from another paper missile. He bent to pick up both bits of trash and tossed them in the can with his free hand. The other held a suspiciously delicious-smelling, grease-spotted paper sack. "So, what's up?"

Alicia leaned back in her chair. "Why don't you tell me? Since you've shown up unannounced again."

He looked embarrassed. "I guess I could call or text first, huh?"

"You could. But no worries. I'm just trying to keep this place from falling down, that's all. The usual. Your brother's back to work, by the way."

"Yeah, he was gone when I left this morning."

She waited, but that was all he said. She hated having to drag out the words, like pulling a splinter from a wound. "Nikolai."

"So, I feel like an asshole." Nikolai held up the bag. "I brought doughnuts from the Donut Shack."

"Far be it from me to turn down a doughnut," Alicia said, but made no move to take the bag, or motion for him to take a seat. "But I'm kind of over the whole doughnut thing."

He got her. Always had. His gaze flashed. He held the bag up higher, but his voice dipped lower.

"Yeah? You sure? They're really . . . really good." He let the tip of his tongue dent his bottom lip for a second.

She was absolutely not going to fall for that bullshit. No way. Alicia lifted her chin, gaze steady on his, not giving away even the tiniest hint that she'd just imagined that tongue someplace else.

"Oh, I'm sure they're delicious. I'm sure that even a day or so ago you might've convinced me to gobble up the entire bag." She paused to narrow her eyes but couldn't stop the corners of her mouth tilting into a small, tight, and humorless smile. "But like I said. I'm over it."

Nikolai opened the bag and peeked inside, then at her. "Mmmm. Just one? Just a taste?"

"Nah," Alicia said coolly and leaned back in her chair to prop her feet on the desk. "I'm not hungry."

His face fell. He closed the bag and set it on the edge of the desk. The good bakery smell was enough to make her stomach rumble, but she pretended she hadn't heard it. Nikolai obviously had, though, because his crestfallen expression turned sly.

"Sure I can't convince you?" he asked. "Just one little bite?"

Alicia tilted her head to make sure he saw how she was looking him up and down. Then, she shrugged. Without taking her gaze from his, she said, "Too many sweets make my stomach hurt."

"Allie."

"You know, I prefer to be called Alicia," she answered in a clipped tone. She set her feet on the floor with a thump and turned toward her computer, putting her hands on the keyboard not only to wake the monitor from sleeping but also to hide the fact that her hands were shaking.

"Alicia," Nikolai said in a low tone full of apology and longing.

She didn't turn. She let her fingers hover over the keyboard, though the truth was she couldn't focus on the screen in front of her. She gave up after a second, folding her hands in her lap, twisting her fingers together. She didn't answer him. He said her name again. Rougher. Raspier.

At last, Alicia twirled in her chair to face him, but that wasn't enough, so she got to her feet to walk to the side of the desk. She took the bag of doughnuts and thrust it at him, forcing him to take it. Making him back up a step toward the door.

"Don't bring me something you're not ready for me to eat," she told him. "Don't do that to me again."

"I'm sorry," Nikolai said.

She shrugged. Chin up. Voice steady. Back straight. "That makes me feel so much better. Thanks. You can leave now."

"Don't do that. Please," he added. "Don't shut me out like that. Look, you know we . . . we can't."

"Right," she said around the lump in her throat. "Of course we can't. I guess it doesn't matter that we already *did*."

Nikolai cleared his throat. "He's my brother."

"He was my husband. You think I don't know how messed up that makes this? Do you really think I don't know?" When he didn't answer her, she crossed her arms over her chest. With a sigh, she looked away. "Just go, Nikolai."

This time when he said her name, she couldn't hide the shiver that rippled through her. Grateful for the thick sweater and her crossed arms that hid her tightening nipples from his gaze, Alicia frowned and closed her eyes. If he touched her, she thought, she would knee him in the junk. She would punch him in the face. She would . . . she would . . .

She would let him kiss her mouth, softly, but with determination. She would let him put his arms around her and pull her close. She would let him tickle her lips with his tongue until she opened for him, and when he threaded his fingers through her hair, tipping her face to his, she would let him do that, too.

"I don't want to want you," he said, his mouth on hers.

She'd have pulled away but for the grip of his hand in her hair. "So stop, then."

"I can't." He kissed her again, harder this time.

She pushed herself against him, her thigh going between his to nudge upward. Not to hurt him. She wanted to feel him getting hard for her. She wanted to touch him. When she tried, he captured her arm at the wrist and stopped her an inch from his body—for no longer than a heartbeat or three, however, before he was moving her hand to cup his thickening erection through his jeans.

"Touch me," he muttered into her mouth, then against her cheek, her throat, as he slid his lips along her skin. He moved her hand slow, slow, curling her fingers over the bulge in the denim.

He groaned aloud when she yanked open the button and slid the zipper down, notch by notch. She freed him, pushing at the waistband of his jeans and briefs until she could hold his bare flesh in her palm. She stroked him as their mouths found each other's again.

"I've been aching for you . . . couldn't stop thinking about how you felt. How you sounded when you came . . ." Nikolai's voice rasped, stuttering to silence when her grip circled the head of his cock.

He was so hard it was like gripping iron. The angle was wrong. The position, awkward. She wanted him in her mouth, but she couldn't force herself to stop kissing him, not when the taste of Nikolai's mouth was so tantalizing. Her tongue slid along his, mimicking the stroking rhythm of her hand. He pulsed in her grip.

It was her turn to slide her hand along the back of his neck. To grip him there, to hold him still while she nibbled at his lips and kept up the steady, demanding pace of her fingers gripping him. His fingers loosened on her wrist. His hips thrust forward, at least until she closed her fist tight around him, just below the head.

"No," Alicia whispered into his ear, then took his lobe between her teeth. "Don't move."

She laughed breathlessly when he let out a muttered curse, but she didn't relent. She pulled away enough to look at his face. He kept his eyes closed. His mouth, wet and open. His hands went flat against the filing cabinets, but he didn't move. Not even when she slowed the stroking to what must have been an infuriatingly slow pace.

Nikolai's brow furrowed. A soft noise slipped out of him. Then another when she gave in to the desire streaking through her and moved her hand faster. Faster. Until finally, he tensed. Warmth coated her hand, but she kept her gaze focused on his face. Waiting for his eyes to open, for him to look at her when his pleasure overtook him.

He did.

Alicia waited another half minute before she stepped away from him and grabbed a couple of paper towels from the shelf next to her desk. They busied themselves with cleaning up, neither of them speaking. She had her back to him, waiting for him to leave. Because of course he would, right? And he'd probably take the doughnuts with him, too.

Nikolai didn't leave. He came up behind her and put his arms around her to draw her back against his chest. He nuzzled the back of her neck, and Alicia let herself melt into the embrace.

"Alicia . . ."

"I don't want to talk about it, Nikolai."

"We have to talk about it."

She turned to face him. "Why? Why do we have to talk about it? This thing has been going on between us for a long time, and I guess it's just something that we have to deal with. But please . . . let's not talk about it if all you're going to keep saying is that you can't and don't want to."

He let her step away from him. He'd buttoned his jeans, but the zipper was still down, and she took a certain satisfaction in that, and the way his hair was still rumpled. His mouth still plump and wet from her kisses.

"You're going to leave again, anyway," she continued. "Right? In what, a month? You're going back all the way to the other side of the world."

Something shifted in Nikolai's gaze. After a second, he nodded. She shrugged.

"You have a life there, isn't that what you said? Anything that will take you away from this place." She gestured at the office, but they both knew she meant more than just where they stood. "You'll go. I'll stay. That's how it works. And nobody has to know this ever happened."

"We'll know it." He put his hands on his hips, brow furrowed. Frowning. He looked pissed.

She smiled, then. "Yes. We will."

He returned her smile, and she wanted to curse herself for letting it warm her. Nikolai sighed. He tossed the paper towels in the trash and smoothed his shirt.

"It's just a *thing*," Alicia said, as though saying it aloud would make it feel true.

He nodded. "Yeah. Just a thing."

"Nobody ever has to know about it," she whispered as he moved closer.

He kissed her. "Nope."

"Just until you leave again."

"Sure," he said. Then, after a second or so, he crushed her against him to bury his face against the side of her neck. He squeezed her.

The embrace felt a little desperate, but she understood that. Wasn't that always how she felt about him? He released her abruptly, and they both stepped away from each other.

"Your zipper's down," Alicia told him.

With a rueful chuckle, Nikolai zipped himself and watched her as she went to the desk to pull out a couple of doughnuts from the bag. She handed him a powdered sugar and took an apple fritter for herself. Alicia settled into her desk chair and waved at him to take a seat across from her.

"How are the home repairs going?"

"The list keeps getting longer. She started this nightly dinner thing, too, where she cooks for us and wants to sit around and talk about our days." Nikolai paused. "Maybe losing her mother has her contemplating the meaning of life or something? Or maybe she's just being manipulative. With her, you can't tell."

Nikolai bit into the doughnut and looked around the office until he spotted the single-serve coffeemaker. Without asking, he got up to help himself, using the pitcher of water she kept there for that reason. "Want one?"

"Yeah, thanks." She watched him for a second before continuing. "I didn't think she'd really stay."

"She shows no signs of leaving. She plans to live there for the rest of her life, I think."

"With Ilya."

Nikolai chuckled. "Yes.

"No wonder he's been such a pain in the ass lately."

"Yep." Nikolai glanced at her over his shoulder as the machine hissed and spit a dark brew. "I heard them arguing. She threw out the fact it's still her house again, so she has the right to stay in it as long as she wants to. Unless he wants to buy it from her, which you and I both know he probably can't do."

Alicia frowned, thinking of the business debt still hanging over their heads. Her parents had paid off their mortgage before retiring early. After her divorce, they'd given her a good deal on buying the house from them, something she'd always appreciated, especially considering the money they'd already given her.

"He *was* paying the mortgage on it and has been since she left. I mean, that was the huge thing. You left," she paused, remembering how sudden and horrible it had been to find out that Nikolai had gone away without saying good-bye. Alicia cleared her throat, continuing, "The next thing we know, Galina's off to South Carolina, leaving everything behind. If he hadn't started making the payments, the bank would've taken it."

"Yeah. Well. Apparently Galina's name is still on the house, not his." Nikolai brought two mugs of coffee to the desk and handed her one. His mouth twisted for a second. "Even if he was the one handling the payments, his name isn't on the paperwork."

She'd been stupid. Married to Ilya for ten or so years, and this was a surprise. They'd divorced as swiftly and amicably as they could, splitting their ownership of the business to the original percentages of when they'd bought it, and taking only the assets they'd each brought to the marriage. They'd never fought about anything material. Still, it seemed like something she ought to have known.

"The mortgage on that house was the one thing Ilya always made sure to take care of. I figured he'd bought it from her the way my parents had sold theirs to me. He never mentioned anything about her name still being on it. And, honestly, he hasn't mentioned anything about her asking him for money or anything else for a long time. I thought she'd stopped."

Nikolai blew on the coffee. "Maybe she's changed."

Alicia laughed. Hard and loud. Nikolai joined her a second later, and the two of them filled her small office with the ringing sounds of their shared hilarity. It faded, leaving him smiling at her.

"I have something to tell you," he began, but stopped himself at the warning look she shot him. "Hey . . . c'mon. I brought you doughnuts."

Alicia very deliberately tucked the last piece of apple fritter into her mouth but spoke around it. "We've already talked about it. There's nothing else to say."

"I was going to say that I don't want to keep sneaking around like this. Furtively doing things in your office, or whatever." Nikolai met her gaze evenly. "It doesn't feel right."

Alicia sat back in her chair, uncertain about what kind of response he expected. "No. It doesn't."

"I think it's clear this unfinished business is real. Something between us."

"Yes," she said quietly. Her heart beat hard enough for her to feel the throb of it at the base of her throat. She closed her fists in her lap, keeping her hands from shaking.

"For a long time. Years."

"Yes," she said again.

Nikolai crossed the room to her in three long strides that startled her enough to push back in her chair. It hit the wall. He leaned across her desk and took her hands in his.

"I've spent too many years of my life trying as hard as I could to get away from Quarrytown, but no matter where I went in the world, no matter what I was doing, I always thought about you," he said.

Alicia gently withdrew her hands from his loose grasp. "Nikolai . . ."

"Just listen, okay? I thought about what happened after Jenni."

"We were kids," Alicia said. "Dumb kids."

Nikolai shook his head. "Was that all it was?"

"I don't know," Alicia admitted in a low voice, looking away from the intensity of his gaze. "It was a long time ago."

"I thought about coming home from Israel to find out you and my brother had run off together," Nikolai continued. "I was such an asshole about it . . ."

She looked at him, wishing she could tell him how devastated she'd been when he left. Wishing she could tell him that one of the reasons she'd turned to Ilya was that he was the only one there. "Were you wrong?"

"I was wrong to be such a prick. It was obvious you believed you were doing the right thing. You'd bought the quarry. You were both talking about making this happen." He waved his hand around the office. "It was a great goal."

"We didn't need to get *married* to start the dive shop." Alicia sighed. This time, she was the one who reached for his hands. She moved around her desk so she could stand in front of him. Close. Touching. Their fingers linked.

Nikolai turned his face toward hers. "But you did."

"Yes. It happened. And you weren't wrong to tell me it was a mistake, even though I didn't want to hear it." She let herself press against him. Her face tucked perfectly against his neck beneath his chin. She took a chance. "You weren't here, Nikolai. You ran off, not a word, nothing . . ."

His arms went around her. "I never meant to hurt you."

"But you did," Alicia said on a grating cough, words from a razor-shredded throat. "You left without saying good-bye, like I didn't matter to you at all. You made me feel like I meant nothing."

And there it was.

Alicia had been in her sister's shadow her entire life, and Jennilynn's death had not brought her into the sunshine. She'd never been able to capture her parents' attention, or Ilya's heart, and none of that had mattered much, really, but this did. Nikolai had gone away and left her as though he'd never even known her. He'd made her into nothing, and she'd never been able to convince herself she'd ever been more than that to him.

She wasn't sure she could ever believe it now.

A hitching, throbbing rasp seared her throat and boiled out of her in scalding tears. She shook, fighting them for only a moment before it became too much to hold back. She sobbed.

Nikolai stroked her hair, which at some point during their escapades had come out of the loose ponytail she wore for work and now lay tangled over her shoulders. He didn't say anything. He offered the comfort of his embrace and his silence, which was what she needed. He fixed everything else, but he wasn't trying to fix her, Alicia thought as she pressed her face to the soft flannel of Nikolai's shirt and wept for the past, for the present—still a mess—and for the future she could not begin to even think about.

It was exactly what she needed, and in a minute or so the tears tapered off. He grabbed a tissue from the box on her desk and tipped her face up to dry her cheeks. She laughed at that and squirmed away from him when he jokingly tried to wipe her nose.

"I got this." She took the tissue from him. After she'd gotten herself under control, she hugged him again. She did not point out that his brother never would have known how to handle her sudden burst of grief, not wanting to once again remind them both that she and Ilya had been married. But she noticed it. "Thanks."

"Any time."

Alicia cleared her throat. "So. What happens now?"

"What do you want to happen?"

"That's a good question," she answered honestly. "I don't know."

"I meant what I said about these random 'things.' I don't want that anymore. If we're going to be together, even if we both agree it has to be a secret, I don't want it to be like this."

Alicia wasn't sure she did agree it had to be a secret, even if she knew that made the best sense. "So what's the solution?"

"I'll think about that," Nikolai said.

She chewed the inside of her cheek for a second. "Nobody will blink an eye if you and I hang out together."

"They'll do a lot more than blink if they know we're a couple," he said.

"Are we a couple? Or are we just screwing?" Alicia asked bluntly.

Nikolai didn't smile. He did reach to twirl a strand of her hair around his fingers and tug it to get her to move closer. "I don't know."

Frustrated, she wasn't going to push him for more. Besides, it wasn't like she knew what the hell they were really doing, either, she told herself as she pushed up on her toes to press her mouth to his. The kiss deepened. His hands roamed across her back to settle on her ass, pulling her closer to him.

"You should go," she said against his mouth. "I have work to do."

"Right. Sure. Of course." He looked at her, but if there was something else he meant to say, he was keeping it to himself. "I'll . . . so, I'll see you? Later?"

She sat in her chair to study him. "I guess we'll see about that."

He didn't say anything after that. He gave her one of those slow, smoldering smiles tinged with just the right amount of smugness to make her want to pinch him someplace tender. Kiss him first, then pinch him, she thought as Nikolai gave her a little wave on the way out the door.

This was going to hurt like hell, she thought, but she was going to keep doing it anyway.

CHAPTER TWENTY-SIX

Then

All Ilya wanted to do was see her, one last time.

He thought he'd have the chance. Everything he'd ever seen about funerals on TV or in the movies showed a satin-lined casket, the deceased with hands folded on the chest. Like they were sleeping. That was what he expected to see today, but they went and closed the lid on the coffin. They trapped her inside.

He was never going to see Jennilynn again.

From his place toward the back of the room, Ilya had a clear view of the black casket up at the front, but his vision was anything but clear. He'd been drinking vodka since nine in the morning. First from the bottle. Then from the water bottle he filled before they left the house. Niko had to help him with his tie.

Now the room threatened to spin, but screw that, he wasn't going to let it. He was going to stand up. He was going to walk up there. He was going to open up that lid. He was going to see her so he could say good-bye. So he could say he was sorry.

"Sorry." The word muttered out of him aloud.

Too loud by the nasty look he got from one of the old ladies sitting near him. Slowly, deliberately, Ilya took another long pull from the bottle while making eye contact. She looked away first.

His mother sat closer to the front. Theresa beside her. Barry next to Theresa. Niko, however, was in the back with Ilya.

"I wanna tell her I'm sorry," Ilya said.

Niko frowned. Good little brother. Always thinking of the right thing to do, right? Except he wasn't so good; he was no better than Ilya. Niko had done his share of shit. He just never seemed to get caught.

"We should go outside. C'mon." Niko grabbed Ilya by the sleeve of his dress shirt. "Be quiet."

Outside the funeral home, Ilya paced. He drained the bottle and tossed it with a curse into the bushes. He bent, hands on his knees, waiting to puke, but even though he wanted to—he wanted to sick up everything inside him—nothing happened but a few heaves and a strand of thick drool.

"Get yourself together." Niko pulled a pack of cigarettes from his pocket and tucked one between his lips. He lit it.

Ilya staggered upright. "Since when do you smoke?"

"Since the girl across the street was found dead." Niko's reply was flat, but broken after a second by the coughing and hacking he did when he took a drag on the smoke.

"Pussy." Ilya's grin peeled back from his teeth, making him a snarling dog.

Without thinking about it, he stepped forward. One, two. His first punch connected directly with his brother's face—a lucky shot. The next missed as Niko shouted and turned, and Ilya staggered forward. Fell on his face.

He rolled onto his back. The sky was an ugly shade of gray. The first spatters of rain hit him in the eyes, and he wanted to close them, but he couldn't seem to do anything but lie on the ground and let the clouds cry for him.

Later.

Darkness. Mouth tasted like shit. Head pounding, he swam up from desperate dreams but couldn't seem to wake. He was in the attic, his cheek pressed to the thin mattress of the army cot. A bucket by his head, though he still couldn't seem to puke.

He heard them. Soft murmurs. The shuffle of blankets, a zipper, the creak of a mattress. He knew what was going on, but he couldn't see anything. Still too drunk to react.

Later.

Ilya woke to the stab of morning light spearing him through the attic window. Niko snored in the sagging double bed, alone. When Ilya sat up to look around, everything came slamming back to him, everything that happened, and his stomach revolted. He retched into the trash can for what seemed like years and then fell back onto the cot with a groan.

His brother pressed a glass of clear, chilly water into Ilya's hand. "Drink this."

He did. Puked again. It hurt less this time, but the taste lingered long after. He tried to wash it away, but it wouldn't go.

He looked up. "She's gone, man. She's really . . . gone."

"I know." Niko sat next to him. Shoulder to shoulder, his warmth welcome in the attic's chill. "I know."

Ilya cried, ashamed not of his tears but because if he'd let himself feel more earlier, he might not have felt this now. Niko put an arm around him. Only for a minute or so before he squeezed, hard, and sat back to let his brother grieve. He handed Ilya a box of tissues and waited patiently for him to finish.

They never spoke of it again.

Downstairs, the house was quiet and empty and trashed. All those people who came over to eat food, and none of them had bothered to help clean up. The smell of leftover pasta and sauce lingered in the kitchen, and his stomach crawled up his throat again as he leaned over the sink, heaving.

"You want some crackers?" The rustle of a package turned him. Theresa held a sleeve of saltines. Her glasses glinted in the light from the windows. "They're good for a sick stomach."

The thought of even nibbling a dry cracker had him doubling over again, hands braced on the sink, while he dry-heaved. An endless minute or two passed before he could control himself. Sweating, Ilya turned on the faucet to splash his face with cool water.

"Here." Theresa took his wrist between her small hands and pressed a spot on the underside of his wrist. "Feel this? Squeeze it. You'll feel better."

He didn't believe it would work, but after another few minutes sitting at the table with her squeezing his wrists, the churning in his stomach got knocked back a bit. He didn't feel better, though. That would have been an impossible task.

"Where'd you learn that?" He asked her.

Theresa withdrew her hands and pushed her glasses up on her nose. Her hair was a wild tangle; her smile, hesitant and solemn. "My dad used to get pretty hungover."

She'd revealed something to him that he didn't know before; knowing it didn't make him like Barry any better than he ever had. Right now, though, Ilya couldn't find it within himself to sympathize with her or even muster the effort to fake it.

Theresa shrugged and looked away. "I'm sorry about Jennilynn. I know you and her—"

"Me and her weren't anything," Ilya cut in. "I mean, she lived across the street. That's it. Me and her were nothing. That's how she wanted it, so that's how it was."

"Sure. Of course. Sorry."

His stomach turned again. "Can you do that thing to my wrists again?"

"Sure," Theresa said quietly and took them both in her hands, her fingers finding the right spots to squeeze.

The pressure eased his nausea. They didn't speak. Ilya closed his eyes and breathed, letting her touch relieve him.

The sound of footsteps in the hallway pulled Theresa away from him. She got up before Ilya could say anything, and disappeared into the dining room, leaving him at the table. His mother, bleary eyed, hair a mess, padded through the kitchen without saying a word to him and went out the sliding glass door with her cigarettes. Ilya watched the plume of smoke drift by the glass; then he stood.

If he was lucky, when he got upstairs to his bed, he would sleep. And, buried beneath his blankets, he did, but only after he pressed his fingers against his opposite wrist on the spot where Theresa had touched him.

CHAPTER TWENTY-SEVEN

Ilya hadn't been in to the office all morning or afternoon but stopped by quickly on his way home to make sure the final details for the dive trip were in place. Allie was still at her computer, typing away, doing whatever she did all day to keep Go Deep running. She didn't look up when he knocked lightly on the door frame.

"I thought you weren't going to come back here," she said.

Ilya stepped through the door to stand in front of her desk. "I wanted to be sure everything was set, since I'm leaving in a couple days."

"Oh!" She turned, looking surprised. "It's you."

"Yeah, last time I checked." He made a show of looking down at himself, then gave her a curious look. "Who'd you think it would be?"

"UPS delivery," Allie answered smoothly.

Ilya eyed the pastry bag on her desk. "You went to the Donut Shack?"

"Grab one. And some coffee. I need to talk to you." She got up before he could answer to make him a mug of coffee.

He opened the bag to look inside, snagging a chocolate frosted with sprinkles. The doughnuts might have been a bribe; the coffee was definitely one. "That sounds bad. What are you going to get on my case about this time?"

She glanced up at him while the coffeemaker hissed and spat. "Why do you always have to do that?"

"Do what?" Ilya shoved the doughnut in his mouth. Chewed. Swallowed.

"Make everything somehow my fault." She handed him a mug of steaming coffee and took her place behind the desk again. "Like I'm some kind of harpy, incapable of being satisfied."

His lip curled a little at her tone. "What's up? Something with the trip? Look, Allie, you know that you can't run the trips, and someone has to stay here to handle business. We can't just close up for two weeks, and we can't afford to cover your costs to go along."

"It's not about the trip, Ilya." Alicia sighed and pinched the bridge of her nose. "It's something else. I wish you'd sit so we can talk about it."

He already knew what it was she meant to bring up. The plain white envelope on the desk told him. Theresa had said she'd talked with Allie about an offer from that real estate development corporation. Days ago. Maybe weeks at this point. She'd been holding out on him.

He didn't sit. "Just hit me with it."

"It's about the quarry. And the shop." She pushed the envelope toward him.

"Yeah. Theresa said something to me about it already." He took grim satisfaction in the way he seemed to have surprised her. "You didn't know that, huh? You thought you were going to sit on this and not talk to me about it?"

"Of course I was going to talk to you about it. I'm talking to you right now."

Ah, there it was. The press of her lips together. The cross of her arms. Allie was getting pissed off at him now. In a few minutes, she'd turn cold and angry, but she'd leave him the hell alone. She'd punish him with the silent treatment, and if he was lucky, it would last until he got back from sunny Jamaica, when maybe he'd be better equipped to deal with all the bullshit that had been happening. Because right now,

Ilya thought as he took a long, deliberate sip of coffee, he had emptied his pockets of any and all fucks he might have had to give.

"You waited long enough," he said. "Theresa told me she'd presented you with an offer, like two weeks ago."

Allie visibly took a breath before she spoke. "The two weeks you didn't come in to work, you mean? The two weeks I handled everything here by myself? Not that it was that much different than any other time, I guess, since I handle most everything here by myself, anyway."

"What are they offering?" He ignored what she'd said so he could push her buttons a little more. Let her keep thinking she was the only one who kept this place running. "Whatever it is, it's not enough."

"It's not enough," she told him. "It will cover what we owe on the mortgage and pay off the outstanding debts for the shop supplies, all of that. But it won't cover what we've put into Go Deep over the years. We won't come out ahead on this deal. We just won't be so far behind."

He tossed the remains of his doughnut in the trash, no longer hungry. He put down the coffee, too, hard enough to slop it onto her desk. "So you want to take it?"

"I want to talk to you about it! Dammit, Ilya, wipe that up."

She yanked one, two, three tissues from the box and started cleaning up the splatters before he even had a chance. The way she always did, stepping in when she thought he wasn't capable of handling whatever it was she then got pissed off at him for not doing in the first place.

"I'm not selling the shop," he said.

Allie made a noise somewhere between a sigh and a groan. She crumpled the stained tissues in her hand. "Ilya—"

"You can't want to sell it. What are they going to do with it?" he demanded.

She pushed the envelope closer across the desk, sliding it through a splotch of coffee she'd missed. "It's all in here. They have plans to develop this side—"

He flapped a hand at her and opened the envelope, curious about what Theresa and her bosses believed his life and dreams were worth. The numbers made him sneer and slide it back toward Allie. "You think this is the first time someone's come up with some bright idea about how they're going to develop the quarry?"

"It's certainly the first time I've ever heard of anything. Have there been other offers?" She gave him an incredulous look.

"Yeah. Couple years ago." He shrugged, determined to downplay it. "I turned it down, and it was more money than these guys are offering."

"I can't believe you got an offer to buy the quarry and you didn't tell me. Ilya, we've been struggling for years! How could you not even discuss it with me?"

"I knew I wasn't going to sell."

She would have taken the money and left him behind, and he would have had nothing.

"It's not only up to you, you know. I own half this business. More than, actually." Allie's mouth thinned. "Dammit, Ilya."

"You want to sell it off? Really? Is that what you want?" He spat the words, wishing he hadn't eaten that doughnut or drunk that coffee. His throat burned.

He'd been trying to push her into anger, but she was quiet for a few seconds. "I think maybe it's time. It wouldn't be the worst thing in the world, you know. We could get out from under the debt. Move on with our lives. You'll need some better credit if you're going to buy a house."

"Who says"—his voice dipped low and dangerous—"that I have to buy a house?"

Allie shook her head. He hated that disappointed look, no matter how many times she'd given it to him. No matter how often he'd deserved it.

He scowled. "My mother isn't going to stick around forever. She says she's back, but you know as well as I do that it never matters, with her. She's going to finish up whatever messed-up thing she's got going on in her head about fixing up the house, and she'll end up leaving again. Probably with me staying behind to foot the bills."

"All the more reason for you to get out from under this place," Allie began, but he cut her off.

"This place," said Ilya, "is mine. I built this place. You can tell yourself all you want that you're the golden princess who waves her magic wand around here to make it happen, but nothing here would've happened if not for me. You've never even dived here. Have you even set one toe in this water?"

She shook her head, eyes glittering with tears, but he wasn't going to feel sorry for her.

"No. Because you can't get over it." Ilya sneered. "She died twenty years ago, Allie. She doesn't haunt anything. She's just dead. And you've never gotten over it."

It would not have been the first time he'd ever made her cry, and he was expecting tears now. Allie didn't cry. She recoiled, briefly, with a small, tight shake of her head and a clench of her fists before she looked him in the eye with a gaze as solid and unyielding as he'd ever seen from her.

"Sometimes," she told him, "you don't get over it. You just get through it."

CHAPTER TWENTY-EIGHT

"So, I've been thinking." Niko said this into the phone while he stared up at the slanted attic ceiling and pondered once again how the hell he'd ended up back here in Quarrytown in a lumpy bed with crappy sheets and too many noises sifting up through the vents.

"Oh, brother." Alicia's low laugh sparked a tingle of heat through him. "About what? Global warming? The reasons why pepper makes you sneeze? The existence, or not, of Bigfoot?"

"Bigfoot totally exists," Niko said, deadpan. "I saw him once in Oregon while I was on a backpacking trip."

He loved the sound of her laughter. There'd been other women in his life. Of course there had. But very few had ever laughed with him the way Alicia did, and when you found someone who laughed with you that way, wasn't that worth holding on to?

"I want to see you," he said, before she could reply.

Alicia didn't answer him for a second or so. "Of course you do."

He stretched in the bed, pushing the blankets down to his ankles. He liked her answer. Confident. Sexy. She was different as a woman than she'd been as a girl, and Niko couldn't get enough.

"I mean I want to see you now," he said.

Again, she was quiet for a few seconds before answering. "You could come over here, you know. I live alone. But you'd have to be careful not to let Dina from next door see you. She's always got an eye out."

"Oh?" Her invitation had set his heart beating just a little faster, but he was going to pretend it hadn't. "What about her?"

"She's a stereotype. Unhappy housewife. Kids, dog, house, husband who travels." Alicia paused. "I'm not sure, but I think she has a thing for Ilya."

Niko grimaced. "Yikes."

"Yeah. He's never confirmed it with me. But . . . yeah."

"So, I shouldn't come over?" he asked.

She laughed again. "Nikolai, seriously. It's almost one in the morning."

"Dina won't be watching," he said, waiting to see if she'd invite him. Hoping.

"And I guess Galina and Ilya are sleeping?"

He thought for a moment. "I assume so. It's quiet. He went to bed a few hours ago. She was out earlier. With friends, she said."

"Is that hard to believe?"

"No. Maybe one of them can help her get a job," he said.

Alicia chuckled. "That might help. Is money an issue again?"

"Not yet, and that's the thing. I don't know where she's getting it," Niko said, "but she seems to have enough, at least for now."

A few beats of silence hung between them before she spoke again.

"What are you doing to me?" Alicia breathed. "What, Nikolai?"

"Whatever you want me to do to you," he whispered in response. "What do you want?"

The sound of her breathing filled the phone. He waited, tense, already hard, for her to answer him. He wasn't sure what he hoped she'd say.

"I want you to touch me."

Six small words that made him shudder. He drew in a breath, his hand moving over his bare belly, feeling the ridges of muscle that would start disappearing soon if he didn't start working out again. Lower, to the rising thickness of his erection. He gripped himself through his briefs.

"Where?" he asked.

"Everywhere."

Niko arched a little into his own touch. "That's a good start."

Alicia laughed again, softly. "It's late. I have to be up early in the morning. The bus to the airport leaves at five."

"Ilya should handle all that. It's his trip."

"He gets to go on the trip. I get to handle all the last-minute details. That's how it works. And it does work," she put in, but if she was trying to convince him or herself, Niko couldn't tell.

"So you're saying good night?"

She groaned. "Ugh. Yes. No. Yes, I am. If I'm going to be tired in the morning, it's going to be for real, full-on sex. Not phone sex."

"I see," Nikolai said. "So you're telling me you want to have sex with me."

This time, her laugh included a snort he found so endearing it made him put a hand to his chest to press against the suddenly swifter beating of his heart. She didn't answer right away. It wasn't a question that needed a real answer.

"Go to sleep," she told him finally. "We'll talk about this later."

She disconnected before he could say anything else. He stretched in the darkness, the light on his phone going out, but in the last few seconds before it went black, he glimpsed a shadow at the top of the attic stairs. Startled, Niko dropped his phone onto the bed and sat up, running his hands over the blankets to find it.

"Shit, Ilya?"

"Yeah, sorry, I didn't mean to scare you. I came to see if I could borrow that solar phone charger you showed me." Ilya moved closer.

Niko's eyes had adjusted enough so he could see. "Yeah, it's on top of the dresser. You getting ready to head out soon?"

"Couple of hours. I'll sleep on the bus. Can't usually the night before a trip. Can I turn on the light?"

"Yeah, sure."

The soft glow of the old dog-shaped lamp illuminated the top of the dresser. Ilya found the charger right away and held it up. "Thanks."

"No problem. Hey, I wish I was heading off to Jamaica," Niko joked.

Ilya turned. "Sounds like you have enough going on to keep you busy here, bro."

Niko didn't say anything. He hadn't used Allie's name . . . had he? Ilya held up the charger again and turned off the lamp.

"Have fun fixing our mother's messes," Ilya said.

CHAPTER TWENTY-NINE

It wasn't what Alicia had expected. She hadn't really known what to expect, actually, but a room in the hotel on the far edge of town that catered to business travelers had not been on her list. It was good, though, she thought as she dropped her purse on the sofa. More than good. It was perfect.

"We don't have to worry," Nikolai said. "Not about your nosy neighbor or Galina or anyone else seeing us. Just you and me and this big old bed."

She'd noticed that as soon as she'd come into the room, no doubt about it. But now she feigned innocence. "That one? There? That one?"

She'd been with guys who didn't get her sense of humor, but even though she and Nikolai had surely had their share of conflicts over the years, there was never any question that he totally understood her jokes.

"Oh, yeah. That one." He tipped his chin toward it. "You know. If you wanted to try it out."

She burst into laughter, covering her face with her hand before peeking through her fingers at him. "So . . . are we really going to do this?"

"God, I hope so." He moved to take her in his arms. "I really, really hope so."

She should've felt more shy. Nervous? Guilt should certainly have poked its greasy head in there somewhere, too.

He didn't kiss her, not at first. Instead, Nikolai stroked a hand over her hair. It was a familiar gesture, one he'd done many times, but even so, Alicia shivered at the touch and turned her face so she could touch her lips against his palm. They stayed that way for a moment, in silence. When he drew her closer so her cheek pressed to his chest, she closed her eyes and breathed him in as the beating of their hearts aligned.

"It's always a little awkward," Nikolai said after a minute. "The first time."

Alicia laughed softly and pulled away to tip her face to his. "It's not the first time."

He stroked his thumb along her lower lip, urging her to open for him. He kissed her. Hot and wet, a slanting pressure on her mouth that echoed an electric thrill through every part of her. His hands moved down her body to slide beneath her ass, lifting her so that she let out a startled yelp, muffled inside his mouth. They both laughed, and Nikolai walked them back toward the bed, where they fell in a tangle of arms and legs and open, kissing mouths.

She moved, or he rolled, but somehow Alicia ended up on top of him. Straddling, she pressed her knees to his hips and pushed his shirt up, revealing the taut strip of belly and curly dark hair leading from his belly button into the waistband of his jeans. She bent her head to nuzzle him there, and Nikolai arched at the pressure of her lips on his skin. She pressed her teeth there for a few seconds, grinning at the sound of his gasp.

She looked up at him through the fall of her hair. "You like it when I bite."

"Girl . . ." Nikolai breathed out with a small groan. "Yeah. I like it when you bite."

She crawled up his body to settle herself against his crotch. She'd dressed carefully for tonight. Soft leggings, and a sheer tunic top over a clingy tank. No bra. Silky thong panties. Everything soft and flowing and easy to get off. Now she tugged the tunic over her head and let it fall in a flutter of fabric off the side of the bed. Sitting up straight, she took Nikolai's hands and slid them up her body to cup her breasts.

He thumbed her nipples, teasing them into tight points. "This body. Mmm, mmmm, mmm."

"I like it when you touch me." She rocked against him, loving the pressure of his hardening cock on her. She tugged the neckline of the tank down, exposing more cleavage but not yet exposing her nipples.

Nikolai dragged his fingertips over the new expanse of flesh. Then over her nipples again, first one, then the other, tweaking each gently so it was her turn to gasp. His gaze burned into her as he licked his lips.

She wanted his mouth on her. All over her. Alicia leaned forward. When he buried his face against her flesh, she shook. Eyes closed, mouth open. Hair hanging all over the both of them. She gripped the headboard with one hand and used the other to cup his chin, urging him to feast on her.

Nikolai tugged her shirt down farther, at last, yes, freeing her to his hungry mouth. Wet heat skidded over her skin. His lips closed on one of the sensitive peaks he'd already teased with his fingertips. His hands cupped her, keeping her close.

She muttered something incoherent and ground herself against him. Nikolai released her nipple to flick it with his tongue. She wanted to move, she wanted to kiss his mouth, she wanted to pull off his clothes and get him naked, but right in that moment, all she could do was give up to the serious waves of desire coursing through her from the expert efforts of Nikolai's lips and tongue . . . and teeth . . .

"Ah!" She yelped, sitting up straight and covering herself with her hands. "No, no . . ."

He laughed, rolling them both so he was on top of her. "No? You don't like it when *I* bite, huh?"

It hadn't hurt, of course. Just surprised her. She pulled her knees up to grip his hips as he kissed her.

"I guess not," she said into his mouth, and sucked his tongue before letting him pull away.

Nikolai braced himself on his arms to look down at her. "So much to learn about you, Ms. Harrison."

"You know a lot about me already." She slipped her hands beneath the bottom of his T-shirt again, warming her chilly skin against his heat and laughing at the way he hissed in a breath.

"You have cold hands—I know that," he agreed, and shifted to cover her with his weight so she didn't have room to get her hands on him again. "But there's a lot I don't know."

"Hmm, oh, yeah? Like what?" With someone else she would've pushed him off her, feeling trapped or squished, but Nikolai's body fit hers with perfect precision. And that was with their clothes on, she thought with another thrill of sensation rolling through her. What was it going to be like when they were both naked?

"Oh, for example . . . do you like this?" He traced his lips along her jawline, making her shiver.

"Yes."

She felt his grin pressed against her. He tugged her earlobe with his teeth. "This?"

"That's good, too," Alicia said. "But I think you need to move a little lower."

He laughed, and she loved that he did. For sure, there'd been lots of times over the years when Nikolai Stern had not laughed with her. To have this now, here, was more surprising to her than wanting to get naked.

"Ah. Gotcha. Here?" He nibbled lightly at her throat, and when she sighed and shifted beneath him, he chuckled again. He feathered kisses over the slopes of her breasts. "Here."

She let her fingers wind in the thickness of the hair at the nape of his neck. "Oh, definitely there, yes, but . . ."

"Lower?" His tongue swirled over her nipples, one at a time.

She sighed out a slow, aching breath. "Yes."

He shifted her to pull off the tank top, then knelt to pull his shirt over his head, using that sexy over-the-shoulder grab that always looked so casual but had to be deliberate by the knowing grin he gave her. Oh, yeah, she thought. Nikolai knew exactly what he was doing. And she was totally going to keep letting him, at least for as much time as they had.

He popped his button and nudged the zipper down, but only a notch or so before bending back to press a line of kisses over the curve of her ribs. The hollow dip of her belly over her navel. He mouthed a hip, then looked up at her.

"Lower?"

Alicia smiled and, by way of an answer, let her fingers rest on the top of his head. No more laughter now. Nikolai's gaze went dark and liquid. Consuming her. He dipped his fingertips below the elastic waistband of her leggings to ease them over her hip, revealing more and more of her. Making her naked for him.

For a moment—a single, terrifying moment—she almost told him to stop. There'd be no going back after this. Everything that had happened between them in the past could never go away. But this—this was moving forward into something new and different and potentially dangerous.

She had never been the first one to jump off the rope swing, she reminded herself. She'd always had to push past the fear to leap. But that had been a long time ago, before Jennilynn died and everything changed. Alicia wasn't that girl anymore.

Now she pushed her leggings over her hips and thighs, giving Nikolai the room to pull them off, leaving her wearing only the wispy silk panties that left nothing to the imagination. She touched herself, a small circling motion, then tapped. Once. Twice.

"Lower," Alicia said.

"You're killing me, girl," Nikolai told her as he moved between her legs. He closed his eyes. His mouth hovered over her panties, which were so thin they did nothing to keep the heat of his breath from washing over her. "You. Like. This?"

He molded his mouth to her over the silk, sucking gently. She arched. The pressure was amazing—delirious, but teasing. She waited, holding her breath as Nikolai nuzzled the insides of her thighs.

When finally he pulled the fabric aside to kiss her nakedness, she tried to take another breath and found at first she could not. All she could do was sip—gasping—at the air as he slid his hands beneath her ass to lift her to his stroking tongue.

"So . . . good," she managed to say, though she couldn't be sure the words weren't garbled.

Nikolai gave her another lick. "You taste amazing."

Giddy, she tipped her hips to offer him more of her, and he took it. Tender, teasing strokes with the flat of his tongue alternated with tight circles. He had her hovering on the edge so fast, so easily, all she could do was let the waves of pleasure sweep her away.

"That's it," Nikolai said against her. "Yeah, come on."

She wasn't about to deny herself this ecstasy nor him the joy of giving it to her. Her climax rocked her, and she shook with it. With the last gasp she was able to take, she cried out his name.

In the silence that followed, Alicia thought she should say something else. Make a joke, maybe. Lighten the mood. She couldn't quite rouse herself to the effort, though. Not with the aftershocks of her orgasm still rippling through her.

She opened her eyes after a bit to find Nikolai lying on his side next to her. Just looking. He smiled when she looked back.

"I think I figured out at least one thing you like," he said.

She gave a contented sigh. "Mmmm. There are plenty more."

"Damn," he said and cupped his hand between her legs. "I guess I'd better keep going, huh?"

She sat up. "This is fun. Not as much fun as if you were naked, too, but it's fun."

"Hold on." Nikolai hopped off the bed and stripped out of his jeans but left his briefs on. "How's this?"

"You're not naked." Alicia drew her knees to her chest to eye him as he crawled onto the bed to kiss her. He pulled away at the last second, then moved in again, then away once more, before she grabbed his shoulders and held him from moving. "You're a tease."

"I thought maybe you'd like being teased."

She shook her head. "No biting. No teasing."

"Noted." He kissed her harder this time.

"I brought condoms," she said in a low voice, after a minute or so.

Nikolai didn't pull away. "Me, too."

"I want you," Alicia breathed against his mouth. "Inside me."

"Yes to that. Feels like I've been waiting forever for it." He looked into her eyes, mouth solemn. "Are you sure you want this?"

A glib answer was rising to her lips, but his expression stopped it before she could say it. She kissed him, instead. They pressed their foreheads together, quiet.

"I don't believe in regrets, that's all. I don't want this to be something we wish we hadn't done," Nikolai said.

She tucked herself against him so they could both lean back against the headboard. "Did you ever? Regret anything about us?"

"Yes."

It wasn't the answer she wanted, especially not right now. A hundred responses flashed through her mind, but she stifled them all. She kissed the corner of his mouth, instead, then got up from the bed and went to her bag. She pulled out the box of condoms and shook one free.

"Be naked for me," Alicia said, and in that moment she couldn't be sure if she meant merely for him to take off the rest of his clothes or something deeper.

Nikolai, in response, shucked off his briefs and tossed them to the side. She let her gaze drop to take all of him in. It was the first time she'd seen him entirely naked in the light, and she didn't want to miss an inch.

Neither of them said a word as she sheathed him, though Nikolai did let out a lingering, raspy sigh. Alicia let her nails scratch up his thighs and over his belly, watching with fascination the play of emotions across his face. Heat blazed in his eyes before he closed them to writhe and arch under her as she increased the pressure of her nails against his tender skin. She left some marks behind.

If he was going to regret this, she wanted to give him plenty to be sorry for.

She soothed the crescents left by her nails with several swipes of her tongue and, urged on by Nikolai's soft moans, let her hair trail over his body. She moved over him, a hand between them to guide him inside her. She paused with him at her entrance.

"Open your eyes, Nikolai."

He did, and she kept his gaze locked with hers as she eased him into her heat until he was seated so deep she winced at the delicious pleasure-pain. It was her turn to gasp and arch as he filled her. Again, her nails scratched lightly down his belly and over his thighs as she began to move. She tested him again with another, deeper, gouge that became a pinch on the taut flesh above each of his hips.

With a grunt, Nikolai thrust upward, hard. He grabbed her hips as they moved together. She pinched harder, twisting, until he cried out with what might've sounded like a protest except for the throbbing of his cock in response. He moved a hand between them so that his knuckles hit her exactly where she needed the pressure every time they moved.

"Perfect." Alicia gave up trying to speak in any way but without words.

She hadn't thought she could come again, but her desire, coiled tight, low in her belly, grew as easily and quickly by the way he touched her as by the way he reacted when she touched him. She'd always been turned on by bringing her partner pleasure, but with Nikolai everything seemed exaggerated. Enhanced. She touched him; he reacted, and it was enough to send her tipping over the edge of desire's cliff, falling toward the jagged rocks below.

He finished seconds after she did, so close behind her it was nearly the same time. They moved in sync for a few more thrusts, until she let herself fall forward to kiss his mouth before rolling off to sprawl at his side. Nikolai got up and went to the bathroom, but he was back in moments. He slipped into bed beside her and pulled up the sheet to their hips.

There'd been no guilt or anxiety when she got to the hotel, but some combination of unease was rising within her now. Nikolai was far from a stranger to her. They'd known each other for nearly their entire lives. Yet now in the aftermath of that fantastic sex, all she could think about was how little she knew him.

"I should go," she said.

Nikolai rolled to put a hand on her hip, keeping her in place. "Why? I have the room until the morning. We can watch a movie. Order takeout. You don't have anyone waiting for you at home that you have to answer to."

"*You* might," she said.

"Nobody I have to answer to." He took her hand and ran it along the path her fingertips had earlier traced over his body. "Alicia. You don't have to go."

She shifted to trace the small wounds she'd left behind. She didn't want to cut him any deeper than this. She didn't want to get cut.

"This isn't what this is supposed to be," she told him. "Remember? It's just this thing between us until you head out again. When is that going to be, by the way?"

He shifted onto his back, putting an inch or so of distance between them. "I had eight weeks of grievance leave and sabbatical time. So . . . not for another few weeks."

"But you are going." She kept herself from touching him again for the simple reason that she wanted to. "I mean, you will be."

"Sure," he said after a second or two of silence. "Yeah."

Some time had passed, and she thought he might've fallen asleep, but when she looked at him, Nikolai was staring at the ceiling. He'd placed his hands on his chest, one over the other. Like a mummy. It was how he'd always slept, she remembered from the long-ago sleepovers.

"You asked me what I regretted," Nikolai replied without looking at her.

"I asked you *if.* Not *what.*"

He closed his eyes for a second, then opened them to stare again upward. "Well, I did, and you should know what it was."

"I don't need to." She moved to get off the bed, but his hand whipped out and snagged her wrist, stopping her. "Nikolai, I don't want to."

He looked at her and pushed up on his elbow. "I regretted hurting you."

Alicia drew a breath. Then another. She wanted to look away from him, but did not.

"Which time?" she asked, an edge in her voice she wished she'd been able to control, if only so he wouldn't have the satisfaction of hearing it.

Nikolai frowned. "Every time. Every damned time."

She hadn't known it was exactly what she needed him to say until he'd said it. Before she could answer him, he pulled her close to kiss her again. It didn't linger, but it was sweeter for the brevity.

"Stay," Nikolai said.

She did.

CHAPTER THIRTY

The phone had rung so many times Theresa was sure he wasn't going to answer it. She wasn't going to leave another voicemail. Not after the four or five she'd already left.

"Yeah?"

"Ilya, it's Theresa." She started talking before he could answer, not wanting to give him a chance to speak. "I know you've spoken to Alicia about this offer. I want to talk to you about it."

"I already told her the same thing I'm going to tell you," he said. "The answer is no. And, also, right now I'm staring out at a beach and the ocean, so this is the last thing in the world I want to talk about."

"Wait! Please," she added, softer. "When will you be back?"

There was silence, and she was sure he was going to disconnect, but after a long, disgruntled sigh, Ilya said, "The end of next week."

"Will you at least meet with me? You and Alicia. I can outline all the plans and what will happen—"

"None of that matters. You can tell me whatever you want, but you know as well as I do that once they get the property, they'll do whatever they want with it."

"I can make sure the contracts are written in your favor," she said, her fingers crossing that she could make that be true.

Ilya made another of those noises. "What's your deal with this project, anyway?"

"It's a lot of money. I work on commission." He didn't need to know why she needed the money, what she intended to do with it. That was her business, not his.

"I don't want to talk about this now, Theresa. I'm about to head out into clean, warm water and look at beautiful things. And I don't just mean the fish, I meant the women in bikinis," Ilya said.

Theresa felt herself grimace, though why should she care what—or who—Ilya Stern did? It was the way he said it, like he was trying to rub her face in it for some reason. She wasn't going to let it get to her.

"Just say you'll meet with me and Alicia when you get back," she said.

"Fine. If it will get you both off my case. I gotta go," he said again, and hung up.

Maybe it was because he felt bad about what had happened in their family so many years ago. A guilt that had nothing to do with him, but one she would exploit to get what she needed. She didn't have to be proud of herself. She just needed to get him to agree to do it.

She had another call to make: one of less importance, but one that at least had a bit less selfish motivation behind it. She pressed in the numbers and waited.

"Hey," Wayne said, somewhat warily. "What's up?"

Theresa closed her eyes briefly, then forced a smile. People could hear it, if you were smiling. It made them feel better about your conversation. She'd learned that in one of those trust-building classes she'd taken, one that had done very little to make it easier for her to trust and a whole lot better at manipulating people into trusting her.

"Hey," she said. "So, listen. I can come pick up those boxes tonight, if you're going to be around."

"Yeah, sure."

"And, Wayne, do you have some time to also talk about something?"

She heard the hope in his voice when he answered. "Yeah. Sure. I thought you didn't want . . . but sure, of course. I'll see you when?"

"In about an hour."

"Great. See you."

He thought she wanted to talk about getting back together. She knew it. She also knew that when she told him that she'd secured the verbal commitment from the co-owners of the old Quarrytown quarry, along with the existing dive shop and all the accompanying equipment, he was going to move on the acquisition, because if there was one thing Wayne craved, it was always that next deal.

Her phone still clutched in her palm, Theresa allowed herself to take a long, deep breath. Time was closing in on her. If she didn't get this deal signed, sealed, and delivered, it was going to fall through, and while it wouldn't be the end of her career, it felt very much like it might be the end of her rope.

CHAPTER THIRTY-ONE

Dinner and a movie. Nothing terribly special about it. Pretty standard date fare. Pretty normal night out, even if you weren't on a date but simply hanging with a longtime childhood friend, the younger brother of the man you used to share toothpaste with.

This was *so* a date.

With dessert afterward at the coffee shop, right out there in public where anyone in the whole world could see them, Alicia did wonder for half a second if they weren't making a big mistake. If maybe it would've been smarter, better, easier, to keep meeting in hotel rooms and having furtive, fantastic sex. It had been Nikolai who'd asked her to go out with him, and although it hadn't taken her more than three seconds to make up her mind and say yes, Alicia was second-guessing her decision a little bit now.

"Niko! Hey, man!" The guy with the receding hairline who clapped Nikolai on the shoulder shot Alicia a look. "Hey, Allie."

Nikolai looked a little confused at first, so Alicia filled in the blanks for him. "Hey, Mike. Good to see you."

"I didn't know you were back in town. Heard about your grandma. I'm sorry." Mike Taylor, the guy who'd once bragged to Niko about kissing her, glanced at Alicia again and gave her a nod. "Where's Ilya?"

"He's on a dive trip," she answered. "Jamaica."

"Lucky bastard. Here we are freezing our tits off, and he gets to go to Jamaica?" Mike shook his head and, without asking, pulled out a chair and sat. "Niko, man, where've you been? What've you been up to?"

The positive side to this was that Mike clearly did not seem to think he was interrupting anything important, which meant he didn't assume they were together as anything more than old friends. The bad thing was he was totally interrupting, and there wasn't much Alicia could say about it. She shot Nikolai a pleading look, but he was leaning forward to hear something Mike was saying and didn't see her.

In the next minute, she caught a wave from across the room from another high school friend, Tammy Peters. She was sitting with a bunch of her girlfriends. Alicia had seen them all around, of course—she and Tammy had been good friends a few years back, before Tammy had a baby and had sort of dropped everything in favor of being a stay-at-home mom. They still kept in touch, but since all the conversations had started revolving around baby stuff, the friendship had faltered.

"Be right back," she said to Nikolai, and got up to say hi to the table of women clustered in the corner. Each of them had a copy of the same book, some battered and some pristine. Ah. Book club.

"Allie, hey! Hi! Grab a chair!" Tammy said.

"Oh, I can't interrupt book club," Alicia said. "Besides, I haven't read the book."

A woman sitting against the wall shook her pixie haircut so her long silver earrings swung. "You didn't miss much."

"Amy hated it," Tammy said. "Most of us liked it. But what have you been up to? It's been ages."

Amy clearly had other concerns. "Is that Niko Stern over there with you and Mike?"

"Yeah." She remembered Amy now. A year ahead of her in school. She and Jennilynn had been frenemies, both of them on the cheerleading squad.

"He grew up nice," Amy said with a slide of her tongue along her teeth that made Alicia want to slap the smug right off her face.

"His grandma died, right? My sister-in-law works at Country View. She said she'd seen you there." Tammy frowned. "Sorry. I know she was a nice lady. I met her once, that time at your house."

Alicia glanced over her shoulder. Mike seemed to be regaling Nikolai with some complicated story that required a lot of hand gestures. Nikolai was listening, laughing even, but when he looked up and his eyes sought the room for her, the look on his face as his gaze settled on her sent a rush of warmth through her so fierce it made her sweat. This man, with one look, could make her shake.

"Sure you don't want to sit? We have a space. We're all done talking about the book." Tammy grinned.

"I'm actually on my way to the ladies' room," Alicia said.

"Maybe next month you'd like to join us?" Tammy glanced around at the rest of the table, everyone else nodding with varying degrees of enthusiasm. "We're going to read a classic. *Anne of Green Gables.*"

It was one of Alicia's favorite childhood books. "Give me a call, okay? I'll see."

In the bathroom, she used the toilet, and at the sink while she was washing her hands, she wet a paper towel with cool water to press the back of her neck and her temples. February might be cold outside, but in here she was starting to sweat, and all because of that look he'd shot her.

It hadn't been a sexy look, lusting and lingering. No, Nikolai's look had been of . . . relief. As though he'd been worried she'd gotten up and left him, and when he found her there across the room, the sight of her had eased every fear he'd ever had.

"Not sure you can handle this," Alicia mouthed to herself in the mirror. Small tendrils of her hair had escaped the high ponytail she wore, clinging to her damp skin. Her eyes were bright. Cheeks pink. She freshened her lipstick and was searching for the compact in her bag, so she could powder away some of the heat, when the restroom door opened.

Amy joined her at the sink, turning to lean on it as though they'd been besties for years. "Niko Stern, huh?"

"What about him?" Alicia snapped the compact closed and tucked it away in her bag. She looked in the mirror, carefully not looking at Amy, and touched the corners of her mouth to check her lipstick.

"He's hot."

Alicia slanted the other woman a look. "Okay?"

"Is he single?"

Alicia paused. "I . . ."

"Could you introduce us?" Amy turned to look in the mirror, using the tips of her fingers to feather her short cut along her cheeks and spike it over her forehead. She sucked in her cheeks to hollow them, then gave herself a slow, sassy smile.

Clearly, Amy thought a lot about herself.

"No, he's not," Alicia said.

Amy frowned. "Damn, really? Is he married?"

"No."

Amy shrugged and found Alicia's gaze in the reflection. "So . . . not that serious, then?"

"You'd have to ask him, I guess." Alicia shouldered her bag and smoothed her skirt. The entire conversation was making her stomach hurt. She shot Amy a smile, though. "Maybe I'll see you next month at book club."

"Allie." Amy's voice caught her with a hand on the door handle. "Hey, I just wanted to say that . . . your sister was the one girl I looked up to at QHS."

The words struck Allie like a slap, although she kept herself from reacting like she'd been struck. All these years later, and it was no easier to handle the condolences. Time should've made it softer, eased the edges of the hurt, but it hadn't. If anything, it somehow seemed worse than when the pain had been fresh, because for people like Amy, they were only jogged into remembering Jennilynn when they saw Alicia, while she had to remember her sister in a dozen different ways every other day. Alicia felt her shoulders trying to slump, but she straightened them. She nodded, glancing over her shoulder.

"Thanks. That's a nice thing to say."

"It's hard to believe she's gone, I guess."

"It's been a long time," Alicia said, with a yank on the door to emphasize the conversation was over, not caring if she came off as rude. Back at their table, she didn't take a seat. "Can we go?"

Mike looked up with disappointed confusion, but Nikolai stood at once. "You okay?"

"Headache. Can we head out?"

"Sure, of course. Mike, buddy, it was good to see you." Nikolai shook his hand but kept the exit moving toward the door, even as Mike tried to call after him. "Yeah, call me! We'll get together!"

In the parking lot, around the corner from the front doors and big glass windows, he pushed Alicia gently against the wall and took her by the upper arms. "What's going on?"

"Nothing. It's stupid. That girl, Amy . . ."

"What about her?" Nikolai pulled her close for a moment, his lips pressing the top of her head. At the sound of someone coming out the doors around the corner, he put distance between them.

She noticed. Of course she did. He was as cautious about revealing the truth about them in public as she was, and he hadn't even lived in this tiny town where everyone knew your business for a long time. What did he care if gossip started? Soon enough, he'd be long gone.

Alicia put another few inches between them, then started walking toward the car without answering him. She pulled her coat tighter around her, wishing she'd brought a scarf. The temperature had dropped—it was an uncharacteristically frigid late February—and all reports were pointing toward at least one blizzard, maybe one as late as March. Figured: no snow all winter until it started to be time for spring. In fact, when she tipped her face up toward the pitch-black sky sprinkled with a few bright, sparkling stars, a lone snowflake drifted down and landed on her cheek.

"Alicia. Hey. What's wrong?" He caught up to her.

She turned. "Maybe you were right. We can't be doing this, Nikolai."

"Having coffee?" He was smart enough to know what she meant, but he was playing innocent.

She didn't want to laugh, so she poked the front of his coat. "Anything."

"Nobody knew anything. It's not like I had you spread out over the table . . . though . . . mmmm, that is something to think about—"

"Shut. Up."

She poked him harder and pushed past him to get to the driver's side. When they were both in the car, Alicia turned on the ignition and punched the seat-warmer buttons. She didn't want this to become an issue between them, and certainly not an argument, but she'd come away from the coffee shop feeling as though something needed to be discussed. She could feel Nikolai looking at her as she drove.

"It's snowing," he said quietly. "Be careful."

"Sure, because I'm usually so reckless," she snapped, both hands gripping the wheel tight enough to hurt her fingers.

The single flake that had kissed her cheek had been joined by a few dozen million or so, thick sheets of fluffy whiteness slanting out of the sky. It covered the road within minutes so that their half-hour drive became forty-five minutes as Alicia slowed to keep from sliding. Their conversation quieted so she could concentrate. By the time she pulled into her driveway, it had become questionable whether she'd be able to get into the garage, even with her car's front-wheel drive. Sitting in the silence unbroken by the shush-shush of the falling snow, she turned off the ignition and let out a sigh of relief at having made it safely. She unkinked her fingers from the wheel and rubbed them to ease the ache, turning to say something to Nikolai about the weather.

He kissed her before she got a word out. Long, slow, steamy. His hand slipped around the back of her neck. They strained to get at each other over the center console. Her seat belt choked her. They broke apart with a gasp, both breathing hard, fogging up the windows.

"We should at least go in the house," she said.

Nikolai sat back in his seat, licking his lips. "Yeah. Give me a second to get up, though."

"What . . . ? Oh. Oh." She laughed, heat flushing her cheeks as she looked at his crotch. The long coat hid any sign of his erection, but the fact he had one just from kissing her gave Alicia a thrill.

They looked at each other, both grinning. Nikolai reached to brush a few curling tendrils away from her forehead. He traced his fingertips along her jaw.

"Amy wanted to know if you were single," Alicia said.

Nikolai's hand drifted to rest on her shoulder. "What did you tell her?"

"I said you weren't. She tried to ask more questions, but I got out of there. She wanted to talk to me about Jenni, and I wasn't . . . I just couldn't." Alicia drew in a breath, looking into his eyes.

The overhead garage light that came on when opening the door went out, plunging them into darkness lit only by the house's outside lights and the lamppost at the end of the driveway. Alicia blinked in the dimness, watching the way Nikolai's face fell into shadow. His fingers squeezed gently, then ran down her arm to take her hand. Their fingers linked.

His phone rang, and he dug it out of his pocket. "Yeah. Yes, I see it. No, I'm actually—I just got home. A few inches . . . yeah, Mom. I heard. Well, are you okay? Do you need me to come get you? Are you sure?" He glanced at Alicia, who made wide eyes. "It's not really my business, is it? So long as you're someplace safe, I guess. Oh, does he? Well . . . that's . . . awkward, but okay, thanks for telling me. Yeah. Fine. Yes, fine."

He disconnected and leaned back against the seat with a groan that turned into a laugh. He looked at Alicia. "My mother."

"I figured."

"She's not coming home tonight. She's with a *friend*." The way Nikolai said the word made it clear what he thought about that. "She says the weather's too bad for him to drive her home."

"Hmmm," Alicia said.

He shrugged. "She's a grown-up. The roads were getting bad. Not for me to judge."

"Speaking of the weather, we should get out of the car. It's getting cold, and snow's coming into the garage."

They both got out. In the short time they'd been in there, another inch had fallen, drifting into the detached garage so that she had to kick the snow away from where the door came down. It wet her shoes and her ankles through her tights, making her wish she'd worn boots. With the door shut, all they had to do was make it across the snow-covered drive and sidewalk up to the front door, unless they wanted to cut through the breezeway and around to the back. Though the path there wouldn't be any clearer.

"I could carry you," Nikolai said with his hands on his hips, face tilted to the sky so that soft white flakes gathered in his eyebrows and over his mouth, making a kind of mustache, before he smiled and shook his head to make it fall away.

"It's just a few feet. I'll have wet shoes, that's all." From next door, the outside light came on, and the Guttridges' door cracked open, so Dina could peek out.

"So . . . your neighbor," Nikolai said. He carefully didn't look toward the Guttridge house or raise his voice below a murmur, but his eyebrows went up. "She's totally staring me down."

"Wave at her." Alicia demonstrated, teeth chattering in the chill. "Hey, Dina! Hi!"

Grinning, she looked back at him when Dina went back inside the house without returning the greeting. "I'm not afraid to name and shame her. She's nosy as hell. Come in?"

They slogged through the snowfall and managed to get inside the front door, where they kicked off their shoes and watched the small piles of snow already beginning to melt. Nikolai bent to put his shoes and hers on the small mat next to the door, an action that warmed her for all kinds of nonlusty reasons. Because he knew it mattered to her that shoes came off inside the house, a habit left over from her childhood that had never been matched at the Sterns'. Because he made sure to respect the rules of her house without having to be told. Because standing there in her front entryway, Nikolai looked like he belonged there and always had.

"You know what would be really great right now?" he asked.

Alicia breathed in. "What?"

"You. Me. The couch. A couple glasses of wine. Something stupid on the television. Maybe one of those old creature features we used to like." Nikolai tilted his head to study her. "Just hanging out, you and me, the way we used to."

"I have a couple bottles in my kitchen. C'mon." She paused to peek around him at the door's sidelight, saying over her shoulder, "It's snowing even harder now."

Nikolai had already started toward the kitchen, finding glasses exactly where they'd been for so many years. She grabbed a bottle of Pinot Grigio from under the cabinet and a corkscrew, and handed them to him. She watched him open the bottle, admiring the shift and bulge of his muscles beneath the formfitting plaid shirt. He poured them each a glass.

They clinked them.

"Cheers," Nikolai said.

She sipped hers, wanting to move into his arms so he could kiss her. She watched him take a drink. The slide of his tongue over his lower lip. When he smiled at her, it felt right.

"What is *this*, Nikolai?"

His smile faded. His gaze shuttered. He took another deliberate sip of wine before answering. "It is whatever it is. Whatever it's going to be. Do we have to put a name on it?"

"A woman stopped me in the bathroom to ask me if you were single," Alicia said wryly. "I think we need to at least talk about it. At least as long as you're back home. I mean, obviously when you leave again, it won't matter."

Together they moved toward the den, where she turned on the television without bothering to set the channel. She took a seat on the couch, Nikolai beside her. It was chillier in this room, which had been built onto the back of the house, and she reached behind them to grab a crocheted blanket.

"Babulya made this," Nikolai said. "I remember it."

"She gave it to me when she went into the home. I've always loved it." Alicia ran a hand over the blocks of orange, brown, and green.

He inched closer to get the blanket over his lap, lifting her legs so she could settle her feet on him. "I'm here with you. Now. I don't know what's going to happen in the future, but if you want me to tell you that I won't see anyone else while I'm living here, I can do that."

"Hmmm." Alicia wiggled her toes and sipped wine, eyeing him over the rim of her glass. "You sure?"

Nikolai laughed. "Umm, yes, Alicia. I'm sure. I've been home a month now. If I wanted to go out sowing my oats all over, don't you think I might've done it sooner?"

"You came home to be with your grandmother. I'm not sure you'd have had time to go out and sow anything. But now . . ."

He shook his head with a grin. "Girl, you know I'm not going to do that."

"I don't know, actually, which is why I think we should talk about it," Alicia said, hating to be that girl, the one who insisted on having "the talk."

"Look, I don't think it's a great idea to just out ourselves, okay? That's going to cause a lot of issues that neither you nor I want to deal with, especially you, since—"

"Since I'm the one who'll stay behind and have to face everyone," she said, finishing the sentence for him when he didn't. The guilty look on Nikolai's face told her she'd hammered that nail all the way home on the first try. Alicia sighed.

Nikolai leaned to kiss her. "We don't know what might happen. That's all I'm saying. Why should we rush into making some kind of announcement?"

If this wasn't going to become something permanent, he meant. Something worth facing the surprise, the comments, the backhanded talk. Worth facing his brother over. She understood it, but it still didn't settle that great inside her, not even when his kiss turned more fervent, and her body responded.

"I'm not seeing anyone but you, Alicia," he said against her mouth. "Can that be enough for now?"

She withdrew just enough to catch her breath, aware that she'd almost spilled her wine. She sipped some and put it on the side table before leaning to take his glass from him to do the same. She kissed him again. "Yes, sure. Of course."

Nikolai paused the kiss long enough to cup her face in his hands for a few seconds before letting go. "What about you?"

She laughed, hard and loud. "Me?"

"Yeah. Have you been seeing anyone?"

She pressed her lips together to hold back another round of chuckles. "God. No. I mean, I have gone on some dates and stuff, but not for a long time."

"How come?"

He twined a long strand of her hair around a fingertip, a gesture that would've driven her out of her skull with annoyance had anyone else tried it. Much like the way he'd cupped her face moments before. At the gentle tug, she let her head tip toward him before he released her.

"Quarrytown," she told him, as though that were enough of an answer.

Nikolai laughed. "The pool's very shallow, huh?"

"If you're not related to someone, you went to school with them," she pointed out, and scooted closer so he could put an arm around her. "Or you've known them since you were, like, three."

"Gross," he said with a laugh, since of course they'd known each other that long. He squeezed her closer.

She propped her feet up next to his on the coffee table, and they sat that way for a few minutes. She tapped his foot with hers. He returned the motion. She snuggled closer, at last paying attention to what was on the television but not willing to give up this closeness to grab the remote.

"This is nice," Alicia said.

Nikolai made a murmured, sleepy reply. She twisted to peek at him and saw his eyes were closed. A faint smile played on his mouth. She didn't want to wake him. She wanted to watch him, just this way.

Time had brought him back to her in a way that she guessed neither of them could've imagined. Whatever that meant, she thought, as she traced the curves and lines of his face with her gaze. Fate? Destiny?

A shared desire for eventual and mutual self-destruction?

Leaving him to sleep on the couch, she took their wineglasses to the kitchen, where she flipped on the outside light to look at the falling snow. It was still coming thick and fast. Heavy curtains of white that blocked out the sight of anything else. At least half a foot had layered on top of the picnic table in the backyard. She clicked off the light and turned, letting out a soft yelp as she connected with a solid male body.

"Sorry. Didn't mean to scare you."

She let herself be enfolded. Her cheek pressed the softness of his flannel shirt. In the dark of her kitchen, they moved slowly. Not quite dancing, but definitely not standing still.

"Are you tired?" she asked.

"A little."

"Are you going to go home?"

"No," Nikolai said.

She smiled against him. "Good."

CHAPTER THIRTY-TWO

Nikolai woke with the taste of her still on his lips. They'd made love slowly, leisurely, taking their time, and it seemed impossible now, after sleeping, that it wasn't yet morning. Not even the hint of light peeked through Alicia's soft curtains, so he contented himself with curling up against her back. Naked. Warm. He pushed aside the fall of her hair so he could press his mouth to the back of her neck. His hand curved over her hip.

She didn't say anything, but she wiggled against him in a way that was definitely going to cause a reaction. He waited to see if she'd speak, or move again, but with a sigh, it seemed Alicia had fallen back into dreams. Nikolai closed his own eyes, no longer tired. He'd grown used to sleeping comfortably in any kind of bed, any kind of situation, but it seemed as he got older, he needed to sleep less, and without the clock to tell him it was nowhere near time to wake up, his body was considering starting the day.

He relaxed into the warm cave of the blankets and Alicia's skin, instead. If he couldn't sleep, at least he could enjoy this moment. He wanted there to be a lot more times like this.

It wasn't going to end well.

How could it? Even if he could put aside the rise of jealousy that clenched his fists every time he thought about Ilya doing even one of the multitude of things Nikolai and Alicia had done, even if he could get past the incestuous tumult of being with his brother's wife, there was no getting beyond the simple truth that he and Alicia had always been more like oil and water than air and fire.

No woman had ever made him so angry or pushed him so far beyond the limits of his temper. None had ever made him laugh so hard or feel so protective. He kissed her bare shoulder, tasting her. Breathing her in. It seemed that Nikolai could remember easily dozens of times when he'd been convinced he hated Alicia, but there was no time when he could not remember loving her.

"Are you awake?" he whispered into the darkness, half hoping she wouldn't answer.

She wriggled against him. "Mmffff."

It was enough of a response for him. He slipped his hand lower, over the softness of her belly. Lower still to the heat between her legs. A small, inquiring stroke of his fingers against her had Alicia arching with a sigh.

"Again?" Her voice, husky and low, sent a tendril of desire curling through him.

He dipped low to find sleek wetness, then drew it up and over her sensitive flesh. "Sure. Let's give it a try."

He loved the way her throaty chuckle turned into a rasping sigh when he circled his fingers against her. Loved the tense and release of her muscles as his touch aroused her. He could lose himself in the sound of her voice muttering his name and in the smell of her hair as he buried his face in it.

He loved her.

She'd been getting close—he knew it by the way her body had smoothed and formed itself to him—but at the stutter of his caress, Alicia tensed in a different way. She shuddered but did not go over. She twisted in his embrace to face him. Her heart pounded hard enough for him to feel it between them. When she spoke, her voice was ragged.

"Nikolai? What's wrong?"

He kissed her so he didn't have to speak. There weren't words for what he wanted to tell her. Or rather, there were plenty of words, but none that he could make himself say. He wanted to fit himself inside her and move, to let their bodies have the conversation instead of their words. It was too soon for him, though. He couldn't quite manage.

"Shhh, stop," she said with her hand at the small of his back to hold him close but stop him from trying to make it happen.

"I want to, for you," he said. Stubborn. Proud.

Alicia kissed his mouth. "Shhh."

Minutes ticked past as she kissed him. After a few, she eased her mouth from his. She kept her hands on him, though.

"Are you worried about this?" she asked. "Because it's not—"

"No." He took her hand, fingers curled around him, and stroked to show her the way his body could respond.

It was faster this time than it had been earlier in the night. Harder. Fiercer. He'd tried to focus on her, to finish what he'd started, but he couldn't manage to do that and finish himself. When the pleasure filled him, he bit back her name.

After, she pushed herself up on her elbow to trace circles on his chest with her fingertips. Over his heart. Across his ribs and up again, not tickling, though he did eventually put his hand over hers to keep from continuing.

At some point, the sun had started to come up. Pale, fresh light filtered through the curtains and lit the lines of her face. She wasn't smiling.

"Nikolai. I want you to know how glad I am that you came home. How happy I am that you and I . . . that we're here. Together, like this." She paused. He stayed quiet. "I think you're amazing and wonderful and all of this is great. I want you to know that."

He wanted to tell her that he felt the same way. He wanted to tell her more than that. But when he tried to form the words, nothing would come.

"And I want you to know," she added carefully, "that it's all right if you have to leave. I would never expect you to stay where you didn't want to be."

When you loved someone, Nikolai thought, you gave them the power to hurt you. Worse than that, you made it possible to hurt them. To disappoint them. The last thing in the world Nikolai wanted to do was hurt or disappoint Alicia, at least not more than he already had in this lifetime.

So he didn't say anything. Not with words. He kissed her and hoped she would be able to understand what he meant to say, even if he couldn't manage to say it.

CHAPTER THIRTY-THREE

Snow. So much snow. Easily four feet of it, piled high in all directions. At least the power hadn't gone out, and she'd gone to the grocery store a couple of days ago, so they weren't going to run out of food.

"And the pipes won't freeze," Alicia said, tongue in cheek, as she pointed with her spatula at the still-dripping faucet. She was making French toast with apple chicken sausage.

Nikolai was in charge of the coffee, and he looked to where she was pointing. "I can fix that for you, you know. I should've done it already."

She thought of how Ilya had promised the same thing, time after time. Nikolai, she reminded herself, was not Ilya. "I bet you could. You could fix it so hard."

"So hard," he agreed as he set out mugs, cream, sugar. He gave her a grin that lit her up inside. "I'd fix it for you so hard you'd forget it ever leaked."

Flipping the toast in the skillet, Alicia guffawed. "Perv."

"That smells good." He came up behind her to nuzzle at her shoulder, bared by the edges of her robe. "I like that you cook."

"Trust me, it's no big thing," she scoffed, but his praise warmed her. "It's just eggs, milk, bread, sugar."

"I like that you're cooking for me—how's that?"

She slid the slices onto the platter she'd already filled and turned off the burner. "I'll cook for you. You fix the faucet. It'll be a love straight out of 1952."

Love. The word had slipped out of her before she could stop it, but there was no calling it back. She didn't want to think about this morning, how she'd spilled her emotional guts all over him and had received only silence in reply. She focused on the French toast instead.

At the table, she sat across from him and watched as he loaded his plate with food. He'd already poured her coffee, though he hadn't added anything to it. She did: sugar and cream enough to turn the liquid to a light-caramel color. They ate in companionable silence. She could look over his shoulder to the window behind him. Snow still falling.

"This is nice," Alicia said. Trying again. Stupid, she thought. Don't be stupid, Alicia.

Nikolai looked up, his cheeks bulging with food he chewed carefully before swallowing. He washed it down with a long swig of coffee. "What, the coffee?"

"Us. Here." She'd forked a bite of food but set it back on the plate. "Together."

"Yeah," he answered after a few seconds' hesitation and a quick glance at the windows. "Snowbound."

"It would be great to do it even without the snow," she said, and when he didn't answer, she sighed. She shook her head. "You can't even say that it would be great?"

"Alicia . . ."

"What?" she challenged, and got up to take her plate to the counter. She'd hardly touched a bite of her food and set about packaging it up to put away in the fridge. She wouldn't look at him.

"I don't want to give you the wrong idea."

She turned at that. "About what?"

"Us."

"I'm not asking you to marry me," she said finally, her voice steady. "But what are we doing, if you can't even tell me that you want to be with me?"

"You should know that I want to. I wouldn't be here if I didn't." Nikolai frowned and pushed his plate away.

"So why can't you just say so?" She leaned against the counter and pulled her robe closer around her. She was naked beneath it, and felt it.

"What do you want me to say?"

She sighed. "Anything. Something. Never mind."

His phone buzzed from where he'd left it plugged in on the counter, and Nikolai got up to answer it. "Yes. No, it's fine. I haven't . . . I'd have to check. Well, I'm not there right now. I'm across the street."

She straightened, looking at him. He looked back. She waited.

"I came to check on her, yes. She's fine. I will. Where are you?" He paused, looking away from her. "Okay. You know it could be a while before the plows come back here. I think everything's going to be shut down for a while. Yeah, I will. Okay. Sure. Yes . . . yes, Mom. You, too."

He disconnected with a sigh and put the phone back on the counter. Alicia turned away to busy herself with putting away the extra food she'd made. She'd lost her appetite. When he came up behind her to put his hands on her hips, she didn't push him away, but she didn't lean back into him, either.

"How about we pick out some old creature feature, make some popcorn, and spend the day on the couch. We're not going anywhere, not until the roads are plowed. And there's not much point in shoveling while it's still snowing." He spun her slowly to face him.

"I'm sure you could make it across the street if you really had to."

He smiled. "But I don't want to."

"You sure about that?" She eyed him. "It's right across the street."

He moved closer, one step. "But, all that snow, Alicia. So much snow. It's really, really deep."

"You're a big, strong man. You lived in Antarctica," she said, remembering.

Nikolai shook his head, those gray-green eyes wide and falsely innocent. "We didn't go outside."

"You didn't—" He was on her then, his arms around her, and she let him kiss her. "You're so full of bull, Nikolai. You know that?"

"I've heard that once or twice." He nibbled at her jaw and tickled her sides until she squealed and tried to get away, only to have him draw her back close to him. He looked into her eyes. "There's nothing else I'd rather do and no place I'd rather be than on that couch with you today. Okay?"

She nodded after a second or so. She could wait for him to give her pretty words, but how could she really expect them? She knew him—didn't she?—even after all these years. Some things about him had changed, but not all things.

"Fine, but I get to pick the movie," she said.

CHAPTER THIRTY-FOUR

Then

There were no days when Alicia woke up without remembering what happened, but there had to be one someday, right? One morning when she would open her eyes without looking at her sister's empty bed and being hit all over again with the reminder that Jennilynn was not out late. Jennilynn was never coming home.

Her mother waited barely a week after the funeral before she came in the room with a box of plastic garbage bags and started throwing things away. Clothes, makeup, sheets, old stuffed animals. She tore down the posters of Jennilynn's favorite bands and cleared out the closet. There were things Alicia would've kept, not because she'd coveted her sister's faded jeans or her Doc Martens, though she always had. She would've clung to them as a way of making herself feel as though Jennilynn wasn't totally gone.

The house was quiet in the gray dawn, and Alicia could no longer sleep. She listened for the sounds of her parents getting up, moving around. Getting ready for work. Moving forward with their lives one day at a time in a way that seemed impossible to her, even now, almost a year later. She'd lost a sister, but they'd lost their daughter, and she couldn't begin to imagine how they could function. All she knew was that they seemed to.

All she knew was that nobody talked about Jennilynn at all.

They took down the photos that hung in the hallway. The framed school pictures lined up on top of the cabinets. The magnetic cheerleading-team photos on the fridge. There were empty spaces where the pictures used to hang. Dust outlines on the walls. If something happened to her, Alicia thought, they would erase her just as easily as they'd done to Jennilynn.

If she hadn't died, Jennilynn would still be gone. Off to college, home only for holidays and vacations. Her seat at the table would still be empty. Her side of the room, relentlessly clean. The bathroom, always free.

It was Alicia's turn to be the one to go away, but how could she? She was the only one left. If Jennilynn hadn't died, if she'd just gone off to college, and it was now Alicia's turn, it would've been the natural order of things, but everything was a mess and had been for a year, so even though the college acceptance letters had been piling up, the scholarship awards coming in one by one, there was no way Alicia could possibly leave home.

◆ ◆ ◆

"It wasn't until much later—recently, even—that I figured out a few things," Alicia said. "First, that my parents had not gotten *over* losing Jenni. They just got *through* it. I hadn't realized that was a thing, you know? That sometimes you don't get over something. You just get through it. And second, that my decision to stay home and go to business college instead of leaving them made no difference, in the end. They didn't need me to stay for them. They were ready for me to leave, to get on to the next phase of their lives as parents of children who'd grown up. And third, that they did me no favors by not insisting I go away to school, get a four-year degree. I just think they were so numbed by what had happened, so focused on their grief, that even though it was a year later, they couldn't really make the right choices. And I . . . didn't want to go away. I've held on to the idea for a long time that somehow I wasn't able to go, but the truth is, I made my choices back then because it was easier to stay than try to figure out what I wanted to be. So here I am."

Nikolai tucked his arm behind his head as he stretched out his legs to prop his feet on the coffee table. "Is that such a bad thing? Being here?"

"You tell me." She pulled the crocheted afghan over her knees, against the house's chill. "You're the one who couldn't wait to get away from here. You were out of here right after you graduated, and you never came back."

"Of course I came back. I'm back right now."

She shrugged. "Not really. Not without waiting every second to leave again."

"Is that what you think I'm doing?" He twisted to look at her, the movie they'd put on about half an hour ago forgotten.

"Isn't it?" Alicia shrugged again.

Nikolai frowned. "I'm not going anywhere right now."

"Right." She looked toward the television but couldn't remember what they were even watching. "What happened? I missed something."

"We don't have to watch this." He pressed the remote to pause the movie.

She wanted to curl up against him with her head on his chest and listen to the sound of his heart beating. She wanted to cover them both with this ugly blanket and keep the world away. She did not want him to leave—that was the stupid truth of everything—and since there was no way she was going to ask him to stay, all she could do was bite her tongue until the pain was enough to choke her into silence.

"Again, already?" She made her tone light. Teasing. "You're going to wear me out."

"No, that's not what I meant."

She frowned, looking at him. "Oh. You don't want to?"

"I always want to," Nikolai said. "That's not it."

"So, what, then?" This tasted like the beginning of an argument, a flavor Alicia knew well when talking with Nikolai.

"Do you really feel like I'm just waiting to leave?"

She withdrew, putting some space between them. "Yes. I do."

"Alicia . . ."

"Aren't you?" she asked, not sure what she expected him to say. Or even what she *wanted* him to say. "Just hanging around here counting the days until you're off to someplace far more exciting?"

She watched his expression and waited for him to answer, but he didn't.

"It's what we knew from the beginning. It's the only reason why we're doing any of this at all," she added quietly. "Isn't it?"

Nikolai frowned, then scrubbed a hand across the top of his head. "Yeah. It's what we agreed on. For sure."

There was a certain relief in hearing him say it, so she didn't have to wonder anymore. "So . . . when?"

"I haven't decided. There's a lot to do around the house. And something's up with Galina. I'm not sure what."

"So you're staying until you're finished with the house repairs. For your mom." She couldn't fault him for that. Not really. It wasn't the reason she wanted to hear, though.

Nikolai didn't answer at first. "You know how she is. She could decide tomorrow that she doesn't want to bother with anything new, or that she's going to head back to South Carolina. Or Arkansas, or, hell, the moon for all I know."

"Gee, I wonder where you get it, then." She meant to sound light and teasing but failed. She cleared her throat and took up the remote to start the movie again.

When he stretched an arm out along the back of the couch, she let him pull her closer. When she put her head on his shoulder and he stroked his hand along her hair, she let him do that, too. When he turned to tip her face to his to kiss her, she gave him her mouth as eagerly as she ever had, without hesitation or reservation, because this time could be the last, and she knew it the way she'd known it every other time he'd ever kissed her.

"You don't have to stay here, you know." Nikolai traced her bottom lip with his finger.

She pulled away from the tickling touch, irritated. "Sure. I know. I just have a business to run and debt to handle. And besides, where would I go, and what would I do?"

"Anything you wanted. Anywhere you wanted. You could work on a cruise ship," he said. "You could teach English in China."

Alicia gave him a look.

"You could do anything you wanted," he repeated.

"You make it sound so easy."

Nikolai smiled and shrugged. "It can be, if you want it to be."

"I can't just up and leave. I have the business. I have responsibilities." She thought of the offer Theresa had made her. How tempting it would be to take it. How free she would be to do exactly what Niko was describing. She almost told him about it but at the last minute held her tongue, wanting him to ask her to go with him. To be with him. To give her that choice, at least. "I lost my chance for those options."

"There are always options, Alicia."

His phone buzzed. Alicia took the chance to get up and use the bathroom while he talked. By the time she got back, Nikolai was off the couch.

"Galina got a ride home."

"How'd she manage that?" Alicia went to the window to look out. No sign of the street being plowed, though the snow at least had stopped. She wasn't looking forward to hauling out the snowblower.

"Her 'friend' has a four-wheel drive." Nikolai made air quotes. "Maybe he got so sick of her that he had to get her out of his house."

Alicia feigned a disapproving look. "Maybe she wanted to get home, make sure you're okay."

He rolled his eyes. "Whatever. She's over there now and wanted to know where I was. I didn't tell her I've been here for the past two days."

"Of course not." Alicia took off the afghan and folded it over the back of the couch. "You should get home."

"Yeah." He stretched. Cracked his neck in the way that made her cringe and wince, then laughed when he saw her. "Sorry."

There was more to be said in that moment, but she wasn't about to start up that conversation now. She'd left it open for him to ask her to go with him, and he had not. She wasn't going to pursue it. She walked him to the front door. They didn't kiss there, suddenly awkward as though Galina could see them from all the way across the street, through a closed door.

"Thanks for putting up with me while we were snowed in," Nikolai said.

She smiled a little. "You can pay me back by fixing my faucet."

"Right. The faucet." He made no move to leave. His phone buzzed again with a text.

"You should go."

"This was fun," Nikolai said.

Fun.

Nothing more than that. Fun. Casual. Fleeting. Not meant to last.

"It always is, isn't it?"

He nodded. "Always."

"How will you feel this time," she said suddenly, no longer able to hold it back, "when you leave?"

Something in his eyes gave her hope, for the barest second. A faint spark. The barest twist of a smile. At the last second, everything went blank, and he cut his gaze from hers.

"I don't know," Nikolai said.

A thin and fruitless fury overtook her. "Can't you even just once tell me how you feel? Can't you even tell me you'll miss me?"

"I will. I will miss you."

She nodded stiffly, not satisfied, not with having to put the words in his mouth. Not surprised, after all this time and knowing him so well, but what had she expected? What was it, exactly, that she even wanted him to say or do that would make her happy? There was probably nothing, she thought as she searched his expression for something, anything at all that would give her reason not to close the door behind him and never open it for him again.

She stepped aside to let him pass and held the door open. She cleared her throat. In the absence of any further words from him, the sound of it was very loud. "Good."

Nikolai paused to brush a kiss over her lips as he moved past her. The snow came up to his knees, and it took him a long time to push through it, across the yard and the street, marked by the path of the truck that had brought Galina home. Alicia watched, shivering in the chilly air, until he made it all the way to his house. He didn't look back at her before he went inside his own front door, but then she supposed he didn't need to do that, either.

CHAPTER THIRTY-FIVE

Being snowbound hadn't bothered Galina at all. Since getting home yesterday, she'd been baking. Piles of cookies. Bread. A pie. It hadn't seemed to matter that the freezer, both in the kitchen and the ancient chest unit in the basement, were both still stuffed to overflowing with leftovers from the generosity of the neighbors after Babulya's death. She'd covered all the kitchen countertops with pans and plates and platters.

"What are you going to do with all of this?" Niko set the toolbox on the table, which so far remained free of the burden of baked goods.

"Feed you with it." She leaned against the countertop with one arm crossed over her belly to cup a hand beneath her elbow, the posture lacking only a cigarette that she clearly was missing.

Niko laughed as he sorted through the mishmash of tools in the box, looking for a wrench and some plumber's tape. He'd been trying to sort the plethora of junk from the basement workbench, pulling out what he needed.

"I can't possibly even make a dent in that."

"Fine. You don't want this? I'll donate it to the home."

He glanced up at the flat tone of her voice. "Do they let the residents eat stuff like that?"

"The nurses and the staff will eat it. They'll appreciate it, if you won't." Galina waved her fingers in front of her face. "Where are you off to, Kolya, with all of those tools?"

"I'm going over to Alicia's to fix her kitchen faucet." He held up the wrench.

Galina snorted lightly. "How nice of you. Will she pay you?"

"Sure, the same rate I've been charging you." He meant to tease her, but his mother didn't smile.

"I'm your mother. I feed you. Give you a roof over your head. What I ask of you shouldn't be anything to complain about, especially since it's all going to benefit you in the end."

Niko turned his attention back to the toolbox, feeling his shoulders hunch and forcing himself to straighten. Here it came. The sour comments. Maybe the rage, if he couldn't defuse it.

"Not complaining, Mom. I'm happy to help out around the house."

She muttered a reply that he didn't catch, then said, louder, "Where is your brother?"

"He's in Jamaica." Niko shut the lid of the toolbox with a click. "Remember? He'll be back at the end of the week. He's leading a dive trip."

Galina frowned. "I like it when you boys are home, where I can keep an eye on you. So I don't have to worry about you."

"You don't have to worry about us. We're grown men."

She hacked out one of her standard harsh cackles. "You think that means I don't have to worry about you? Mothers never stop worrying. Where you are, what you're doing, if you're happy, if you're going to ever be happy . . ."

With an inward sigh, Niko went to her and took her by the shoulders. "I'm just going across the street to fix a faucet. Ilya will be back in a few days, after his trip. We're okay, Mom."

Galina frowned. "You and your brother are not very okay, I don't think. What did I do wrong, Kolya? Was I really so bad of a mother?"

The words, barbed, hooked him in a tender spot and stung. He knew there'd be no sufficient answer for her. Nothing he could say would be good enough.

"Of course not," he said.

She looked at him with narrowed eyes, head tilted. In the past, Galina had often played the martyr. There was something different in her expression this time. A kind of blankness that unsettled him.

"We all make mistakes. If you ever had children, you'd know. It's not too late."

Niko shook his head. "I already told you that I don't plan on having kids, Mom."

"Well," Galina said briskly, "I didn't plan on having any, either, and look what happened."

She was also fond of rewriting history, so he shouldn't be too surprised, but this was the first time he'd ever heard her mention anything like that. Galina's story about meeting her first husband and starting a family had been mostly consistent through the years. She'd met Steven Stern at the hospital where she'd been working as a registered nurse. He'd been an orderly. They'd fallen in love. Gotten pregnant.

"Children take so much out of you," she continued. "You could ask your Babulya about that. What a trial I was as a child. How she told me all the time that she wished upon me the same tribulations I'd put her through."

"If children are such a pain in the ass," he said finally, not pointing out that he couldn't ask Babulya anything, "why do you keep wishing Ilya and I would have some?"

Galina smiled. "So I can be the granny who wishes the tribulations you put me through to come back to you through your kids. Of course."

He laughed, though it wasn't that funny. "Well, I don't think you need to worry about it."

"No. Maybe not." She looked oddly sad and gestured at the baked goods. "I learned to cook, finally. Your Babulya would be proud of that, at least."

And then she was crying, burying her face in her hands, shoulders shaking in silent, racking sobs. Disturbed, Niko went to her. The way she clung to him, clutching at the front of his shirt, made him uncomfortable, but there was nothing to do but let her. She shook. Not for the first time since he'd been back, he noticed that Galina seemed thinner. Brittle. She'd never been a woman who held on to weight, but her shoulder blades were very prominent even beneath the thickness of her sweater.

"Mom . . . is there something going on with you? Are you all right?"

"I'm grieving." She pushed away from him to go to the sink to splash water on her face. She kept herself turned away from him, her fingers gripping the sink's edges as her shoulders hunched. "More than you will, I'm sure, when it's my turn to die."

"Stop that," he said sharply. "That bullshit worked when I was a kid, but it doesn't anymore."

She twisted to look at him with a grim smile. "Eat a cookie. You're too thin."

His mother chucked him under the chin and pushed past him to go out the back door onto the porch. She reached behind her to close the door with a firm click. The flare of her lighter flashed a moment later.

Hefting the toolbox, he headed out through the front. It still jarred him, a little, to see the new houses lined up along the street. Dina Guttridge was pulling her van into her driveway as he crossed. He made sure to wave, letting her know he saw the way she was straining to catch a glimpse of him going into Alicia's house.

"Ilya?"

"No, it's me, Niko. Ilya is . . ." He paused, not sure why it was Dina's business where Ilya was. "How are you tonight?"

"Cold. But at least they plowed the roads, am I right? Thank God. I was going to go crazy, stuck in the house for another day with this crew." She opened the van's sliding door to reveal the bags of groceries and car seats inside.

He couldn't let her handle all that by herself. The kids, the bags, the slippery driveway. He set the toolbox on Alicia's stoop and slogged through the snow over to the Guttridges'.

"Let me give you a hand."

"Well, aren't you nice?" Dina dimpled. "Thanks."

"You get the kids. I'll take care of this stuff." He hefted two double handfuls of plastic grocery bags and set them inside the front door while Dina dealt with the kids.

"You want to come in for a minute?" She held the door open for the last load.

Niko shook his head. "Ah . . . thanks, but no. I have to get next door. I'm fixing Alicia's faucet for her."

It wasn't any of Dina's business, of course, but with Alicia's fair warning about Dina's interest in her neighbor's business ringing in his ears, he wanted to make it clear what the purpose of his visit was. He could tell by the look on Dina's face that she didn't believe him, but he figured that would be the case even if it was the truth. He hopped down the couple of front porch steps and crossed the yards. She was still looking when he picked up the toolbox and gave her another wave.

"That woman has no shame," Alicia said when he came inside.

Niko laughed. "No. Not too much. Thanks for the heads-up, or I'd probably be drinking a mug of hot cocoa right now and fending off her lustful advances."

"You still have time. I'm sure she'll still be up once she puts all those kids to bed." Alicia gave him an arch look and crooked her finger over her shoulder as she led the way to the kitchen. "Just do me a favor and fix this leak first. It's making me nuts."

He settled the toolbox on the table and put his hands on his hips. "That's it, huh? This is what it's come down to?"

She'd been pulling a pair of mugs out of the cabinet but stopped to give him a look over her shoulder. "Hmm?"

"I'm only useful for fixing things?" He eased closer to her, moving up behind to nuzzle the back of her neck. She smelled so good it was all he could do not to get on his knees right there in front of her.

She didn't turn, though her sigh told him she liked what he was doing. "I can think of a few things you're good for. Anyway, you haven't fixed the faucet yet . . ."

"Later." Niko moved his hands over her belly and lower to find the heat between her legs. Brushing his lips down over her shoulder, he pressed his fingers against the denim.

Her response was to press her ass back against him, grinding. He was already hard. All it took around her was the simplest thing to get him that way.

"Promises, promises." Her voice hitched as she put her hands flat on the countertop and leaned forward.

He unbuttoned and unzipped her, pushing her jeans over her hips. Down her thighs. She wore a pair of gigantic cotton panties beneath, and the sight stumped him for a moment.

Alicia laughed as he paused. "I thought you were coming over later. I didn't shave my legs yet, either."

"Oh, how fast the magic fades." He cupped the perfect globes of her ass through the cotton, then ran his fingers down the backs of her thighs. "Prickly."

"I'll prickly you." She started to turn, but he put a hand on her shoulder to keep her facing front.

His other hand slipped between her legs from behind, urging her to widen her stance. "I like it."

"Mmm." She bent forward again, pushing her ass into his touch. "You have a granny-panties fetish?"

"And a thing for Sasquatch, remember?" He laughed and ducked as she turned to swat him again. He grabbed her hands, holding her still even as she struggled. She quieted when he kissed the side of her mouth.

"You're mean," Alicia said, her voice breathy. "So mean to me . . ."

"Aww, baby, I don't want to be mean. I wanna be nice to you." He stroked over the white cotton, circling against her. He reveled in the sound of her moan. "Are you gonna let me?"

Her only answer was another moan as he tweaked the tight knot of sensitive flesh with his thumb and forefinger. When he eased her panties to the side, he found her already slick for him. He kissed her, letting his tongue slide in at the same slow, steady pace as his fingers. Then out. One, then another, until the heel of his hand could rub her at the same time.

"I love getting you off," Niko said as he kissed her. "I love it when you make those sounds."

Her fingers dug into his shoulder as her head fell back. He got his mouth on her neck, nibbling, finding all the places he knew would make her squirm against him. Her hips moved. He slid deeper inside, aching to replace his fingers with his cock but wanting to draw this out until Alicia was shaking and crying out his name.

"We should go upstairs." She made no move to leave.

Niko withdrew to move his slippery fingers up and over her sweet spot. "In a minute."

"It's only going to take me a minute . . ."

He couldn't stand it any longer. He had to taste her. Swiftly, he pulled her panties down and got on his knees to spread her open for him. Feasting on her, teasing with the flat of his tongue, until he felt her body swell and tremble under his lips. He kept his mouth held to her while she shook and grabbed at his head, holding him close to her. He wanted to draw it out, make it go on forever, even as he finished her.

She looked down at him, her eyes glazed over and her lips plump and swollen from where she'd bitten them. Her tight grip loosened, though she kept her hand on his head. She shook her head the tiniest bit, drawing in and letting out a breath, but no words.

Niko gave her another slow, long lick, all the while keeping his gaze locked on hers. He could make her come again, just like this, with him on his knees on the hard kitchen floor and her sweetness coating his tongue. He wanted to.

Alicia groaned, her fingers twisting again in his hair. "Wait, wait . . ."

"Mmm, no. Let me."

"I want you inside me." She didn't push him away, though. Her thighs widened. She cried out when he licked her again.

"First, this." His cock was so hard it ached, pressing against the front of his jeans, so he undid his button and zipper, freeing himself into his fist. Just a few strokes, Niko thought. He wouldn't go over, not until he could be inside her, the way she wanted. But for now, licking her, bringing himself to the edge . . .

They were moving. Turning. He was behind her, then inside her. Pumping gently, then harder until she cried out and her hands skidded against the countertop. He followed her half a minute later, losing himself in ecstasy.

Panting, he pressed himself to her back, holding her for as long as he could before it got weird, which was about thirty seconds before the tensing of her muscles alerted him to move. They disengaged, cleaned up, buttoned up, and zipped up.

"Hey." She snagged his arm as he went to the sink to wash his hands. "Kiss me."

He did, gladly. When she tucked herself against him, Niko closed his eyes and lost himself in the scent of her hair. The rise and fall of her shoulders told him she sighed, but when she pulled away to look at him, her smile gave away nothing of what she might've been thinking.

He could just ask her, he thought as he watched Alicia rearrange her clothes to erase all signs of what had just happened. But if he did, then she'd want to know what he was thinking, and it would become complicated. Messy. It would upset the balance. So he kept his mouth shut and took up his tools so he could fix her faucet.

It didn't take long. He held up the broken part to show her. "All it needed was a washer."

Alicia glanced at him from the table she'd been setting with two of everything. She'd pulled her hair up on top of her head in a messy bun, tendrils hanging down all over the place. She wore no makeup. He thought about the giant cotton underpants and her prickly shins, about beauty, about comfort and safety and expectations. He thought about love.

"I made meatloaf," she told him. "If you want to stay. And we could watch a movie—I mean, unless you have other plans or something."

He did not, of course. Not unless you counted working on more home-repair projects for his mother. "Scalloped potatoes?"

"Ummm, duh." She grinned over her shoulder as she bent to look inside the oven; she opened it and let out a waft of something delicious. Her grin faltered for a second as she straightened. "What?"

"What, what?" He tested the faucet, running the water and then turning it off to make sure the dripping had stopped.

"You looked weird." She reached for a hot pad hanging from the drawer next to the oven.

He'd been admiring her ass; that's what he told himself. Nothing else. "No idea what you're talking about."

"It was a really weird look," she said.

"French toast. Meatloaf. You're so domestic. That's all. I remember when you could barely make microwave nachos." He hefted the spanner and shrugged.

Alicia made a face. "Wow, thanks. You don't need to sound so surprised. I'm all grown up now."

"And a woman of many talents," he said.

She studied him again, more thoughtfully this time. "And you're a handy handyman."

"Seems like we make a good team," Niko said.

Alicia's grin had always been sunshine burning away the clouds to him, probably because for most of their lives, he'd spent as much time earning frowns from her as smiles. He said her name, thinking he would tell her that. How beautiful she looked to him just then.

But when she tilted her head to give him another assessing, curious look, all Niko managed to say was, "I'm starving. Dinner sounds great."

CHAPTER THIRTY-SIX

He'd left sunshine, warm waters, and the pervasive scent of coconut tanning lotion for this bullshit? Ilya watched the bus pull out of the Go Deep lot. At least Alicia had managed to cajole someone into coming to plow out the lane and the parking lot before the bus arrived, and even then, there'd been a few minutes when he was sure they were going to get stuck. When everyone had gone, he let himself into the office.

It was cold.

It was dark.

It was nothing like Jamaica, and Ilya muttered a few choice words as he let himself into Allie's office to grab the phone, since his cell had gone dead on the ride home from the airport. When she didn't answer, he tried the landline. At least he thought he did.

"Niko?" he asked at the sound of his brother's voice. "Sorry, bro, I was trying to call Allie. I must've dialed home by accident. She's not answering her cell, and I'm at the shop. I need a ride."

"I can come and get you. Be there in about half an hour."

Thirty minutes was going to feel like thirty hours, at this point. Ilya tried not to party too hard when on a trip, because hangovers and deep dives definitely do not mix. But on that last night in the hotel, with a late-afternoon flight home? He might've indulged a little heavily in island rum and a couple of bachelorettes. He'd managed to sleep a little on the plane and then on the bus back from the airport, but that was why his phone was now dead, since he hadn't thought to plug it in.

He grabbed a bottle of water from the mini fridge and settled into Allie's desk chair. The motion of him nudging the desk shook the computer enough to wake it from sleep, and he took the mouse to see if he could pass the time watching funny fail videos, or something. The screen lit—her e-mail program prominent—and a new message caught his eye.

From Theresa.

He read the message, of course, not caring at all that it wasn't addressed to him. Go Deep was 40 percent his business, and this was the business computer. He sat back, reading the points Theresa had outlined trying to convince Allie that this offer from Diamond Development was going to change their lives.

"Son of a bitch," he muttered.

Ilya drained the bottle of water and tossed the empty into the trash. It didn't do anything to fend off the headache, or his anger. He got up to pace the tiny office. By the time he heard the faint jingle of the bell on the front door alerting him to Niko's arrival, he hadn't managed to calm down.

"Hey," Niko said and stopped at the sight of him. "You okay?"

Ilya gestured at the computer screen—not that Niko could see what he meant. "Allie is totally going behind my back."

"About . . . ?" Niko's voice went cool and steady, and so did his gaze.

Oh, yeah, he knew exactly what Ilya meant. Not only had Theresa talked with Allie about it, but it looked to Ilya like Niko had also been let in on the deal.

"This offer. From Theresa."

Niko's eyes narrowed, and his mouth pursed for a second before he said, "What are you talking about?"

"This offer. To buy the shop and the quarry. Some hotel wants to make it into a water park." Ilya gestured again, confused now by his brother's sudden look of ignorance. "You looked like you knew what I was talking about."

"I have no idea." Niko shook his head.

Some of his ire eased. Ilya stood, moving from behind the desk. "Shit. Are you sure she didn't say anything to you about it?"

"She definitely did not say anything to me about any offer to buy the business," Niko said with a bite in his voice. "But it sounds like something you need to discuss with her, not me. Are you ready to go? It's cold in here, and I have stuff to do at home."

Niko turned without waiting for an answer. Ilya followed him out of the office and into the shop. "They want to come in and build condos or some shit. Do you even have any idea what that means? How about everything I've done over the years? You want to know how hard it is to even find a helicopter, much less get it here and sink it so we have something different and unique to bring people in? They think they can just come on in here and tear down some walls and make it pretty, and that's going to make it better?"

His brother turned at the grasp of Ilya's hand on his coat sleeve. "Back off, man."

"You don't give a damn at all. Why am I even talking to you about it?" Ilya shook his head.

Niko frowned. "Okay, Galina."

Those were fighting words, but all at once Ilya didn't want to fight. "That's low."

"You're coming at me the way she does. It's not that I don't care, Ilya. Okay? It's just that it's not anything to do with me. I can't fix this."

Ilya took a breath and unclenched his fists. "I'm not asking you to fix it."

"I know," his brother said.

"Anyway, you'll be out of here soon, and you won't have to deal with it."

Niko looked guilty.

Ilya paused. "Right?"

"I haven't told anyone else this, yet. But I'm cashing in my contract."

Ilya had only the vaguest idea of how the kibbutz had worked. He knew his brother was part of a collective, that he worked in exchange for food, board, a stipend. Beyond that, he had no clue.

"It means," Nikolai added, "that they'll give me a payout based on my years there, and I'm no longer obligated to work there. It also means I've terminated the rights of living there. So in other words—"

"You're home? For good?" Ilya clapped his brother on the shoulder, happier than he had expected to be at this surprising news. "Welcome home, brother. Welcome home."

CHAPTER THIRTY-SEVEN

Then

Alicia's jaw cracked from the effort of holding back a yawn. She was cold, too, although sitting shoulder to shoulder with Nikolai on the Sterns' battered picnic table, she felt a warmth that had nothing to do with the weather or the layers she wore. She tipped her head back to look up at the sky. Waiting for the clouds to clear.

"How long do we have to wait? It's freaking cold out here." Ilya shrugged deeper into his heavy winter coat and acted like he wasn't watching Jennilynn from the corner of his eye.

He should've just sat next to her. He wanted to. Jennilynn wanted him to. But, instead, the two of them sat on opposite ends of the picnic table, as far apart from each other as they could possibly get.

"It might be too cloudy." Nikolai stretched out his legs and leaned his head back to look up into the winter sky.

There was supposed to be something special up there. An alignment of the planets, nine of them. Something rare. A once-in-a-lifetime sort of thing.

"Just watch," Jennilynn said, her voice uncharacteristically quiet. "It's going to be amazing."

This felt right. The four of them, together, the way they'd been for as long as Alicia could remember. Friends. More than friends. Without thinking about it, she let her head rest on Niko's shoulder, then smiled when he tilted his to rest on hers. Beneath the blanket covering them both, his hand found hers. Fingers squeezed.

"Wouldn't it be great," he said, "if we could travel into space the way we can fly in an airplane?"

Ilya inched closer to Alicia to grab some of the blanket, and as if on cue, she and Nikolai released each other's hands. "Why would you want to?"

"I'd like to," Jennilynn put in. She did not move closer to Nikolai's other side, although the blanket was big enough for all of them. "Just . . . fly away."

Ilya leaned to look at her. "Where would you go?"

"Anywhere."

"I'm with you," Nikolai said. "Get out of this town. See something. Do something important."

The thought of leaving Quarrytown had always seemed like a no-brainer for Alicia. College. A job. Someday a family. Visits home at Christmas and Thanksgiving, the way her parents did with their parents. She hadn't thought much about what, exactly, she wanted to do or where she wanted to go, but the world was a big place. Plenty of choices and plenty of time to make them.

For now, she was content to sit with her butt going numb on a splintery old picnic table in the Sterns' backyard, looking up at the sky, waiting to see something that only came along once in a lifetime.

◆ ◆ ◆

Theresa handed Alicia the pen—a heavy, fancy Parker fountain pen that seemed perfectly made for signing papers of such importance. Alicia carefully wrote her name and the date in all the places she was supposed to. She put the pen on the table gently, so it wouldn't roll into a splash of coffee or a dusting of crumbs.

"Congratulations," Theresa said with a smile. She pushed a thin envelope across the table. The check.

"It's a lot of money," Alicia said with a peek at the contents. "It's going to let me do a lot of things."

Theresa nodded. "Money is freedom, that's for sure."

Alicia grinned. She did feel free. "Coffee's on me, okay?"

"Oh, you bet it is." Theresa also smiled and leaned back in her chair. "I'll get the final paperwork over to you as soon as possible."

"I'll cash this check as soon as possible—you better believe it." Alicia tucked the envelope into her bag, a little giddy at all the zeroes on the check.

Theresa laughed. "I'm sure. So . . . if you don't mind my asking, what are you planning to do with it?"

"I haven't decided just yet. Travel. I know that. See things." Alicia stretched. "Do things. Get out of here. That's all I know."

"Sounds fantastic. Good luck." Theresa looked sad for a moment.

Alicia noticed. "You okay?"

"Oh. Yeah. Just wish I could've sealed the entire deal." Theresa bit her lower lip for a second or so. "Sixty percent is better than nothing, though."

"Ilya is a pain in the ass," Alicia said flatly. "I'm sorry. It's not going to make it easy for you, having to deal with him. My extra twenty percent might end up being more of a hassle than Diamond Development planned for."

"They can build around the dive shop and still develop the property—no worries there." Theresa shook her head and lifted her coffee mug. "Hey, it's not champagne, but I still think we should toast. To freedom!"

"To freedom," Alicia agreed, clinking her mug against Theresa's. "Let it begin now."

CHAPTER THIRTY-EIGHT

This was a bullshit business. Selling the quarry to that real estate development company so they could build that hotel and water park and take over everything he and Alicia had built over the past ten years and turn it into something bland and neutral.

"And profitable," Alicia said when Ilya let this last bit of his rant out. She offered him coffee, but he waved it away so he could pace in her kitchen.

He flung out a hand. "We've done all right. Look at what we started with."

"A cheap piece of property tainted by a high-profile tragedy that made it almost impossible to sell, and we still paid too much for it," Alicia said quietly. "Ilya, sit down or stand in one place, but stop pacing. You're driving me nuts."

He pivoted on his heel. "Fine. You want me to sit here at your kitchen table and talk to you about this like we're, what . . . having tea and biscuits?"

"Like we're partners," she snapped, then softened. "Like we're friends, okay?"

He gripped the back of one of her chairs until his knuckles turned white and the wood creaked in protest. "Right. Partners. That would mean agreeing on things, wouldn't it? Giving me a say on how things should happen?"

"We were married for a long time, and I always thought that meant that I'd get a say in how things would happen, but it didn't. I tried to talk to you about it. I told you what I wanted. You refused. You wouldn't listen." Alicia clinked her spoon deliberately against the side of her mug.

Ilya's lip curled at that old accusation, and he fixed her with a look. "Seems to me that at the end, you were the only one who got any say in how it all went down."

"Here we go again," she muttered, and got up to pour herself another mug of coffee. "Do you want me to call for the wa-a-a-ambulance? Are you going to complain again how I never really gave you a chance to . . . what, be the man I wanted you to be? That I walked out on you without any warning? That if only I'd told you what it was that I wanted, you'd have changed? Is that the conversation we're going to have, again? It's old news."

"Old news for you, because you're the only one who ever got to say a word about it." His fingers curled again on the back of the chair.

Angry, not so much at Alicia as he was at Niko and Galina—hell, at Theresa and the company she worked for that was trying to come in and take away everything he'd worked so hard to build, no matter if Alicia wanted to give him any credit for taking any part of it.

Alicia rolled her eyes. "Oh, we talked about it. Lots of times. You never *listened*."

"I listened to you!"

"Then you didn't do a very good job of hearing me," she told him.

Ilya shrugged, then shook his head. "You're just so hard to understand, Allie. You don't make yourself clear."

He waited for her to make that face, the one that told him she was getting ready to explode. They'd battle it out, go round and round, but he knew in the end he'd give in to her just to keep the fight from turning endless. Allie always had to be right, the way his mother always had to have her way. He'd set his life around giving in to women who nevertheless always found him to be a disappointment.

Now, although her lips firmed into a grim line and her eyes narrowed, Allie kept her voice smooth and calm as the quarry's water on a chilly spring day. She stirred cream and sugar into her mug and sipped while she eyed him over the rim. When he gave her a gesture, wordlessly telling her he expected an answer, she shrugged.

"Not going to argue with you about this," she said simply. Solidly.

Ilya frowned. "What's that supposed to mean?"

"I'm not arguing with you about our marriage or anything else. That's it. If you want to talk about your mother, I can listen and offer some advice, but I'm not going to fight with you about her, either. And if you want to talk like adults about this offer Theresa brought us, well, I'm ready for that."

"Theresa." Ilya shook his head, thinking of the fourteen-year-old girl in braces and ponytail who'd become the sort of woman he knew he would never be able to impress. "I knew she didn't just come back to offer her condolences. She's as sneaky as her creep of a dad."

Allie looked up at that, tilting her head to stare at him. "Huh? What do you mean?"

"Barry. Her dad. He was a creep back then when he started coming around my mom. I always thought so, but she didn't want to hear it, and Niko was always looking off to his own adventures. Didn't give a damn about anything beyond himself." Ilya went to the coffeemaker to help himself. "Don't supposed you have any Baileys to splash in this?"

"It's not even lunchtime." Allie twisted in her chair to face him. "You never said much about Barry before."

Ilya focused on filling the mug as close to the brim as possible without spilling it. A flash of memory slithered through his brain, a snake in wild grasses looking for something warm and scampering to bite. "He was boning my mother. Don't you think that made him creepy enough in my book?"

"What does that have to do with Theresa now?" Allie got out of her chair to cross to him, getting in his space so that he had little choice but to back up against the counter with his mug in his hand to keep her far enough away. "What's your problem?"

"I'm just saying that anyone could've worked for this development company, right? It could've been anyone. But who shows up after all this time but the one person pretty much guaranteed to get in with us, both of us, but especially me, acting like . . . family." His lip curled as he spat the words, thinking of every single conversation he and Theresa'd had before she finally left.

"You think she took that job just so she could convince them to come around trying to acquire our property? Ilya, that's beyond crazy." She reached around him to pull the jar of sugar toward him. "Here."

"Spoon?"

He was well familiar with her sigh.

"In the drawer," Allie said.

"Which drawer?"

"The same drawer that the spoons have been in since about 1983." She yanked open the drawer next to the sink so hard everything inside it rattled. "There. Right there."

"Why do you always do that?" he asked her without taking a spoon.

Allie closed her eyes as she took a few steps back, pressing her fingers to the bridge of her nose before she looked at him. The carefully blank slant of her expression spoke more about her anger with him than if she'd been screaming. It had always infuriated him when she did that. Her sister hadn't been that way. Jennilynn would've let him have it, laid into him. Maybe even smacked him a little, never enough to hurt even though he'd been sure she meant it to.

"Do what?" Allie asked finally.

"Treat me like I'm an idiot."

She looked at him. "Stop it."

"Is that what you think of me? That I'm an idiot?" Ilya poked her, to get some goddamned kind of rise out of her. To make her see him, to at least give him that.

"Yes," Allie snapped and slammed the drawer closed. "Yes. Yes, I do, sometimes, think you are an idiot. Worse than that, I believe you make yourself deliberately obtuse as a way of somehow getting out of doing the things that an adult person should just be able to do. Like find a freaking spoon in a drawer, in the place where the spoons have been for as long as you and I have known each other. Why do you do *that*?"

Ah, this. Here it came. The fury, the fire. She would look at him instead of through him or around him.

"I don't understand what the big deal is. I forgot, okay? Why couldn't you just give it to me, without all the hassle?"

Alicia shook her head and turned, walking away. "Get your own spoon. Or go home. Your choice."

He stared after her for a second. "Hey. Don't walk away from me."

"Did you come over here to start an argument with me or to talk about this offer?" she shot over her shoulder as she headed toward the living room. "Or is talking about the offer just a reason to pick a fight with me? Because I'll be honest with you right up front. I have too much of my own shit going on right now to have any desire to go battling with you. Okay?"

He followed her. "Hey. Allie."

She took a seat, her usual, in the rocker facing the television. She put her mug on the side table and covered herself with the faded, ugly, orange-and-green afghan that was always draped over the chair. She picked up the remote and lifted it with an arch of her brow.

"What's going on with you?" he asked.

She looked faintly surprised before everything in her expression closed up tight. He'd always hated that look. The one that told him he'd gone too far, pushed too hard, and now she was going to shut him out.

"We don't have to take the money. I know it looks like a lot of money, right there on paper like that, but babe—"

"Don't call me that," she warned.

"Allie," Ilya said, "I know you think this deal is the best thing, but it really isn't. The money's not even enough to cover what we sunk into the business."

She tapped the remote gently into her fist and then let it rest there. She sighed. "It's not just the money. It's the business, as a whole."

He sank into the couch across from her. "What do you mean?"

"I mean that I'm tired of working at Go Deep."

He shook his head. "So . . . so we hire someone else to come in, run the numbers, and handle the books. We can find someone to do that, no problem. You can start taking over some of the trips. You always complained about how I was the one who got to do all the exciting things—"

Her harsh bark of razor-blade laughter shut him up quick.

"Yes. That's exactly it," Allie said in a voice thick with tears. "I want to go and do exciting things. I want to go and do anything but stay here in this house, in this town, with—"

"Me."

Her second wave of laughter was harder to hear than the first, sharp-edged and jagged. Poised to shred. Allie dropped the remote and leaned forward to hang her head, to drop it into her hands.

"No, Ilya. My God, no. You have nothing to do with what I want or where I want to go or who I want to do it with."

He knew he should get up off the couch, but a sudden pressure at the base of his neck kept him from moving. He let it push him forward, echoing Allie's position, his elbows on his knees. Fingers clasped, palms together.

"No," he said. "I know that."

Her quiet sniffle made him want to run. He could never handle a crying woman, especially if he was in any way responsible for the tears. And he had to face the facts: he almost always had a hand in it, somehow. Yet he couldn't make himself move—not to get up, not to leave, not to go across the room and put a comforting arm around her—hell, if she even wanted that from him, and he was sure she wouldn't.

"It's time to give it up, Ilya."

He shook his head, not able to look at her. Not able to see anything at the moment, not through the cloudy gray haze covering his vision. He wanted to blame it on a bottle of vodka, a couple of six-packs, but he hadn't had so much as a shot of liquor. It would be better if he could pace, but in the kitchen she'd told him to sit or go, so now he was sitting, and he couldn't make himself get to his feet.

"No. They're just offering us money, Allie. It's only money—"

Her voice rose. "It's not money! It's not about that!"

He found the strength to stand, then, by pushing too hard and too fast, the way he always did about everything else, and he took a few stumbling steps forward to catch his toe on the edge of the coffee table. It flipped over, spilling the candy in the dish, a spread of magazines. He kicked those, too.

"I've put everything I have into building that business!" he cried, whirling on her. "And you . . . you of all people, should understand that! It's not about the money!"

"No," she said. "No, it's about her! It's always been about her! Everything I've done since the day she died has been about her!"

He ran. Or tried to run. But the coffee table was in the way. So was Allie. She'd stepped in front of him, trying to pick up the candy dish. He didn't mean to kick her arm, and he didn't mean to shove her out of the way when she stood with a yelp. She lost her balance and fell back, knocking into the chair and then the table next to her chair. Her coffee spilled. The mug shattered.

He didn't know how it happened or what was going on, but all at once he was on the floor with the broken pieces of her mug in his hands and lukewarm coffee staining the knees of his jeans. Allie was beside him, an arm over his shoulder. He turned and pressed his face into the familiar warmth of her, closing his eyes to let the fall of her hair cover him up, for her perfume to fill his lungs.

"We've both held on for way too long," Allie said into his ear. "We have to let go, Ilya. We have to let *her* go."

She held him while he shook and shuddered; she kept holding him even when he fought her. He stopped after a few seconds. He sank into himself.

The weight of the afghan covered them both. Light through the holes. The floor was hard and chilly, but Ilya didn't move. Beneath the blanket's embrace, he twisted to look at her.

"I can't," he whispered. "I want to, Allie. But I just can't."

She rubbed his back. "Honey. She's gone. We did this together, and I know why we did, believe me, but back then we never talked about why we decided that buying the quarry was what we needed to do. We told ourselves—and each other, I guess—that it was a great business opportunity."

He coughed, but couldn't clear himself of whatever was choking him. "It was."

"Sure. Of course. But it wasn't the reason why we bought the quarry, and it's not why we kept it through everything else. It's not why we put ourselves in debt, Ilya. It's not . . ." Allie sat up, making a tent out of the afghan with herself as the center pole. "That's not why you and I ended up together."

"We ended up together because we loved each other," he said.

Alicia's mouth turned down at the corners, and she gave him a sad shake of her head. "No, honey. No. We got together because we both loved *her*."

"Don't do it, Allie. Please. Don't."

That was when she started to cry. "I'm sorry, honey . . . but I already did."

CHAPTER THIRTY-NINE

She hadn't told him to, but Nikolai had shown up at her door with takeout Indian food and a six-pack of that craft beer she'd started to grow so fond of. She'd already changed into flannel pajamas and pulled her hair up on top of her head, but if there was any point in worrying about that, Alicia had gotten over it a long time ago. She greeted him with a kiss, after he quickly shut the door behind him to keep the cold air from coming in.

"How did you know I was craving curry?" She took the takeout bags from him.

Nikolai shrugged out of his coat and hung it on the hook. "Just a guess. And I was on that side of town anyway. Had to run to the home store."

"Ah. Your mom's projects, huh?"

"I don't mind. Why should she pay someone to do it when I can?" He laughed and pulled her closer for another kiss. This one lingered.

"You're so handy," Alicia murmured. Nikolai's hands shifted, roaming over her back to settle on her ass. She laughed and wriggled away. "Hey, hey. I meant like hammering things . . ."

"I'm great at hammering. Better at screwing." He chased her into the dining room.

It was no difficult feat for him to catch her, although she did make him wait to kiss her until she'd put the food and beer on the table. "Mmmm. Such a funny guy."

She'd been cleaning in the kitchen, her wireless speaker transmitting music from her computer. As she put her arms around his neck, a slow song came on: a new download and one of her current favorites she sometimes kept on Repeat. They eased into a slowly circling dance. Nikolai stepped deliberately on one of her slipper-clad feet, but not hard enough to hurt. Laughing, Alicia kicked his shin lightly.

Nikolai pulled her even closer, tucking her face against his shoulder. One hand smoothed over her hair, tugging it gently from the loose tie. Freed, it tumbled over her shoulders and down her back, and he ran his hand over the tangles to rest it finally at the base of her spine.

"You smell good," Alicia said against his skin.

"Mmm-hmm."

"Like curry and beer and snow," she continued as she breathed him in.

Nikolai laughed into her hair. "Nobody's ever told me smelling like curry and beer was something good."

"It's just you," she told him. "Your skin. You always smell good to me."

Nikolai kissed her again. His hands moved over her, squeezing her ass before moving up to settle on her hips to squeeze her there, too. When he moved up farther to cup her breasts, though, Alicia pulled away.

"Food first. What kind of girl do you think I am, anyway?" she said with an arched brow. "Don't answer that."

Nikolai grabbed some plates and silverware while Alicia set out the food. He'd brought her favorite—lamb rogan josh with basmati rice. She paused as she opened the carton.

"Something wrong?" Nikolai slid a plate in front of her.

Alicia shook her head. "No. It's nice, that's all. That you remembered what I like best."

"Well . . . it's not that hard to remember." Nikolai's grin faded at her expression. "Right? I mean . . . not when you pay attention."

It was no big deal, she told herself as she kissed him. It was just takeout food. It didn't mean anything.

Except it did, she thought, watching him serve the food. It mattered that he'd taken the time to pick up the food and bring it to her, that it was her favorite. That he was choosing to be here with her, here and now, instead of anywhere else in the world that he could've been. She loved him for all of that.

She loved *him*.

"Alicia? You okay?" Nikolai reached to brush the hair off her forehead. His fingers stroked down her cheek. "What's wrong?"

"Nothing." She cupped his hand to her face for a second. "Nothing's wrong. I'm just hungry."

He gave her an odd look but didn't pursue it.

Alicia dug into the food on her plate, although now her stomach was doing rolls and tumbles worthy of a circus act. So were her thoughts. How had this happened? And when?

Watching Nikolai laugh as he told her a story about one of the repair jobs he was doing for Galina, she knew the answer to those questions; they became clear and sharp as diamonds. Not *how*. Not *when*.

But *always*.

"Nikolai . . . ," she began, but stopped herself.

He put down his bottle of beer and wiped his mouth with the napkin. He gave her a curious, wary look. "Yeah?"

The sound of the front door opening turned both of them toward it. It could only be one person, of course. Nobody else would simply come inside her house without knocking first.

"Hey," Ilya said, then stopped at the sight of his brother. "Wow. What's the occasion?"

"It's just dinner," Nikolai said evenly. "What's up, man?"

Ilya held up the packet of papers and looked at Alicia. "Maybe I should be asking you that. Both of you."

"We're eating dinner," Alicia said tightly. "And we can talk about that stuff in your hand tomorrow, at work."

"I want to talk about it now." Ilya slapped the papers onto the table and grabbed at one of the takeout cartons. "Great, I'm starving."

Alicia leaned to snag the carton from him and set it out of his reach. Ilya raised both brows. His smile did not reach his eyes.

"What, am I interrupting something? Is this like . . . a date or something?" He looked from his brother and back to her. "Why don't you tell me what's going on?"

"Nothing's going on," Nikolai said. "I was out getting some stuff at the hardware store. Figured I'd pick up some takeout. I brought it over to Alicia's house because I know she likes Indian food. That's all. You don't need to get bent about it."

"No, I guess not," Ilya answered with a short bark of a laugh. "I mean, except that she's my wife. And you're my brother."

"I'm your ex-wife, Ilya."

He turned to her. "And he's still my brother."

"You didn't seem to think that sort of thing was a very big deal," Alicia bit out, "when you started fucking me after you'd been fucking my sister."

Ilya's fists clenched, resting on the table. Nikolai started to speak, but Ilya's glance shut him up. Ilya fixed her with an unwavering, impassive look. She took a long pull on the beer to wash the taste of bitterness off her tongue, but she didn't look away from Ilya's gaze.

Ilya stood. "The difference is at least your sister was dead before I took up with you."

"Ilya!" Nikolai stood, too. "Don't, man."

Alicia flinched at his words and closed her eyes for a second before looking at him again. "Because of you. Right? Isn't that what you think? Isn't that why you came after me at all? To replace her?"

"You," Ilya said with a sneer, "could never replace her."

Nikolai moved around the table to take his brother by the arm—firmly, but gently. "C'mon, man. You want me to walk you—"

"I'm not fucking feeble." Ilya yanked himself out of his brother's grip and focused on Alicia. His sneer became a sly, nasty smile. "Did he tell you he's not going back?"

"Not going back?" Alicia looked at Nikolai, confused. He frowned and ran a hand through his hair with a sigh. She looked back at Ilya. "I thought you said you were only on a short leave, that they expected you to go back? That you had to—you had a contract."

"He dissolved it." Ilya thumped the packet of papers. "Got a bunch of money, got bought out. He doesn't have to go back to Israel. He can stay here, right here in good old Quarrytown, for as long as he wants to. He didn't tell you that, did he?"

Stunned, uncertain of what to say, she looked at Nikolai. His expression was confirmation enough. Blinking, Alicia stood slowly. Now the three of them faced off, over the remains of takeout food going cold.

"I thought you were going to leave," she said after a few seconds of silence.

Nikolai sighed again. "I was. But I changed my mind."

"Were you going to tell me?" She put her hands flat on the table to steady herself, as if she might fall over at any moment.

"Yes. Of course." Nikolai backed off from his brother but didn't take a step toward her. "Tonight, actually."

Ilya snorted derisively. "Aw, how cute. See, Allie. He brought you dinner to soften the blow."

"It's not a blow," she said after a moment. "It's just unexpected. It just changes things, that's all."

Ilya said something else, but Alicia in that moment couldn't have cared less what he had to say about anything. All she could do was look at Nikolai. He looked back.

"Oh, shit," Ilya said. "So it's like that?"

Without looking away from Nikolai, Alicia said, "Yes. It's like that."

CHAPTER FORTY

Then

Niko didn't want to admit it to himself, but he couldn't wait to see her. Through all the cold, dark nights of Antarctica and all the long, hot days working in the apiary fields of Beit Devorah, he had not missed Quarrytown or, for the most part, the United States. He certainly hadn't missed Galina, whose letters still found their way to him, but which he'd refused to answer. He thought of his brother now and then, but the only person consistently on Niko's mind was Allie.

He didn't regret leaving. He'd seen a chance and taken it, and it had led him to bigger and more exciting things. Leaving had saved his life, but it didn't mean he didn't wish he'd done it a little bit differently.

It was almost a year since he'd been home, and he hadn't noticed until now that he'd grown another couple of inches. His chin and cheeks bristled with scruff if he didn't shave every day. His arms and legs bulged with the muscles he earned fixing broken pipes and dealing with heavy equipment, as well as from all the work he'd done for the past few months back on Beit Devorah, where he went to stay after leaving the science station. He noticed now because he'd been on a plane for something like sixteen hours and on a bus for another five.

His clothes were rumpled, his hair, a mess. He wasn't sure whether he smelled bad or whether he'd become immune to his odor, but a shower would definitely not have been a bad idea.

That wasn't the way the universe worked, though. When the cab dropped him off in front of his house, the first thing Niko noticed was the construction along the street. Then, the flowers in front of the house in window boxes that had been empty for as long as he could remember. He held back, uncertain. He knew Galina had moved away; her last letter to him was postmarked South Carolina and had taken months to reach him. And it was possible Ilya'd gone, too; maybe he found his own place. But surely Babulya would still be there, and his grandmother had never been a fan of planting flowers.

This wasn't his home any longer—hadn't been for a long time—and that was his choice. He'd made himself a stranger to it, so it felt only right that he knocked on the front door instead of simply letting himself inside. He wasn't expecting to see Allie's face on the other side of it when it opened, and clearly by her startled expression she was not expecting him. Then his arms were full of her, the familiar scent of her hair tickling his nose, and she was laughing but also crying a little.

"Come in, come in!" She stepped back into the hallway, welcoming him.

All of this was overwhelming, but he noticed that she wore pajama bottoms and a faded T-shirt. She was talking, but he wasn't really paying attention to what she said as she led the way to the kitchen, where Ilya was at the table, and Babulya turned from the stove to greet Niko with a cry of joy. It wasn't the strangest thing in the world for Allie to be there with them, but still, something about it jarred him even as Niko allowed his grandmother to enfold him into her embrace. His brother got up to clap him on the shoulder, shake his hand, and even hug him, as they all seemed happy and surprised and excited to see him.

Niko wasn't sure what he felt.

Everything was off. Subtle changes in the house. The smell of a different fabric softener. The easy way Allie moved around the kitchen, not like a guest or even a longtime family friend but something more. And finally, ultimately, the flowers in the window boxes outside.

"What's new?" he asked at last, a plate of breakfast in front of him that he didn't want to eat. He looked at his brother, who was grinning, and then at Allie, who was not. "What's going on?"

"Congratulate us," Ilya said. "We got married two weeks ago."

"In Las Vegas," Babulya added, the disdain thick in her voice to show exactly what she thought of *that*.

It wasn't until much, much later that night, after his brother had taken him drinking—even though Niko was not even twenty-one yet—that he managed to have a moment with Allie alone. Ilya had stumbled off to bed. Babulya, too. Allie sat at the kitchen table with a laptop, a paper ledger next to her along with a stack of papers and a checkbook. Work for the dive shop she and Ilya opened together. A dive shop, Niko thought derisively. In the middle of Pennsylvania?

He wasn't sure how the argument started, but it was his fault. He couldn't hold himself back from telling her how wrong she was. Marry his brother? She must be insane, she must be desperate, she must be pathetic.

"You were gone," Allie said in a voice so cold, so distant—yet somehow so broken—that it was a knife right through Niko's heart. "You left. You didn't even say good-bye!"

More words came after that, spilling out. He wanted—needed to explain to her that his brother did not love her. Could not possibly. Ilya was seeking a replacement for Jennilynn, and Allie would never be able to be what his brother wanted because of that. It all came out wrong. Nasty, mean, hurting her, and he couldn't make himself stop, because he was hurting, too.

He had not intended to accept the membership at Beit Devorah, a contract that would require him to work on the kibbutz in jobs they determined were best for him in exchange for room, board, and a stipend. Niko loved working in the apiaries, tending the hives and harvesting the honey, but it was never where he saw himself staying for the rest of his life.

The trouble was that once it became real to him there would be no Allie in his life, moving all the way across the world had seemed like the only option.

CHAPTER FORTY-ONE

Alicia had never imagined that the weight of a pile of papers could have ever felt so much like a stone, but there it was. The envelope in her hand, the paper slick yet rough at the same time. She put it on the table, went to the fridge, and pulled out the bottle of champagne she'd had chilling in there since Thanksgiving. She hadn't bought it thinking she'd have anything to celebrate. She wasn't sure she did, now.

She poured two glasses and handed one to Nikolai without a word. It was in place of a kiss, and if he didn't know that, Alicia did. She sipped and looked at him over the rim.

"So . . ." He lifted the glass to the light spilling in through the sliding glass door to the backyard, twisting it from side to side as though he was studying the bubbles. "Celebrating?"

"I think it's worth celebrating," she said. "It was a big decision, and not an easy one, but I think it's the right one."

Nikolai nodded and put the glass on the table. "I told them I wouldn't be going back after my leave. It was a contract, not a prison sentence. I got my payout. They wished me well. I'm welcome to visit anytime, and if I ever want to live there again, I'll have to go through the same approval process I did the first time. It's pretty cut-and-dried."

"When did you decide you weren't going back?"

"After—" He coughed, then cleared his throat and shifted in the chair. "The night in the attic. It took me a while to admit it to myself. Then I had to work out the details. I wanted to tell you. I really did."

"But you didn't."

"No," he said with a sigh. "I didn't."

"You wanted to stay for me?"

"Yes, Alicia," Nikolai said. "I wanted to stay for you."

"I signed the papers two days ago. Already deposited the check." She took another sip.

Nikolai smiled. "Uh-oh. Is all that money burning a hole?"

"Maybe just a tiny one." She finished her glass of champagne and winced at the sting of bubbles at the back of her throat. She thought about pouring another, but didn't.

She didn't want to be crying, but she was.

"Would you look at me, please?" Niko asked.

She didn't want to look at him. There was nothing in Nikolai's face she would allow herself to see. Still, she turned because he'd asked her to. She could do that, at least.

It was a mistake, of course. How could she ever have thought she would be able to look at his face, the downward slope of his mouth that was not a smile yet fighting bravely not to be a frown? How could she look into the depths of his gray-green eyes without seeing her own reflection?

Nikolai took the glass from her hand and put it beside his. He put his arms around her. He kissed her . . . oh, he kissed her, and there was no way she should have ever even let him in the front door, but she had. She did. She always would.

Somehow, Alicia found the strength to put her hands up flat on his chest to hold him off. "Nikolai. Stop. Wait."

He did, licking his lips as though to keep the taste of her lingering as long as possible. "Don't say it, please. Don't tell me you're leaving."

"But I am." She drew in a breath and wished for a moment that she'd doused herself in a couple of shots of tequila rather than a few sips of cheap sparkling wine.

He stepped away from her and dragged a hand through his hair to push it out of his eyes. "You don't have to."

"How can you say that to me? You, of all people! You're the one who was telling me that I should travel, that I could go anywhere or do anything, but now what? Because you've decided to stick around, I should, too?" She advanced upon him, not wanting to raise her voice but doing that anyway. Helpless to stop herself from wanting to rage at him. "Every time we were together, you could never tell me really how you felt. You let me think that it was nothing. It wasn't permanent. You let me believe that it was all going to end, because you were going to leave again. You lied to me!"

"Oh, like you were so up front with me? You knew about this offer and what it could mean, and you never said a word about it to me, not even when I was telling you—yeah, I was—that you could go anywhere or do anything. You said you had no choice but to stay!" he shouted. Toe-to-toe. Face-to-face. He didn't grab her or shake her, but that's how it felt.

She almost wanted him to, if only because it meant his hands would be on her body. If he hurt her, all the better. If he bruised her, there would be marks she could look at when she was far away, to remind her of this moment here in her front hallway, when Nikolai Stern had last touched her.

Because this *was* the last time he was going to touch her, and if it didn't hurt now, it was going to hurt later, and for the rest of her life. He didn't have to cut her for his touch to leave behind scars.

"Now I have a choice," she spat. "And I'm going to take it!"

"But . . . why now?" Nikolai asked her, and for that, Alicia had only one simple answer.

"Because I didn't then."

She was the one who reached for him. To take his hand, linking their fingers. She pulled him closer, one, two, three steps, and she kept pulling him, toward the stairs and up to her bedroom, where she led him to her bed and pushed him gently down.

She let him watch her as she undid the buttons on her blouse, one at a time. This was no striptease, but it was a show, put on for him so that when time and distance had once more come between them, he would have something to remember.

Alicia eased open the fabric over her collarbones, drawing her fingertips over the hard curves beneath the softness of her skin. Lower, she traced the lacy edges of her bra, then cupped the fullness of her breasts. Under the heat of his gaze, her nipples tightened. She ran her thumbs over them, emphasizing the shape of them through the lace. Making sure he could see.

She turned as she shrugged out of the blouse and tossed it to the side. Her hair came down with a few tugs at the pins that had been securing it, and she shook her head to feel it brushing her back. She pushed the elastic waistband of her skirt over her hips and stood in her bra and panties for a moment, half-afraid to look around, to see his expression. The low, agonized sound of his voice saying her name nearly sent her to her knees. Instead, she reached behind her to unhook her bra and let it fall away.

But when she moved to hook her fingers in her panties, Nikolai said, "Wait. Let me look at you. Just for a minute."

She stood still, not moving. Letting him drink in this last sight of her. When he made another noise, she turned to look into his eyes. She slid a hand between her legs, over the lace, stroking for the joy of watching the way his pupils dilated. Her breath caught in her throat at the pleasure she brought herself.

"Take them off," Nikolai rasped. "Please."

She smiled and did as he'd asked, as slowly as she'd done everything else. When at last she stood fully naked in front of him, the instinct to cover herself rose up as it always did. She refused to give in to it. If nothing else, this last time, she wanted to feel as beautiful in front of him as he'd always told her she was.

"You're a goddess," he told her.

She blushed then, heat rising up her throat to paint her cheeks that had nothing to do with being embarrassed. She could dispute him, but she did not, because it was so easy to believe he meant it. She crawled up over his body to kiss him, and he rolled them both so they could get him out of his clothes a lot faster and with less fanfare than she'd taken getting naked.

They made love slowly. Almost with caution. He touched her as though she were fragile, the lacework of a spiderweb hung heavy with dew and ready to shred at the slightest touch. And wasn't she? Ready to tear? Over and over again until there was nothing left of her but broken threads.

When it was over and they'd both settled onto their backs with the blankets pulled up to cover them against the chill, Alicia thought they might sleep. She didn't want to. It would waste the time they had left together before daylight came and she was ready, at last, to finally go. And, having him there in the morning would make all of this more awkward and painful than it was already going to be.

She tucked herself against him, her hand over his heart. "You should leave."

"Ilya already knows about us," Nikolai answered. "It doesn't matter if I stay all night."

"That's not why."

He didn't reply at first, but the skipping beat of his heart pounded harder against her palm. "Why, then?"

"I'm getting up early. I need to be at the airport by four. My flight leaves at six. It's late, and I won't sleep if you're here . . ."

He covered her hand with his, curling the fingers tight around hers. When he looked at her, the darkness of his pupils had nearly swallowed up all the gray green. She could see nothing of herself reflected there.

"You're leaving . . . tomorrow?"

"Yes." She waited for him to ask her where she was going, but he didn't. She thought he might at least ask how long she'd be gone, but he didn't ask her that, either.

"Were you going to tell me?"

She pressed her lips to his skin. "No."

"That's . . . I can't even think of what that is. It's bullshit, Allie." He sat, pushing her hand away from him hard enough for it to smack against the covers before she withdrew it. "But seriously, what the hell, you were just going to . . . leave? Without saying anything?"

"I don't want any long, drawn-out good-byes. Okay?" Irritated at the waver in her voice, Alicia sat, too, and swung her legs over her side of the bed. She found a T-shirt and tugged it on over her head. It hit her midthigh and meant she could feel covered up without finding a pair of panties, but . . . it was his.

"You want to leave without *any* good-bye."

This time, with her back to him, she felt exactly like she was shutting him out and not drawing him in. The best truth now was still mostly a lie, though. "Yes. The way you did to me."

"Fine." Nikolai didn't sound angry anymore. He sounded resigned. She heard the soft thump of his feet on the floor on the other side of the bed. "I'll go, if that's what you want."

Ask me to stay.

Irrational. It was all he had to do, wasn't it? Say the words out loud. Tell her that he loved her and he wanted her. All he had to do was ask her to stay, but of course, Nikolai didn't.

He didn't ask her to walk him to the front door, but she did. He turned before he opened it, and she hadn't thought she would kiss him again—why drag this out? Yet her mouth found his, and she backed him up against the wall, and his hands were in her hair, and her tongue was in his mouth, and all she could do was try not to devour him where they stood.

She didn't try very hard.

He was the one who broke the kiss, panting. Nikolai wiped the wetness of her kiss off his lips with the back of his hand. With his back against the door, there was no place for him to go, but he turned his head and held up his hands, pushing her away as effectively as if he'd shoved her.

"You wanted me to go. Let me go," he said. "That's what you want, isn't it?"

Alicia could still taste him. She could still feel him against her, though inches of space now separated them. So many words left unsaid, and she was as much at fault as he was, if not more. How could she hate him for not asking her to stay when she hadn't been able to ask him to go with her?

"Sometimes you love someone who can't give you what you want, so what can you do but love them enough to let them go?" she said.

"Bullshit," Nikolai answered. "If nine planets in this universe can align, why can't we?"

For that, Alicia had no answer. This time, Nikolai was the one who bent to kiss her. The briefest brush of his lips on hers, nothing more than that.

"Close your eyes," he told her, and she did, waiting for another kiss that never came.

She heard the click of the door. Felt the rush of winter air that started her teeth chattering. Then silence.

When she opened her eyes, Nikolai was gone.

CHAPTER FORTY-TWO

"I should punch you right in the face," Ilya said. "But to be honest, I've run out of energy."

Niko hadn't bothered to sneak into the house, but he hadn't expected to find his brother sitting at the kitchen table with a full bottle and an empty glass. "Pour me one?"

"You can have mine. I tried, but it doesn't taste good to me. Hell if I can figure out why." Ilya filled the glass halfway with amber liquid and pushed it across the table toward Niko.

It didn't taste good to Niko, either, so after a single, grimacing sip, he pushed it away. He looked at his brother, not sure what he expected to see. Ilya leaned back in the chair with a shrug, when he caught his brother's look.

"I don't know what you want me to say," Ilya told him.

"You could say congratulations. That's what I said to you," Niko replied, knowing the response was shitty but saying it anyway.

Ilya snorted rough laughter. "Why? You guys running off to get married?"

"She's running off. I don't know where."

His brother's laughter faded, and he tilted his head, brow furrowed. "What do you mean she's running off? Where's she going?"

"I don't know."

Ilya sat up straight. "What do you mean you don't know? What's wrong with you? You didn't ask?"

Niko stood, scraping the chair on the linoleum hard enough to almost knock it over. "She's leaving tomorrow morning. She said she'd be at the airport by four. Does it really matter where she's going? She's still going to be gone."

"That's in about two hours," Ilya said. "You should get your shit together and go after her. Fuck's sakes, man. Don't tell me you came back here and did all this just to let her go?"

Niko's fists clenched, then unclenched. "She has the right to go wherever she wants. I know it's what she wants, Ilya. She wants to leave."

"She doesn't want to leave *you*," Ilya said. "And if you can't see that, you're an idiot. Now I really might punch you in your face, for being stupid."

He might welcome the punch, if only because a fight would get rid of at least some of this anxiety. He put his hands on the kitchen counter, his back to his brother. "Shit."

"Yeah, it's a mess of it. You'd better figure it out."

Niko looked over his shoulder. "She could be going anywhere. She didn't say anything to you?"

"You always were the pretty one, not the smart one." Ilya shook his head with a sour expression. "Because, right, Allie absolutely confided in me about her plans. Sure. Again, what the hell is wrong with you? She's taking a trip, not moving across the world to join a commune."

Niko frowned. "It was *not* a commune."

Ilya waved a hand, clearly not caring. "Whatever. You're afraid she's going to do to you what you did to us, but that was you, not Allie. Go to the airport and find out where, how long she'll be gone, when she'll be back. But go after her, Niko. Or she will come back, but it won't matter, because you'll have lost her. And trust me, brother. You'll spend a long, long time wishing you'd stepped up when you had the chance."

CHAPTER FORTY-THREE

The drive to the airport normally took about forty minutes, with traffic, on the winding back roads from Quarrytown. At three in the morning, there wasn't any traffic. The car she'd hired to take her made the trip in twenty-five minutes, and the driver didn't speak, so that was a bonus. Alicia wouldn't have been able to hold much of a conversation.

All she'd brought was one small suitcase and a backpack, both meant as carry-ons. She had money in her pocket and more in her bank account. She had a ticket to Barcelona, and from there she intended to spend the next four weeks traveling to wherever the desire took her. Places she'd read about or seen in movies but had never imagined she would actually visit. She would take planes and trains and buses and walk along cobblestoned streets and try adventurous foods from street vendors.

She didn't want to go.

She was afraid to go; that was the embarrassing truth.

She tipped the driver and got out of the car. All Alicia could think of was that long-ago night, staring up at the night sky and watching those planets align. She'd never imagined back then that she wouldn't get out of this town, that she wouldn't live the life she'd dreamed of, so why now that she had the opportunity was she so terrified to actually try?

She hefted her pack on her shoulder and turned back, ready to hail the driver, but he probably wanted to get back home and into bed before the sun rose. He'd already pulled away from the curb, his brake lights barely blinking. Her fingers tightened on the handle of her suitcase.

And there, across the drop-off lane, standing with his hands shoved in his pockets, was Nikolai.

She didn't believe it, not at first. She had to be conjuring him out of wishful thinking . . . but no, there he was, crossing the street, looking both ways so he wouldn't get struck by a car. He was in front of her before she knew it.

"I couldn't let you go without saying good-bye," he said. "Not ever again."

Alicia put down her bag, then the backpack. "What . . . ?"

He kissed her. Or she kissed him—she couldn't be sure who moved first. Maybe they moved at the same time, urged by mutual desire and the urge to be in each other's arms. All she knew was that the taste of him flooded her. His arms around her warded off the early-morning chill.

"I love you," Nikolai said. "I should've told you before. I should've said it every time you asked me and every time you didn't."

Stunned, blinking away tears, Alicia swallowed the ache in her throat. "I love you, too. Are you asking me to stay?"

Nikolai shook his head, looking surprised. "Huh? No. Of course not."

"But . . ." Confused, she tried to step out of his embrace, but he held her still.

"You should go. You need to go," he told her. "You deserve this, Alicia. Go out there. See the world. Just . . . if you decide you want to . . . come back to me."

Come back to me.

It was better than if he'd asked her to stay. She smiled, sniffing back tears, and kissed him again. People passing stared. She didn't care. Let them look. Let them see what it was like to be loved.

"I'm only going for four weeks," she said. "Then I'll be back."

"You might decide you like traveling so much you'll want to leave again," Nikolai told her, his expression serious even though the corners of his mouth quirked the tiniest bit. "That's how it works, sometimes."

Alicia laughed, giddy with this, the two of them. "You could decide you want to come with me."

"Stranger things have happened," he said and kissed her again.

They stayed that way for a few seconds before she became mindful of the time and pushed away enough to look into his face. "Maybe I shouldn't go . . . I mean . . ."

"You're going. This is what you want, and I want it for you. You should take this trip. You'll always be sorry if you don't. And I'll be right here waiting for you," Nikolai told her.

"Right here? Right at the airport? The entire time?"

He laughed. "I'll be at home, dealing with my mother and Ilya, but I'll be there. I promise."

She believed him; that was the crazy thing. All these years and all the things they'd gone through together, yet she knew with every part of her that he was telling the truth.

"I'm nervous. And scared."

"You got this," he told her. "I never knew a woman who could make things happen the way you can, when you want them. You're going to have a great time. But while you're gone, don't forget something."

She studied him for a second. "What's that?"

"I'm going to miss you," Niko replied. "Every single day."

One more kiss, and she stepped away from him, but not apart. There was a difference, and she could feel it. She would go on this adventure, and she would come home, and they'd figure out what that meant when she did—but whatever it was, they were going to discover it together, with whatever journeys lay ahead for both of them.

READ ON FOR A SNEAK PEEK OF

All the Secrets We Keep

Editor's Note: This is an early excerpt and may not reflect the finished book.

CHAPTER ONE

Theresa Malone had made a lot of mistakes in her life, but that didn't mean she wasn't capable of making a few more. One of them was sitting across from her right now with a glass of whiskey on the table in front of him and a smirk that looked like every kind of bad idea. She'd invited Ilya Stern out tonight, so she had nobody but herself to blame. She ought to have known he'd be no different with her than he was with anyone else. Charming and difficult.

"You are bound and determined to make my life miserable, aren't you?" She frowned. "C'mon, Ilya. Why? What good is any of this going to do? You're delaying the inevitable."

"It's not at all inevitable, Theresa. And it'll make me feel better." He sipped from the glass with a grimace and set it down before leaning back in the chair to link his fingers behind his head. His grin was hard and didn't soften his expression at all.

Theresa drew in a slow, calming breath. "They're not going to offer you more money or any kind of guarantees beyond what they already have. You're coming across as greedy."

"Oh," Ilya said with a purposeful leer, "I'm very greedy."

Theresa pressed her lips together to keep from smiling. This wasn't funny, and though it was easy to see exactly how her former stepbrother had earned his reputation for being an alluring rogue, she wasn't going to succumb. He could treat her the same way he treated every other woman in his life, but that didn't mean she was like any of them.

She leaned forward. "You're going to screw yourself over. That's all that's going to happen. They're going to build that hotel and those condos up all around you and not put one cent toward developing the dive shop or diving area, and in fact, they will do their very best to make sure that you can't do anything, either. Your business," she said, "is going to wither and die and leave you with nothing."

Ilya's brows rose, and that tilting smile vanished. "Damn, that's harsh. Why you gotta be so cold, Theresa? What do you have wrapped up in all of this, anyway?"

That was a good question. She had put her reputation on the line to get this deal together, gambling on all the pieces falling into place just right so that maybe she could come up for air instead of drowning in years of debt. She'd first convinced her former boyfriend Wayne Diamond to sign off on the offer to buy the dive shop and quarry Ilya and his ex-wife, Alicia, had owned together by telling Wayne the owners were eager to sell. Then, offer in hand, she'd encouraged Alicia to sell her 60 percent. Ilya was the only one she hadn't been able to convince, and she was running out of both ideas and time.

"I mean, why do you care," Ilya asked when she didn't answer, "if my business crashes and burns or I end up in the hole, or what? What's it to you, really?"

"Why wouldn't I care? It's not like we're total strangers. You act like I should just sit back and watch you screw yourself out of what could be something really good for you." The words slipped out of her, almost so low she couldn't be sure he'd be able to hear her over the ambient noise in the bar, even with her leaning closer.

Ilya frowned and leaned across the table. "You don't owe me anything, you know. If anything, my family's the one that owes you. My mother's the one who kicked out you and your dad without more than a few hours' notice, then erased you from our lives like you'd never been a part of them."

She couldn't say anything about that; it was true, even if Ilya didn't quite understand the entirety of what had happened back then. The truth was, Theresa didn't, either. She'd given up trying a long time ago, even if some small part of her had always remained tied to the Sterns and that time when she'd been part of their family.

"Of course," he said with another of those grins that had laid waste to women for years, "considering what a pain in the ass my mother is, maybe you guys got lucky."

Lucky was far from what Theresa would've considered herself, but she shrugged and dipped her chin in response. They shared a look, longer than necessary. His gaze held hers, dropping for a second or so to her mouth, before his lips thinned and he looked away. Ilya sat back, raising his glass and draining it before setting it down even harder on the table.

"You're buying, right?" He waved over the waitress for another. "One for me. Not for her. She doesn't drink. Right?"

Theresa sighed. "Yes."

Ilya shrugged. "Suit yourself."

Theresa gathered the papers she'd spread out in front of them both shortly after arriving, before Ilya had waved them away and told her flat out he wanted more money and written promises regarding the plans for Go Deep and the quarry property. She put them neatly into the folder she'd brought along, then closed it and slid it across the table toward him. He gave her a look.

"I'll take the requests to them," she said. "But you should realize this isn't a negotiation. They've settled with Alicia for her major share, and they're going to move ahead with the project no matter what."

"Screw them," Ilya said evenly. "And you know what? You, too."

That was it; she was done.

Theresa got out a pair of twenties—all the cash she had in her wallet. All the cash she'd have for the next couple of weeks until her commission check from the first part of the sale cleared. She tossed the money on the table and stood. She didn't bother saying good-bye. Her heart was pounding, her throat closing, her eyes burning. The last thing in the world she wanted to do was give him the benefit of seeing her get upset—and how familiar did that feel? Years had passed, and the difference now was that instead of Ilya teasing her about the posters on her wall or stealing the last slice of pizza, holding it above her head so she couldn't reach it, he was actively pushing the point of something sharp into her soft places in order to get a reaction out of her.

Outside in the parking lot, she gave herself a few seconds to breathe in the night air, fresh with the promise of spring. At her car, she opened the trunk to sort through a few of her bags, looking for her pajama pants. At the sound of a male voice behind her, she jumped, hitting her head on the edge of the trunk and letting out a cry.

Blinking against the pain stars blooming in her vision, she whirled. *Pepper spray, dammit, where is . . . oh.* "You scared the hell out of me!"

Ilya had backed off a step, hands held up. "Sorry. Shit, Theresa, ease up."

She took in a breath and put a hand on her head, rubbing away the sting. "What do you want?"

"I was hoping you'd give me a ride home."

"After what you said to me?" She laughed harshly. "You *must* be drunk."

"If I wasn't, I wouldn't need a ride. And I'm sorry," Ilya said in the tone of a man for whom apologies had always worked in the past. "I shouldn't have said it. I didn't mean it, really. I know you're just doing your job."

She hesitated, wishing she could tell him to screw off. There weren't any ready cabs in this rural town. None of those phone-app car services. There was no way he'd be able to walk home, and that meant risking his deciding to drive himself if she refused. She didn't want that on her conscience.

"I know it's out of your way," Ilya said while she was weighing her answer. He shuffled his feet in the gravel and had the grace to look at least a little bit embarrassed—that earlier put-on charm dissipating. "I'd owe you. Not enough to agree to that deal. But I'd owe you."

Theresa sighed. "Fine. Get in."

She realized too late that the passenger-side seat sported her cosmetics case, pillow, blanket, and—oh, there were her pajama pants. She bent across the center console to start moving things into the backseat so he could get in. Ilya helped, then slid into the seat.

"What's up with all this stuff? Your landlord still fixing the ducts or whatever he was doing before?"

She'd forgotten she'd told him that lie a few weeks ago when she'd been staying at his house after Babulya's funeral. She shrugged, not looking at him. "I've been on the road for a while. For work."

When he snapped on the radio, she didn't say anything. It was better than trying to make conversation. She felt him looking at her but kept her eyes on the road.

"Was your hair always that curly?" Ilya asked.

Theresa's brows knit. "Huh?"

"Your hair." Incredibly, he reached to touch it. "It's so curly. And soft."

She burst into laughter, shivering at the touch of his fingers and pulling away as best she could while keeping the car on the road. "You're drunk."

"It looks good," Ilya said. "I like it."

She frowned at that. "Okay, well, thanks. I'm glad to know that my personal appearance is up to your presumably high standards."

Ilya laughed, low. "Salty."

She didn't answer that. Again, she felt his stare on her, but she didn't look at him. They drove in silence for the next few minutes until she made the last turn onto Quarry Street.

"Still wigs me out sometimes," Ilya said as they pulled into the driveway. "All the houses."

Theresa peered through the windshield, turning on the wipers to swipe at the faint drizzle that had misted the glass. "Things changed, for sure. That's what they do."

"Yeah," he said quietly. "That's what they do."